The
UNWITTING

Ellen Feldman is the author of five novels,
most recently *Next to Love* and *Scottsboro*, which
was shortlisted for the Orange Prize for Fiction.
She lives in New York City with her husband.

The
UNWITTING

A Novel

Ellen Feldman

PICADOR

First published 2014 by Picador
an imprint of Pan Macmillan, a division of Macmillan Publishers Limited
Pan Macmillan, 20 New Wharf Road, London N1 9RR
Basingstoke and Oxford
Associated companies throughout the world
www.panmacmillan.com

ISBN 978-1-4472-5216-0

The Unwitting is a work of historical fiction. Apart from the
well-known actul people, events, and locales that figure in the narrative,
all names, characters, places, and incidents are the products of the author's
imagination or are used fictitiously. Any resemblance to current events
or locales, or to living persons, is entirely coincidental.

Grateful acknowledgment is made to Edward B. Marks
Music Company c/o Carlin America, Inc. for permission to reprint
an excerpt from 'Fine and Mellow', written by Billie Holiday.
Used by permission of Edward B. Marks Music Company.

1 3 5 7 9 8 6 4 2

A CIP catalogue record for this book is available from the British Library.

Printed and bound by CPI Group (UK) Ltd, Croydon, CR0 4YY

Visit **www.picador.com** to read more about all our books
and to buy them. You will also find features, author interviews and
news of any author events, and you can sign up for e-newsletters
so that you're always first to hear about our new releases.

For
Liza Bennett
and
Richard Snow
and again, always
for Stephen

If I had to choose between betraying my country and betraying my friend, I hope I should have the guts to betray my country.

E. M. FORSTER

Love, by its very nature, is unworldly, and it is for this reason rather than its rarity that it is not only apolitical but anti-political, perhaps the most powerful of all anti-political human forces.

HANNAH ARENDT

The
UNWITTING

Prologue

November 22, 1963

THE CURIOUS THING about marriage, one of the curious things about marriage, is that the same habit that moves you to indulgent tenderness one minute can make you want to pack a toothbrush and a change of underwear and walk out the door the next. That morning I was in the walking-out-the-door mood, though I knew I wasn't going anywhere. Not about this. Not about anything. I wasn't a fool.

Charlie sat across the kitchen table from me reading the morning papers, drinking his coffee, and humming. No, not humming. I wouldn't have minded a bit of Beethoven or Bach or a few bars of Gershwin or Cole Porter. He was keening, quietly, through his coffee. Sometimes I find the habit endearing, my own movable serenade. Occasionally I can tune it out. But when I'm annoyed, it becomes as intrusive as a buzz saw.

A shaft of sunlight streamed through the kitchen window and lay between us on the table like a sword. I glanced down at the headlines. Reading upside down is a largely useless skill I picked up working in book and magazine publishing. Charlie is even better at it.

CONGO OUSTS SOVIET AIDES
SUSPENDS TIES TO MOSCOW

My eyes moved to the left-hand column.

KENNEDY PLEDGES

SPACE ADVANCES:

OPENS TEXAS TOUR

Charlie looked up from the paper. "Want the *Trib*?"

I shook my head no. On most mornings I love the conjugal intimacies of shared newspapers and swapped opinions, but in the wake of last night I would not be so easily seduced.

His eyes went back to the paper, while his hand groped for the coffeepot. I picked it up and poured coffee into his mug, further proof that I wasn't going anywhere. A woman on her way out the door doesn't pour coffee into her husband's mug. His lap perhaps, but not his mug.

He folded the paper in half, peeled back the front page, and tucked it into the fold—the prescribed method for reading broadsheets on crowded subways and buses and at small kitchen tables. I've never been able to master the art, but Charlie's a whiz at it.

He looked up again.

"Stop brooding. She'll be fine."

He had caught me off guard. Did he really think I was worried rather than wounded, or was he pretending so he could get out the door unscathed?

"I'm not brooding," I snapped, then caught myself. I have a fear I've never confided to anyone, not even to Charlie, especially not to Charlie. One day someone will bug our apartment, and I'll hear the snippiness in my voice. I keep making resolutions to moderate it. Sometimes I succeed for weeks, or at least days at a time.

"You were the one who was worried," I went on more gently.

He looked up from the paper again and arched one eyebrow.

"You were," I insisted.

Abby had come up with the idea a few weeks earlier. If we trusted Susannah, who lived two floors below us in the building, to babysit her, surely we'd let her take Abby across the park to school. But when it came to potential harm to those he loved, Charlie worked from a grim actuarial table of his own. He had insisted on grilling Susannah, talking to her parents, and extracting promises from Abby about waiting for traffic lights, steering clear of strangers, and sticking to Susannah's side like glue, though he knew as well as I that she wasn't likely to stray. The cachet of arriving in the company of a girl from the upper school was too heady.

I'd had my own reservations, though I'd kept them to myself. I knew my tendency toward overprotection had more to do with my childhood than with my child.

That morning Abby had gone off to school without me. I was handling it splendidly. I had followed her to the door without expressing last-minute worries and warnings. I had not had to fake allergies to cover tears. There had been no tears. I was fine.

Charlie took the last bite of English muffin. He rarely leaves food on his plate. A man who has grown up to a constant chorus of reminders of children starving in Europe, and not anonymous children either, isn't likely to. Then he stood and, holding his tie with one hand as he bent over the table, lifted his mug with the other and took a last swallow of coffee. I waited for the sigh of satisfaction that always followed the final gulp. He sighed. I would pack only a small suitcase. He started down the hall to the front door, talking about the weather—the weather!—and how it was so nice he thought he'd walk to work through the park. I followed him along the corridor, though I knew I should let him go. It wasn't the old saw about picking your fights. That was too coarse a view of marriage. It was simply that the incident was not that important. We would both have forgotten it by tonight. Only I had a feeling I wouldn't forget it. I wondered if I'd be as offended if someone other than Frank Tucker had made the remark. He'd said it the night before, then lurched out of the apartment, the adoring long-haired waif he'd brought to dinner tucked under his arm like a crutch.

Charlie reached the door, turned back, and leaned down to kiss me. We usually kissed goodbye on the mouth, nothing smoochy, just enough to keep the franchise. I turned my cheek. I will never forget that.

One tweed shoulder was already through the door.

"So that's it? We're going to pretend nothing happened?" I had sworn I wasn't going to say anything.

He stopped and stood with his head down, his eyes closed. It was his patient stance, and it was a ruse. Everyone thought he was un-flappable. I knew what it cost him.

"Nothing did happen."

"Where were you last night?"

He turned back to face me. "You know what he's like when he gets in his cups."

"If we know what he's like, why do we keep inviting him to din-ner?"

I waited through another long-suffering pause. He thought those moments of silence demonstrated his reasonableness. I found them more provocative than a taunt.

"Because he's an old friend. And because I want to persuade him to start writing for the magazine again. Anyway, I thought you thought he was a stand-up guy."

"That was a long time ago. For one specific act. All I'm saying is that the comment was insulting, and you could have called him on it."

"Now there's an idea whose time has come. Get into a fight with a drunk who, when he's fried, likes nothing better than taking swings at old friends and busting up the premises."

"What if he'd said those things about negroes?"

"He didn't."

"Or Jews? Would you have called him on it then?"

"That's different."

"Why?"

He stood staring at me from the depths of his murderous patience.

"Look," he said quietly, "I'm not suggesting you had an easy time of it, but your ancestors were not auctioned off in a Southern slave market. Nor did your entire family go up the chimneys of Auschwitz."

"This has nothing to do with me. It's about principles."

"Okay, let's talk about principles. Frank Tucker, our guest, made a boorish remark. He's a bad drunk. We all know that. But he didn't murder anyone. Or sell out his best friend, which is more than you can say about some people we know. In fact, if you remember, and I'm sure you do, he went to jail for not selling out his friends. So can we just keep some perspective on this particular principle?"

I wanted to. But the memory of Tucker's lubricious voice and oily smirk as he leered into my face—the comment was made to rile not the waif under his arm or Charlie but me—distorted my perspective as grossly as a fun house mirror.

"I have to go to work," he said.

"Fine."

"I'll see you tonight."

I imagined him walking into an empty apartment. I'm home, he'd call. The silence would mock his words. Red, he'd shout. The sound would echo through the empty rooms. Nell, he'd try. Still no answer.

"Will you call me when Abby gets home?" he asked.

"Someday she's going to grow up to be a woman."

"What's that supposed to mean?" he asked, though he knew. Each of us knew how the other sparred. That's the part the love songs don't tell you.

"Then she, too, will be, according to your good buddy Frank Tucker, too dumb to do anything but type, file, and fuck."

He turned and started down the hall toward the elevator.

"See you tonight," he called without looking back.

I closed the door and stood listening to the elevator opening, then clanging shut and beginning its descent. The sound was the gnashing and whirring of ordinary life going on.

I made my way down the hall to the kitchen. I was already regretting my outburst. The sword of sunlight still lay on the table, but it had inched around so it was pointing at me. I glanced at the clock over the sink. Abby and Susannah would be getting on the crosstown bus.

As I started clearing the breakfast dishes, I caught a glimpse of myself in the side of the coffeepot. Like most people, I usually manage to arrange my face when I know I'm approaching my reflection in a mirror or window. Held at the right angle, my nose isn't long but retroussé. The heavily browed raccoon eyes I had hated as a teenager struck me now as a nice foil for my hair, which all those years ago my mother's friend Mr. Richardson had compared to the reflection of fire on burnished copper. Who would have thought that Mr. Richardson, who was in what he called the insurance game, had a poetic streak? But when I'm not on my guard, my mouth gives me away. Some boy in my past, not Charlie, not even Woody, someone with no staying power, had once called it sensual, but even then I knew it was a line. My mother had it right. Stop pouting, she used to say. You have a discontented mouth, she sometimes added. Look at yourself in the mirror, I wanted to shout at her, but never did. My job was to soften the blows she thought the world rained on her, not deliver more.

I poured the last of the coffee into my mug, put the pot in the sink, and stood listening to the silence. The apartment was never so quiet as just after Charlie and Abby left. Some mornings the hush was a buoyant peace I could float on; others it ached like hunger. This morning it had a gnawing feel. I never should have brought up Tucker's remark.

I looked at my watch. The bus would be on its way through the park now.

I carried the mug into the small room behind the kitchen, the maid's room in an earlier time for swankier tenants, now my study. The space was barely big enough for a desk, a chair, a typewriter table, shelves along two walls, and an old set of wooden library steps to reach the books at the top. A tall narrow window opened onto a miserly slice of sky.

I put the mug on the desk and stood staring at the mess of open books, uncapped pens, and scribbled notes. I usually tidied up when I stopped work for the day, but the previous afternoon I had been under the gun with the grocery shopping to do, the chicken in lemon cream to get started, the flowers to arrange. Flowers for Frank Tucker!

A sheet of paper hung limp over the typewriter roller. I leaned down and lifted it between my thumb and forefinger.

He lay on a wooden plank in a small room in the basement of the clinic, his skin ashen in the glare of the single bare bulb that swung overhead. His body . . .

I had stopped in midsentence because I hadn't made up my mind how to continue. The paragraph was part of a piece I was writing on Richard Wright. The rumors that Wright had succumbed not to a heart attack, as listed on the death certificate, but to foul play were still rampant, though he had died three years earlier. Some pointed a finger at the communists, because Wright, who had been an active party member before the war, had turned on them; others at the CIA, which could never decide whether Wright was a useful tool in their fight against communism or an outspoken negro thorn in their side. His friends were sure the CIA was behind his death; his daughter suspected it; his wife did not want to hear about it.

I stood staring at the unfinished sentence. Stopping in the middle of a thought wasn't necessarily a bad idea. It often made it easier to get going again the next morning. Who said that? Hemingway? Frank Tucker's hero. Two posturing bellicose buffoons who just happened to be good writers. The thought of so much talent residing in a couple of overgrown bad boys made me turn away from my own stalled essay and start back down the hall, past the kitchen, to the dining room.

The hardwood floor creaked under my loafers, then went silent again as I stepped into the deep hush of the abstract patterned rug. Everything was in place: the round walnut table with the sickle-shaped pieces that slid in and out to make it bigger or smaller, the matching curved chairs, the weighted Dansk candleholders that could be angled one way or another. When we'd finished furnishing the place, Charlie had said it wasn't an apartment, it was a Scandinavian manifesto, and we'd laughed at ourselves, but with secret pride. The memory was another pinprick to my conscience. Would I prefer the place in shambles and Charlie with a black eye, assuming Frank Tucker had been sober enough to land a punch?

I kept going through the dining room to the entrance hall and took the single step down to the living room. This really was ridiculous. I should be getting to work, not prowling the premises, taking inventory of everything I'd never leave, not for something as foolish as this, not for anything.

I crossed the room to the windows. Overhead, the wind was herding the clouds like misshapen sheep. Below, the trees in Central Park licked the air like flames. On the opposite side of the street, pedestrians the size of large insects hurried along Central Park West, moving from deep shadows into sun-drenched pools of light. I glanced at my watch again. Abby and Susannah would be boarding an uptown bus, unless they'd decided to walk.

The traffic light at the corner turned green, but the line of cars didn't budge. A taxi driver leaned on his horn. The shriek of fury rose twelve floors and shattered the silence. I went on standing at the window, imagining Charlie striding beneath the flaming trees, his briefcase thumping against his leg. Once, a few years earlier, I had looked out the window of a traffic-stalled taxi and caught a glimpse of him walking up Fifth Avenue. The experience had been disorienting. The man I slept beside every night and awakened next to every morning was, for a moment, a stranger, loping along the sidewalk toward a destination I didn't know, thinking thoughts I could only guess. The realization had been frightening, and seductive.

I really did have to get to work. I turned away from the window and started across the living room, but instead of veering right to go back to the study, I went left down the hall to our bedroom. It overlooked the park too, and the morning light flooded in, glinting off the blond wood of the dressers, puddling in pools on the pale carpet, reflecting off the shiny dust jackets of the piles of books on the night tables on either side of the bed. The top book on Charlie's table was Frank Tucker's latest. I could not get away from the man.

I walked around the bed, picked it up, and turned it over. Tucker stared up at me. Better cut down on the booze, Frank, I warned him, before the nose begins to look like J. P. Morgan's.

I put the book back on the pile, front side up, crossed the room to the television that sat on a wooden stand facing the bed, and switched it on. I never watched television during the day, not even the news. People were always telling me that they couldn't do what I did because they didn't have the discipline to stay home alone and write all day. Discipline was not one of my problems, though it seemed to be this morning.

I stood waiting while the television warmed up. On the screen, a convertible was making its way slowly down a street between crowds of cheering, waving men, women, and children. There were so many children; they must have been given the day off from school.

"Jack! Jackie!" the crowd howled. "Jack! Jackie!"

From the backseat, the President and First Lady waved back, his mouth stretched into that dazzling grin with almost too many teeth, hers curved into a more demure smile.

"The President and Mrs. Kennedy begin their two-day tour of Texas," the announcer said, "after these messages."

I sat on the end of the bed and waited while a woman swooned over freshly laundered sheets and towels, children wolfed down soup that was just like homemade, and another woman stood under a pounding shower with an expression of such ecstasy on her up-turned face that it always made me wonder what was going on below the camera's frame.

The first couple returned, still sitting in the back of the open car, still smiling and waving to the cheering crowd.

"Yesterday," the announcer resumed, "President Kennedy, on the first leg of his two-day tour of Texas, announced in a speech at Brooks Air Force Base in San Antonio that the space program would continue, despite congressional cutbacks."

"This research must and will go on," said a voice-over with an exaggerated Boston accent that would have been laughable if it had come from anyone else. "The conquest of space must and will go ahead."

"From San Antonio," the announcer continued, "the first couple went on to Houston."

Now the President and the First Lady were coming down the steps of a plane, an absurdly boyish-looking man and a maddeningly glamorous woman in a white suit with a black belt and black hat, carrying a bouquet of red roses. Didn't they ever stop smiling? Behind them, the words AIR FORCE ONE were visible on the side of the plane.

Frank Tucker had flown on Air Force One. He had a pack of cigarettes with the presidential seal and a menu with the same seal in gold at the top and the words AIR FORCE ONE in gold at the bottom to prove it. According to the menu, which I swear he carried around with him for weeks after, he'd had a sloppy joe on a roll, Fritos, coleslaw, and an oatmeal cookie for lunch. The fare wasn't much, but the thought of the misogynistic Tucker, who just happened to write like a dream, flying and eating even that meager meal on taxpayer dollars, and with that golden couple, annoyed me. Except that Tucker insisted they weren't so golden. JFK was monumentally unfaithful, he said. All the reporters knew it, but none of them would write about it. It was a gentlemen's agreement. Some gentlemen, I'd said when he'd told the story, but he'd only smirked.

"In Houston," the announcer continued, "the first couple made an unscheduled stop at the League of United Latin American Citizens, where Mrs. Kennedy gave a brief speech."

Now Jackie filled the screen, smiling her impeccable smile, and in her improbably breathy voice charmed the crowd in Spanish.

I sat watching her and thinking about Tucker's gossip. I was pretty certain Charlie was faithful, but I wasn't stupid enough to swear to it.

"Today," the announcer went on, "the President and First Lady will wrap up the Texas tour with a breakfast speech in Fort Worth, a luncheon talk in Dallas, and dinner in Austin."

I stood and switched off the television. The President couldn't be the wolf Tucker said. He didn't have the time.

I started back down the hall, then stopped again in the doorway to Abby's room. Volumes of Betsy-Tacy and Anne of Green Gables, childish Winnie-the-Poohs and precocious Mark Twains marched down the bookcase shelves. There were even the touch-and-feel books that I had turned the pages of for her in infancy and the illustrated volumes that Charlie had read to her a few years later. Above them sat a line of dolls and stuffed animals that she no longer played with.

I glanced at the clock on the night table. I had watched the news for longer than I'd thought. Abby had been safe at school for a good fifteen minutes. The muscles I didn't know I had tensed unknotted. My nerves stopped jangling.

I sat in the chair where I had spent so many hours feeding and rocking and singing to her, gazing at the books we no longer read to her and the dolls she no longer played with, and saw my daughter moving away from me, her long legs scissoring into the future, her coltish body morphing into womanhood, her silky auburn hair streaming behind her as she broke into a run. So long, Mom. See you around. I was nothing like my own mother, but I still had to be abandoned. If I weren't, I had failed. But I hadn't expected success to feel so bleak.

I had to get to work. I stood and started back through the apartment to my study. The framed photograph on the desk caught my attention as soon as I stepped into the room, though I rarely noticed it anymore. That's what happens when you live with objects day in and day out.

The film was black-and-white, but the sharp contrast between the almost overexposed playground and the deep shadows of the tree-shaded benches indicated that the picture had been taken on a day much like today. Light glinted off Charlie's dark hair, making it sleek as an otter's. He was wearing a crew neck sweater and a pair of khakis that sat low on his hips. The image sent a sudden erotic charge through me.

Beside him in the picture, Abby came rushing toward the camera on a swing seat, hands gripping the chains, torso cantilevered back, corduroy legs stuck straight out in front of her, hair streaking behind. The thrill of flying free and the faith that those big Daddy hands would be there to catch her when she returned, caught by the click of a camera shutter, were frozen on her face for eternity.

What was I doing fighting with this man about a drunk's inane remark? Suddenly, for no reason at all, or maybe for every reason in the world, I remembered a morning about a year earlier. I'd been in my study working, and I'd had the radio tuned low to WQXR. The news had come on, and a phrase had broken into my consciousness. *Congress for Cultural Freedom,* then the word *bomb.*

My hands had hovered over the typewriter keys. I'd reached out to turn up the volume, but I was too late. The announcer had moved on to the weather. I'd tried to remember what time Charlie had said his meeting there that day was scheduled for. I had been so busy telling Abby to hurry or we'd be late for school that I hadn't paid attention to what he'd said. I'd tried to call him, but the line had been busy. A moment later, the phone had rung. He'd heard the news in his office and knew I would be worried. He was fine, but his meeting at the Congress for Cultural Freedom that afternoon had been canceled.

I leaned over the desk now and reached for the telephone. My hand closed around the receiver. I felt the vibration before I heard the ring and glanced at my watch again. If he had walked, he'd have only just arrived at his office.

I picked up the receiver. "I was just about to call you."

"Pardon me?"

The voice on the other end of the line belonged to a man, but not Charlie.

"I'm sorry, I thought you were someone else. Who is this, please?"

The voice answered with his own question. "Is this Mrs. Benjamin?"

"Yes."

"Mrs. Charles Benjamin?"

I still did not recognize the voice, but I knew the tone instinctively. It was muted with pity and grave with the knowledge of the many ways life could turn on a dime.

BOOK ONE

1948–1963

One

I HADN'T PLANNED TO go to the party that night, but as my room-mate, Natalie, was leaving for the evening, she stopped in the doorway, turned back, and said, "Fine. Don't go. Stay here and feel sorry for yourself."

Until then, I'd thought she didn't know me at all.

Sometimes I torture myself with the idea of what my life would have been like if I hadn't gone that night. Charlie always said he would have found me somehow, but life is a tricky proposition. Happenstance trumps fate every time.

The apartment on 119th Street was packed with young bodies in search of one another. The heat they gave off cooked the temperature to a tropical high, despite windows open to the rainy January night. Smoke from forty or fifty cigarettes swirled through the air. The fumes made me queasy, and the queasiness revved up my fear until my pulse raced like a hopped-up engine. Could you have morning sickness at ten o'clock at night?

On the record player, Billie Holiday was warning that love could make you drink and gamble and stay out all night long. And Charlie, though I didn't know his name at the time because I hadn't been listening when he'd introduced himself, was leaning over me with one hand propped against the wall half a foot northwest of my head. It was a proprietary stance, but I was too preoccupied to care. All I knew was that he was not my type. Beneath a trim dark mustache, his mouth was wide but thin-lipped, a sign of a lack of generosity, I thought. His mouth made me remember kissing Woody.

Love will make you do things that you know is wrong, Billie sang.

He was talking about the antidraft rally on campus the day before and getting incensed about the unconscionable insanity of gearing up for another war. Under different circumstances, I would have agreed, but the draft was the last thing on my mind that night.

I could tell he was a vet. The war had been over for three years, but the campus was still swarming with them, though not still in their uniforms as they had been that first year. Correction: the campus was swarming with male vets. As far as I knew, I was the only girl.

I stood with a rag of a smile on my face, pretending to listen, while I berated myself for my naïveté. I should have been wary of Woody the day I met him. But all I'd noticed was his creamy milk chocolate skin and the sign he was carrying on the picket line protesting the revival of the movie.

BIRTH OF A NATION

PREACHES RACE HATRED

NAACP

We had been perhaps ten protesters apart in a picket line of about twenty, which meant that we kept passing each other as we circled the sidewalk in front of the theater. I was the first to smile. It took me five or six passes to work up to it. When he smiled back, it was like the beam of a headlight swerving by. After a few more passes, we began exchanging comments. The demonstration broke up early, when a contingent of American Youth for Democracy arrived. Everyone knew they were a communist-front group, and the last thing the NAACP wanted was to be associated with communists. That was when Woody asked if I wanted to go for coffee. I said I did.

I'd assumed we'd go to a diner around the movie theater, but

Woody was less naïve. He steered me to an out-of-the-way place on the border between the Columbia campus and Harlem. I suppose I should have known then that the romance was doomed.

Love is just like the faucet, Billie sang. *It turns off and on.*

Charlie was still talking. Beyond his shoulder, rain streaked down the window and made dark stains on the brownstones across the street. In the distance, the reflected lights of Broadway hung like a halo in the mist. I wanted to be away from the party, away from New York. I imagined myself roaming the world, an unwed mother with a beautiful mocha baby in tow. Only I knew I never would. The story would be too close to my mother's, though she had married and stayed put with her white baby. Some of the more worldly girls in the dorm whispered about a reliable doctor in Pennsylvania. He performed the procedure on principle, unlike the back-alley butchers who were in it for the money, though he was not cheap, despite his principles. Woody had said he would get the money somehow. He wasn't behaving badly. He had gone home to Philadelphia for the weekend to see his brother who would probably lend him whatever was necessary.

We hadn't discussed the possibility of having the baby. If Woody wanted to save the world, he had to finish Columbia, then law school. I didn't blame him for that. I'd fallen for him for that. But rationality did not enter into it. My sore heart, my fragile ego, my punctured pride wanted him to offer to throw it all over for me. Then I could stand on principle and refuse to ruin his life.

The sheer unholy injustice of it rankled. We had known each other for three months, but our entire sexual history consisted of two furtive, though protected, late-night encounters behind the locked door of the veterans' affairs office, where he had a part-time job.

The thin ungenerous mouth was still moving. It made me think of kissing Woody again, and the memory made my stomach turn over on itself.

Sometimes when you think it's on, baby
It has turned off and gone.

I felt the dampness between my legs. It took me a moment to realize that the sensation was not recollected passion. It was unmistakable, but it was probably a mistake. I was three weeks late and had had half a dozen false alarms. Only I could tell this was real. Maybe the nasty little discovery that love had turned off and gone had shocked my body into action, the way an icy bath or a fall down the stairs was supposed to but never did. A trickle of dampness was seeping down my thigh.

I mumbled an excuse, ducked under Charlie's arm, and, clutching my handbag containing the sanitary pad and belt that I'd been carrying around for a month, started down the hall. That was the logical place for a bathroom, unless it was off the kitchen. You never knew in the makeshift apartments for vets and graduate students that had been hacked out of the respectable brownstones built for the solid families of another century.

I pushed opened the first door in the hallway. A bed heaped with coats seemed to be writhing in the darkness. A couple took shape. I slammed the door and kept going down the hall. The second door opened onto more beds and coats. I reached the third door just in time. As I slammed it behind me and pulled down my pants, several drops of blood hit the yellowing floor tiles. The relief made me sit down on the toilet seat hard.

Charlie was waiting in the hall when I emerged from the bathroom.

"Are you okay?"

I told him I was fine.

"You mean it wasn't the booze or a sudden case of the vapors that sent you running, just my company?"

"No. I'm sorry. I mean . . ."

"It was a joke." He hesitated for a moment. "I just wanted to make sure you were all right." He started to turn away.

Perhaps it was the euphoria of my escape, but the idea that anyone would worry if I was all right made me want to cry. "Thank you."

He stopped, turned back, and stood staring down at me. For the first time, I noticed his eyes. They were brown, nothing to write home about, but if you looked hard, you saw green lights going off like pinpricks of curiosity.

"I mean it," I said. "That was kind."

"Ouch. *Kind* is for Boy Scouts and maiden uncles."

"So think what happens when it comes in a different package."

I was flirting. I could not believe it. I had either a fierce drive for survival or no scruples at all.

He leaned his right shoulder against the wall. "If that's an invitation to stay, I accept."

I leaned my left shoulder against the wall, mirroring his stance. He was coming into focus now. He had the long lean look of a man who lopes through life carelessly. The look, I would learn, was a lie. His hair, like his eyes, was dark. It was also receding, leaving two half-moons of skin above his high forehead. Maybe that was why he still wore a mustache. Most of the men who had come home from the war with them had shaved them off by now. His face was long too, with sharp cheekbones and that thin-lipped ungenerous mouth.

The image of what he was seeing in return suddenly occurred to me. For weeks I had been walking around in an un-made-up face to reproach the world for the mess I had gotten myself in. But even as I stood worrying about my appearance, I looked back with pity on that girl who had worn her misery like a billboard, and with a shameful hard-hearted glee that I was no longer she.

He was talking again. Now I could follow what he was saying. He was asking if I wanted to get out of there and go somewhere quiet.

The idea was indecent. How could I go larking off with someone new when my heart sat in my chest like a piece of cracked china? But someone had put on the Billie Holiday record again, and I was tired of hearing what love could make me do.

His coat was in one bedroom, mine was in the other, with the writhing couple.

"I'm not sure I ought to go in there," I said. "When I opened the door before, I think I caught someone in flagrante delicto."

"Can some*one* be in flagrante delicto?" He asked me what my coat looked like.

"A camel polo."

"Right. There shouldn't be more than ten or twenty of those."

"Peck & Peck label," I said and immediately regretted it. The coat was the most expensive article of clothing I owned, and my relationship with it was as complicated as any I'd ever had with a man. The fabric was soft and beautifully cut, and I loved being inside it, but my mother had wheedled it out of Mr. Richardson as a going-away present for me.

"Ah, the rich girl," he said. "With apologies to F. Scott Fitzgerald."

I winced. He took it for bewilderment.

"'The Rich Boy.' It's a long short story by Scott Fitzgerald."

"I know what it is." I was wondering if it was too late to change my mind about leaving with him.

Before I could, he pushed open the door. "Coming through," he shouted and stepped inside. He was back in a minute with a polo coat in each hand. I took the longer one from his right hand. He hung the other on the doorknob, then helped me on with mine. We fought our way through the crowd in the living room and started down the stairs.

Outside, the rain had let up. The night was mild for January, but mist hung from the streetlights and steamed up from the pavement. Trees dripped overhead.

He had a long stride, and I had to stretch mine to keep up with him. When we reached Broadway, he took one hand from the pocket of his Navy-issue trench coat and closed his fingers around my arm to steer me across the street.

As we made our way south, signs flashing DRINKS, BREAKFAST LUNCH DINNER, CHEMISTS, and HARDWARE burned through the haze. Tires of cars speeding past sizzled on the wet pavement like cartoon electricity. When we reached the West End Bar, I expected him to turn in, but he kept going. Several blocks farther, he stopped in front of a plate-glass window with two neon blue cocktail glasses tilting toward each other.

He held the door for me, and as I went past him from the acrid exhaust-fumed street to the sour-smelling bar, I lingered for a split second in a fragrant patch of soap and aftershave. He was not my type, but in all fairness to him, he smelled good.

He began shouldering through the crowd, holding my hand to keep me close behind him. When he spotted a couple getting up from a booth in the back, he managed to guide me into it an instant before another group reached it.

"Nice maneuver," I said.

"You ain't seen nothing yet."

He asked what I wanted to drink. I told him bourbon and sat watching him make his way to the bar. There was nothing wrong with the way he moved. He even had a kind of loping on-the-balls-of-his-feet grace. But it wasn't Woody's swivel-hipped saunter, which had turned picketing for a good cause into an indecent exercise.

He returned carrying two glasses in one hand and a bowl of peanuts in the other, settled in across from me, and went through the business of fishing a pack of cigarettes from one pocket and a lighter from another. He cupped his hand over the flame as he held it to my cigarette, then his own, though there was no wind in the bar. I couldn't decide if it was a habit or a pretension. We inhaled, exhaled, and got down to the dicey business of discovering if we had made a mistake leaving the party together. His explanation of the Fitzgerald reference still rankled, in more ways than one. I did not like being patronized. And I was not what he thought.

We began with books, moved on to music, detoured into movies, edged a little closer to the personal. I asked him what he planned to do after graduation. I wasn't checking prospects, merely curious.

He said he was hoping for a job on a magazine.

"Writing?"

"Editing."

I told him I hoped to write, though he hadn't asked. Men never did. But I had to give him credit. He didn't laugh, or tell me I'd give up the idea once I was married and had children, or ask me if I had anything to say. The last was the worst, because I wasn't sure I did. Nonetheless, I was determined to find out.

We sidled into our pasts. I admit I did not play fair. I let him go on about enlisting in the Navy and serving on a destroyer escort in the North Atlantic. He didn't brag, far from it, but there was the attitude. All the vets had it, except the haunted ones who walked around with wounds you couldn't see on the surface. It wasn't arrogance, merely an air of being on intimate terms with the dark underbelly of humanity that was unknown to those who hadn't served, especially girls like me, or girls like the one he thought I was. The rest of the story brought him to Columbia on the G.I. Bill. He'd already had a year at City College when he enlisted. He raised the last piece of information like a red flag, and I knew he was thinking about the Peck & Peck label in my coat. He was telling me he was poor, because he thought I was rich. Only when he finished did I tell him that I was here on the G.I. Bill too.

"I don't understand," he said.

"You know, the G.I. Bill of Rights. It pays tuition and . . ."

He grinned. His mouth was ungenerous, but the smile was anything but stingy. It was wide and a little crooked, the way vulnerable smiles often are. "I know what it is. What I don't understand is how you're on it."

"This is going to come as a shock to you. Heaven knows the government tried to keep it a secret. The information about female vets being eligible was buried somewhere in the small print."

"You were in the service?"

"I wasn't exactly at the front. Unless you call a sweltering vermin-infested office on a sickeningly bigoted base in Alabama the front."

"You were a WAC?" I heard the incredulity in his voice. He was trying to put this new piece of information together with the Peck & Peck label.

"It was one way to get away from home," I explained, and didn't add that the idea had not been entirely my own. That was a secret I didn't give away so easily. Instead, I asked about his family.

"Dress British, think Yiddish is my motto." He was trying to get that out of the way as soon as possible too.

He went to the bar and returned with two fresh drinks.

"I knew I'd seen you around," he said as he slid back into the booth across from me, "and I just figured out where."

"It's a small campus."

"No, not around here. It was in midtown. The Republic Theatre. You were picketing *Birth of a Nation*."

"I didn't see you in the picket line."

"I wasn't there. I just happened to be walking by."

"Fifteen million Americans are second-class citizens, and you walk by?"

He held up both hands, palms toward me. "Mea culpa. I probably had a paper due or something."

"That's no excuse."

"You're right. Next time you picket, let me know, and I'll go with you."

"It's not funny."

"You've got a conscience like a G.I. asleep in a foxhole. Make the slightest noise and it comes out shooting."

"Tell me it's cute, and you're going to have a drink in your lap."

"Cute is one thing I would never call you."

I started to reach for my coat. "This wasn't a good idea."

He put his hand on my arm. "Actually, it was. But just for the record, I'm sorry about 'The Rich Boy' comment. It was patronizing."

"Oh, no, I love being lectured on the American canon."

"So I noticed."

"Was I that obvious?"

"Your face is an open book."

"And what's the story now?"

"The plot thickens. You're less angry at me than you were a few minutes ago, but you don't want to admit it. In fact, you're beginning to like me."

"You have to get over that excessive modesty."

"You're drawn to diffident men?"

I had to smile, finally. "No."

"I didn't think so."

We were still sparring, but something else was going on beneath. Not innuendo. It was more primitive than that. He reached across the table to stub out his cigarette, and his tweed jacket and shirt cuff pulled back from his wrist. I noticed the dusting of fine dark hair that curled around his leather watchband. Woody had been as smooth and hairless as a baby. I went on staring at his wrist. It struck me as grown-up; as more than grown-up, as virile.

He asked if I wanted another drink. I looked at my watch and reminded him of the dorm curfew.

"I thought you said you were a vet."

"There's no housing for women vets. All you men and your wives have taken it."

"Don't blame me. No wife in sight." He hesitated. "You could take an overnight. I have a room in a boardinghouse on a Hundred and Twenty-First Street."

The suggestion was impossible. I had just gotten my period. I had just gotten my period! I still could not believe my luck. Besides, I knew what he was thinking. A girl who had been in the service had been around. He was wrong about that. The officers who were shipping out had reeked of desperation. The ones who were staying behind were on vacation from their real lives. I had been careful to steer clear.

I told him I had to get back to the dorm and watched him take in the answer.

"Now you're the one with the telltale face," I said.

"You see heartbreak, right?"

"I see you-can't-blame-a-guy-for-trying."

Outside the bar, a new front had come through and the sky had cleared. He reached an arm around my shoulders. It seemed only civil to fit myself into the curve it made. Besides, a wind had come up, and the temperature had dropped.

In front of the dormitory, several couples clung together in the glare of the lights that were supposed to be as sex-repressing as the saltpeter rumored to be in the Women's Army Corps mess food, and were just as ineffective. He let go of my shoulders and turned to face me. We stood that way for a moment, only inches apart, as oblivious to the other couples as the couples were to us. I was waiting for what came next. He surprised me. With both hands, he opened his trench coat wide, as if he were holding a blanket, and wrapped it around me. I was engulfed.

He bent his face to mine. His tongue tasted of bourbon and peanuts. The flavor was not unpleasant, even secondhand. I could feel his erection through his flannel trousers and my coat and woolen skirt and girdle. Somewhere in the back of my mind, a question floated aimlessly. What kind of a girl starts the day in love with one man and ends it inside the coat of another?

Two

I THOUGHT I HAD learned my lesson with Woody, but I had learned nothing. If I wasn't careful, I would turn into my mother, who had bet her life on a string of unreliable men, starting with my father, who'd disappeared before I was born, though they had married. I hadn't taken her word for it but had gotten a copy of my birth certificate. I never told her that. Most kids keep secrets to protect themselves. I'd done my share of that, but I'd also kept them to protect her. It wasn't altruism, only self-interest. Distraught was my mother's natural state. I didn't want to push her over the line into despair.

Don't misunderstand me. She was not a terrible mother. Lying about my age and dressing me in clothes that were a few years too young for me to make her look younger was not a life-threatening crime. Parking me in movie theaters for hours at a time when Mr. Richardson or one of his predecessors came to visit was not even a scarring misdemeanor. Eventually it turned out to be a blessing, because once I was old enough to find my way around town, and after a man sat next to me in a movie and put a raincoat on his lap—I didn't know what he was doing, but I knew it wasn't pretty—I discovered that libraries were a safer haven. I might have been *de trop*—a phrase I learned from my reading—at home, but in the light-filled reading room of the Epiphany Branch Library, Jo March, Elizabeth Bennet, and Daisy Buchanan were always happy to see me.

And the one time my mother suspected I was in danger, she figured out a way to protect me. When I graduated from high school, she suggested that I enlist in the Women's Army Corps. The idea was timely and practical. I would be helping the war effort. I would be earning a living. And I would not be rattling around the apartment. She had seen the way Mr. Richardson, who paid for the apartment a stone's throw from Stuyvesant Square—thanks to him, we had moved up in the world—had begun to follow me with his eyes.

As it turned out, I was grateful to my mother for urging me to enlist. As long as I'd lived at home, I was a misfit in the world. My mother was not like other mothers. My father was nonexistent. In the Army, my parents did not matter. I stood or fell on my own. The experience had given me confidence. It had also given me, as I'd told Charlie, the G.I. Bill. Without it, and without those long afternoons in the library, I never would have gone to any college, let alone to one of the Seven Sisters. I still marveled at my good luck, despite the fact that Barnard had turned me back into a misfit.

I was different from the other girls, even from my roommate, Natalie, who was supposed to be my best friend. Secretly, I prided myself on the fact. It was partly my past—I was a couple of years older and had been in the service—but it was also my future. They had their lives mapped out. I had plenty of aspirations, but few plans. In late-night talks, their scrubbed faces, framed with freshly shampooed hair set in metal clips, glowed as they spoke of their prospective husbands, some already being reeled in, others still in the fantasy stage. Those men were sure to do well. I was more interested in finding someone who was going to do good, though I wasn't stupid enough to tell them that. They thought I was odd enough as it was, with my picketing and political passions and negro boyfriend.

Then there was the bartering. Those girls in their innocent cotton pajamas with embroidered monograms over their hearts were as crafty as the most seasoned seller in a Middle Eastern souk. A handful of sweatered breast for a fraternity pin. Bare flesh for a promise of marriage. Under-the-skirt privileges for a blue-white diamond on the third finger of the left hand. But I had neither the head nor the heart for haggling. I was reckless. That was what had gotten me in trouble with Woody. That was what would get me in trouble with Charlie. A month after that first night when I refused to go to his room, I went.

Like everything else having to do with sex, the forbidden climb to the fourth floor of his boardinghouse was riskier for me than for him. If we were caught, he might be evicted. I could be expelled. As I said, I was reckless.

I was also, in the weeks since I'd met Charlie, in a state. I was raw with sensation. In class or at the library, I could not sit still. My mind wandered, my senses throbbed. One night when Natalie went home for the weekend and I returned to the deserted room still aching from the thwarted pleasure of being with Charlie, I managed to gratify myself in the privacy of my narrow dormitory cot, but it was no good. I wanted the real thing. By the time I went to his room, nothing short of a natural disaster could have kept me away.

We were quick and furtive as cat burglars on the worn sloping stairs. By the time we reached his room, our breath was coming in gasps, partly from excitement, partly from the race up the steps. He opened the door, pushed me inside, and closed it behind us. We stood for a moment facing each other, just long enough for the potential disasters to begin going off in my head like fireworks. Expulsion. Pregnancy. Abandonment. Then he took a step toward me. I'd like to say that I met him halfway, but I have the feeling I went beyond that.

THE NEXT MORNING, we sat across from each other at a table in Bickford's, addled by physical proximity, bleary-eyed from lack of sleep, gulping orange juice and coffee and downing eggs and bacon and toast. Sex had made us ravenous. Black smudges underlined his

eyes; secret glee was smeared on his mouth like jam. I wanted to lick
it off.

Now and then, I glanced around at the other people in the eye-
achingly bright restaurant. Loners sat reading newspapers or staring
morosely into stacks of pancakes. Couples carried on desultory conversations. My swollen heart ached for the whole benighted bunch
of them. They knew nothing of joy. They were bereft of wonder.

Nonetheless, I was determined to be responsible. I had not been
irresponsible with Woody. If there was one thing you learned about
in the military, it was condoms. The women weren't bombarded
with booklets, films, and kits as the men were—we were expected to
be chaste; the men only had to be careful—but you couldn't possibly
live in that world without picking up some practical information.
Nonetheless, the terror of that false alarm still haunted me. A few
days after my first night with Charlie, who had been prepared, I
made an appointment with a woman doctor in the Village. I had
heard about her from another girl in the dorm, but unlike the other
girl, I did not buy a dime store wedding band for my appointment.
Even while I was acting responsibly, I could not stop thumbing my
nose.

When I left the doctor's office, I went straight to the library. At
that time of day Charlie would be in his usual carrel. He was so en-
grossed in his book that he didn't notice me until I was standing
beside him. Then he looked up.

"I bought you a present," I said and put the brown-paper-
wrapped package down on the desk. "But I wouldn't open it here if
I were you." My grin gave me away.

We made it from the library to his room in record time.

WE DID NOT always court danger in the rooming house. One weekend, an old Navy buddy lent Charlie his car and a shack on a lake in
Connecticut. Nobody would have called the place romantic. Early

Miss Havisham, we agreed, was a more accurate description. But the lake came almost to the door, and no other houses were in sight. On Friday night, we made a terrible racket on the springs of the old iron bed. On Saturday morning, we went skinny-dipping in a lake so icy it sent us back to bed to warm each other beneath the musty blankets.

Twice more that spring, when he was feeling flush, we went away. The first time, we checked into the Marlton hotel on West Eighth Street on a Saturday afternoon and lived on room service and each other until checkout time on Sunday. That was the weekend of our perplexing conversation.

We were sitting up in bed with the room service tray between us. A striped tie hung down his bare chest. I was wearing my imitation pearls, matching earrings, and nothing else. We had decided to dress for dinner.

"Am I your current cause?" he asked as he poured the bottle of wine he'd brought because it would be cheaper than room service.

"What do you mean?"

"The first time I saw you, you were picketing with the NAACP."

I thought about that for a moment. By then I had picked up a few words from him.

"I could ask you the same question. Am I your forbidden fruit? Your shiksa?"

We laughed and let it go, but I wondered if he was worried that he was a passing phase or if I should worry that I was.

A few weeks later, we ended up in the honeymoon suite of the Waldorf-Astoria Hotel. The incident wasn't as sexy as it sounds, though it was romantic, at least for me.

The National Council of the Arts, Sciences, and Professions had organized a conference to promote peace, goodwill, and understanding between Western artists and intellectuals and their counterparts from the Soviet Union and Eastern Bloc countries. In the years to come, meetings like that would multiply like rabbits, but this was the first I attended.

Charlie's thesis adviser, who was a founding member of a group called Americans for Intellectual Freedom, had come down with the flu and asked Charlie to deliver some papers to one of the organizers of the conference. Charlie asked if I wanted to go along. He grinned when he invited me because he knew wild horses couldn't have kept me away.

We took the subway to Fiftieth Street and made our way east through the sooty slush. Above us, skyscrapers pierced the low battleship-gray sky. When we reached Park Avenue, I noticed a crowd outside the hotel entrance on the far side of the street. At first I thought it was the crush of delegates waiting to get in. Then I spotted the signs people were carrying. As we got closer, I made out the words on them.

COMMUNISM IS THE DEVIL'S WORK

DOWN WITH THE GODLESS U.S.S.R

SATAN LIVES AT THE WALDORF-ASTORIA

The men carrying the signs wore dark overcoats, well-brushed hats, and grim expressions; the women were equally well dressed and even more dour. As they circled in front of the entrance, their galoshes crunched on the salt the hotel had spread to keep guests from slipping.

To get to the revolving door, we had to walk a gauntlet of kneeling nuns in black habits praying for our souls. I couldn't help thinking of the salt grinding into their knees.

The lobby was all sinuous art deco swirl and opulent smooth surfaces. I had been inside the hotel twice before. The first time was when my mother persuaded Mr. Richardson to take us to tea the day before I was inducted into the WACs; the second was the previous

year, when the college newspaper had sent me to cover a press conference to introduce the new long-playing records. Now, workmen
rushed back and forth, carrying flowers, lugging chairs, and checking microphones. We crossed to the front desk, and Charlie asked
for Mr. Sidney Hook's room.

"Ten forty-two," the clerk said. "The honeymoon suite."

"If I'd known we were going to the honeymoon suite," I whispered as the elevator glided upward, "I would have come prepared."

Charlie rang the bell to the suite. A man wearing a hat answered
it. Behind him, the room was so dense with smoke that it might have
been on fire. A dozen or so men and women were talking into telephones. The lines lay tangled on the pale blue carpet like a nest of
snakes. Other men and women were arguing and barking orders.
Overflowing ashtrays and plates of half-eaten hamburgers, club
sandwiches, and steaks littered every surface, their metal covers scat-
tered on tables, chairs, and the floor. Beyond the open door to a
bathroom, a girl was standing over a mimeograph machine. Another
girl sat on a closed toilet seat taking dictation from a man perched
on the sink. I recognized a few of the faces. Mary McCarthy was
typing furiously. Elizabeth Hardwick was talking into a phone. Robert Lowell sat in the middle of the chaos, sipping a drink and looking
as if he was in another world.

While Charlie made his way to the bedroom to find Mr. Hook, I
stood in the midst of the pandemonium, spellbound. I was so transfixed that it didn't occur to me to wonder who was ponying up the
money for the honeymoon suite at a plush hotel, the multitude of
phones, the mimeograph machine, and all that room service. All I
knew was that this was where I was meant to be. And one more
thing: Charlie had brought me here. I was still young enough to believe that people fell in love for shared interests, common principles,
and other logical rationalizations. I hadn't an inkling of the more
primitive needs that drove them together. I'm not talking about sex,

though of course that was part of it. I mean the hungers our pasts hollow out of our souls.

IN THE WEEKS following our visit to the Waldorf, I found myself thinking about the conversation we'd had the weekend we'd checked into that other shabbier hotel, when Charlie had asked if he was my current cause, and I'd wondered if I was his rebellion. I still couldn't figure out if he was worried or if I ought to be. The fear that I might turn out to be as bad a judge of character as my mother haunted me. Then, a week before his graduation, we had another conversation, and I knew.

He had found an inexpensive boardinghouse on the East End of Long Island. On Saturday morning, we took a train from Pennsylvania Station, and when it came to the end of the line, we got off and walked the few blocks to the house. Even before we climbed to the room, wallpapered with oversize cabbage roses and cluttered with crocheted doilies, seashells, and china cats, I knew something was not quite right between us. He had been uncharacteristically silent on the train. The less he had said, the more I had chattered. Our timing was off. Even in bed.

Things did not improve at dinner. He insisted we have lobster. I wanted to tell him to stop trying so hard. When the waitress tied the paper bib around my neck, I felt foolish. When I cracked a claw and got lobster juice all over my good linen dress, I was despondent. I told myself it was only a stain, but as I dipped my napkin in my water glass and rubbed, I knew the spot would never come out.

After the waitress took away our plates, the bowl of shells, and our crumpled bibs, he leaned back in his chair, looked at me, then glanced away. The word *shifty* came to mind. It reminded me of the way Mr. Richardson and his predecessors used to say goodbye to my mother. Something about getting ready to walk out the door made them unable to meet her eye.

"I didn't say anything, because I wasn't sure until a few days ago," he began.

I stared at the stain on my dress and knew he was leaving.

"But now it's set. I have a job at *Compass*." He was still staring somewhere over my shoulder. "They got a grant to go from a quarterly to a monthly. That's why they can hire me." He met my eyes finally. "It was a close call. I was sure I was going to end up toiling for the greater glory of *Cattleman's Monthly*."

"*Cattleman's Monthly?*"

"A trade magazine, as if you couldn't guess. I would have had to cover auctions on horseback."

"Can you ride?"

"How many Jewish cowboys do you know?" He tried a smile, but it didn't quite come off; then he looked past my shoulder again.

"The problem is *Cattleman's Monthly* pays better than *Compass*. Hell, just about everything pays better than *Compass*, except maybe sanitation work. Come to think of it, that probably pays better too. Garbagemen have a union." He dragged his eyes back to me. "What I'm trying to say is I won't be making much money. We'll never be rich, but we won't starve."

Perhaps I was not such a bad judge of character after all.

A YEAR LATER, on a clement June afternoon three days after I had graduated, when a cloudless blue sky stretched over us and the air was as soft as down—surely those were omens—we took the subway to the city clerk's office. I wore a white linen suit and a straw hat with a wide floppy brim. Charlie had a white carnation in his lapel. His parents stood behind us, looking slightly embarrassed, as if they should have been able to muster more of a crowd for the occasion. My mother cried.

THE MARRIAGE WAS not supposed to work. Mixed marriages never do, or so people said. In the heat of anger, one partner always turns on the other with accusations of running true to type. But neither of us was a believer, and we did not have to worry about family. My mother had gone to church only when the current man in her life was spending Sunday with his family. Charlie's parents were not religious. They had met at a socialist rally in Budapest, running fast and hard from their own devoutly observant parents, come to America, and never looked back. The Nazi attempt to purify Europe that had begun three decades later and wiped out the relatives they'd left behind did nothing to reignite their faith. The only thing that mattered was that Charlie marry and begin having children. They were less concerned, he teased me after he took me home to meet them, about my religious affiliation than about my narrow hips.

"They may not mind, but what about you?" my roommate, Natalie, had asked. "How are you going to feel walking around with a Jewish name?"

"Nell?" I asked.

"Very funny. Look, I'm not prejudiced—"

"Of course not."

"—but it'll make a difference."

"Being married to Charlie? I should say so."

"I suppose you know you're his passport."

"To what?"

"Becoming a real American."

"Charlie was born here."

"You know what I mean."

I did, but I wasn't going to argue with her.

"I just don't want to see you make a mistake," she said.

The statement was not entirely accurate. Natalie was known as a sympathetic ear for girls with romantic, academic, or parental problems. In other words, she thrived on other people's miseries.

CHARLIE AND I found a quirky one-bedroom apartment in a brownstone on West Eighty-Ninth Street. The climb to the fifth floor left us breathless, and when we were in the kitchen at the same time, we could not help bumping into each other. But the bedroom, which had once been a greenhouse, was made entirely of small panes of glass. We lay in bed at night watching clouds snag on the moon, and snow fall silent as sleep, and planes glide through the stars on their way to and from Idlewild Airport. On fine mornings, the sun pried open our eyes. When it was stormy, rain pounded the glass. It was like making love inside a waterfall. When I padded into the kitchen to make coffee, I wore Charlie's bathrobe or sometimes the shirt he had taken off the night before. He had five inches and forty pounds on me, but his clothes fit me like a glove.

I got a job as a secretary in a publishing house for forty-five dollars a week, the occasional pilfered book, and the chance to write reader's reports on manuscripts from the slush pile. I thought I was lucky they let me do it. Charlie got books at the magazine, too, and sometimes tickets to plays. There were author parties at the publishing house and celebrations at the magazine where we plucked martinis and manhattans from the trays of circling waiters, made dinners of angels on horseback and pigs in blankets, and afterward climbed home to our apartment clutching each other, to tumble into bed and make raucous love as our own private moon swooned overhead.

Each morning we took the subway to our offices together, and sometimes, when Charlie wasn't working late, we met at the Forty-Second Street station and went home together in the evening. As I sat beside him, shoulder to shoulder, hip to hip, thigh to thigh, our good fortune frightened me. Around us headlines screamed of war in Korea, upheaval in Africa, and injustice and malfeasance at home, all of it unraveling in the long shadow of total nuclear annihilation. Two months after we'd married, the Russians had successfully exploded their own atomic bomb. Diplomats lurched from crisis to crisis. Armies stood ready to match devastation for devastation. Even our little cerebral corner of the universe was rent by warring factions. Communist-front organizations spread propaganda in the guise of information. The CIA, the State Department, and other less official groups put out their own versions of the truth. Plots hatched and conspiracies simmered. Books were banned from American libraries overseas, sales of suspect writers like Faulkner, John Steinbeck, and Richard Wright were subverted, and reputations were destroyed. It was called the Cold War, and as in any war, both sides played dirty. Surely, Charlie and I had no right to be so happy in the middle of it.

I do not mean to make us sound like fugitives from one of those sunny television sitcoms. Charlie was no Ozzie, and I was no Harriet. We did not embody the zeitgeist of Togetherness as touted in *McCall's* and *Ladies' Home Journal*. We were two strong-minded articulate people, of different sexes to boot, living cheek by jowl. We found plenty to fight about. Here is a partial list of recurring arguments from those early years together. Toilet seats; old girlfriends— or rather his unwillingness to talk about them; his refusal to straighten the mess on his desk; my straightening the mess on his desk; my irresponsibility in putting his Irish fisherman's sweater in the washing machine so it came out fitting me; his failed attempt to fix the toaster, which wasn't broken in the first place, you just had to know how to use it; Frank Tucker; Tintoretto; my erratic coffee; his refusal to make the coffee; Henry James's sentences; the starch I could not keep the laundry from putting in his shirts; my Manichaean view of the world; his willingness to see a silver lining where there was only smoke and mirrors.

Let me give you an example of the last. One morning on the subway, I called his attention to an article on the front page of the paper. A photograph showed a crowd of citizens, eyes bulging, mouths howling, faces deformed by rage. They were heckling and harassing a negro family who had managed to rent an apartment in a white neighborhood of Cicero, Illinois.

"What kind of a country do we live in?" I demanded.

He went on reading over my shoulder. "One where the governor of the state called out the National Guard to stop the rioting. How many places in the world do you think that would happen?"

Charlie's patriotism always surprised me. It was the chink in his armor of cynicism.

And sometimes we quarreled for no reason at all, or maybe only because we were uneasy in our unexpected happiness. It was my twist on my mother's favorite warning that if I sang before breakfast, I'd be sure to end up crying before supper.

Three

ABOUT THE TIME Charlie went to work for *Compass*, a year before our marriage, the magazine moved from Greenwich Village to a building on the corner of Broadway and Forty-Third Street. The location was louche for a magazine of culture, ideas, and politics, and the office was down-at-the-heels, but the grant that enabled it to go from a quarterly to a monthly, and to hire Charlie, came from the Drinkwater Foundation, and the Drinkwater family owned the building. Charlie insisted that he didn't mind the location. Every time he looked out the window at the hustlers and sailors and tourists elbowing their way beneath the conflagration of neon signs howling KINSEY BLENDED WHISKEY, MAKE MINE RUPPERT, and AUTO-MAT, he thought again how lucky he was to be there and not riding on horseback in the Chicago stockyards.

He was working with writers whose names were sacred, at least to us, writers who had shaped our minds and our taste. And he was discovering new writers, or at least one new writer. About eight months after he began working there, as he was slogging through the slush pile, he came across a short story by a young man who worked as an auto mechanic in Maine. The story was a gem and made up for all the overheated prose and unintelligible poetry he'd had to wade through since he'd started at *Compass*. The discovery made him feel, he said, like a real editor. He also commissioned Frank Tucker, an old friend from his Columbia days, to write a piece on the suppos-edly bloodless communist coup in Czechoslovakia.

When he stayed past midnight, or one, or two, to put the maga-zine to bed, he came home drunk on a blend of exhaustion, accom-plishment, and the scotch or bourbon the staff broke out to celebrate. When the magazine arrived from the printer with the heady, inky hot-off-the-press smell, he'd bring home a copy and hand it to me as reverently as if it were a first edition of Joyce or Eliot.

He even liked the motley staff: Gus, the managing editor, who was too polite and bookish to hound any of them about deadlines, though that was his job; Wally, who wore big round black-rimmed glasses and a floppy hat, and invariably began spouting long unintel-ligible passages of *Finnegans Wake* halfway through his third mar-tini; Sonia, the secretary, who had a magna cum laude degree from Vassar, an aversion to using uppercase letters because, she explained, this was an avant-garde magazine, and a body that looked as if it had stepped off the nose of a B-29 bomber. Charlie didn't tell me that, his old friend from Columbia, Frank Tucker, did. He did not even mind Belle, the dour copy editor whose sole pleasure in life was pointing out other people's mistakes. But most of all, he liked and admired Gideon Abel.

Abel, a big, rawboned man with a mane of white hair, had founded *Compass* before the war, though it was a different magazine in those days, and not merely because it came out only four times a year. Abel had never actually joined the Communist Party, but in the twenties and thirties, he'd been among the most vocal and ardent fellow travelers who toed the party line. These days he was a virulent left-wing anti-Stalinist. The conversion, or perhaps evolution, was not unusual. Many people had traveled the same bumpy road to dis-illusionment. Even Charlie and I had, though I had been a kid, and no one had taken me seriously, or at least not as seriously as I'd taken myself. I had dreamed of a better world, been heartbroken at the Hitler-Stalin pact, and forgiven all when the Soviet Union became our ally against Nazi Germany. Only after the war did we, and Gideon Abel, and so many like us, begin to realize that the totalitarianism of the left was not so far from that of the right. All isms seemed to end in murder.

Abel's conversion, however, had been especially precipitous. Some saw it as an indication of his open-mindedness, others as proof that he was a frivolous gadfly. The fact that he was on his fourth wife, or third, depending on how you counted, because the fourth had also been the second, did not make him appear any more steadfast. He was also rumored to have had affairs with Mary McCarthy, Dawn Powell, and Jean Stafford, among others. In literary and intellectual circles, adultery was not only rampant, it was incestuous. A few years later, when I began doing research on Richard Wright for a series of articles, I would discover that while Wright was compulsively unfaithful, his wife, Ellen, was having an affair with Nelson Algren, who was having an affair with Ellen's friend Simone de Beauvoir, who had an ongoing relationship with Jean-Paul Sartre, who was having affairs with most of his students.

Sometimes political allegiances upped the sexual ante. One of the women Wright was sleeping with frequently went to bed with a man who Wright was sure was spying on him for the CIA. I don't suppose our friends and acquaintances were much different, though if there were CIA operatives among us, I wasn't aware of them. Casual infidelity and literary feuds were the two favorite pastimes. Those who didn't take their adultery lightly got into even more trouble. The unfaithful spouse invariably insisted on dignifying the affair by running off with the new lover. Recriminations, divorces, and bitter custody battles followed like the tin cans and old shoes tied to the bumpers of less intellectual newlyweds.

According to Charlie, when Gideon Abel invited men to his parties, he said, "Bring a pretty girl." Occasionally, he varied the invitation. "Bring a leggy girl," he might say. One afternoon, about six months after we were married, Gideon told Charlie to "bring that pretty, leggy girl you're married to." I said Gideon had probably forgotten my name, but I was pleased. I was vain about my legs. Girls without breasts frequently are. I also knew the way the world worked. At Gideon Abel's parties, girls were window dressing. Men talked; girls listened. Men quipped; girls laughed. Men flirted; girls were flattered. Men made passes; girls made decisions to or not to go along. I wasn't complaining. I was determined to fight injustice, but I knew I couldn't change human nature.

There was another aspect of Gideon's parties I was under no illusion about. They weren't as dazzling as people imagined. Jokes flew. Wit sparked. Intellects sparred. But at all the parties I went to over the years, I don't think I ever heard a truly original thought. Those who had one saved it for a book or magazine piece.

Let me make one thing clear before I tell the story of what happened the night Gideon told Charlie to bring that pretty, leggy girl he was married to. I was not shocked or outraged or even terribly surprised. I wasn't a child. I knew what went on at those parties. From this vantage point, I can even see the humorous or at least the ludicrous side of it. The only troubling aspect was that I couldn't tell Charlie.

I should not have gone to the party in the first place. My throat was scratchy, my eyes burned, and I probably had a low-grade fever. The sensible thing would have been to call Charlie at his office and tell him to go to Gideon's without me, especially since a flurry of big wet snowflakes had begun to fall as I'd walked home from the subway. But the point of Gideon Abel's parties was not to be sensible. Clever, amusing, provocative, flirtatious, but never sensible. So instead of getting into an old flannel shirt of Charlie's that I'd appropriated and crawling into bed, I put on the new black jersey dress that Charlie loved—body-hugging sheaths were beginning to give the crinoline-stiffened skirts of the New Look a run for the money—and my second-best pumps—I was sensible enough not to want to

ruin my best pair, but not wise enough to put galoshes over them—
and headed crosstown.

Gideon's parties took place in his Park Avenue duplex, which
floated above the city like the elusive dream that sucked the hopeful
and adventurous out of every corner of the country and kept natives
like us in place. It belonged to his second and fourth wife, who was
heir to one of those improbable American fortunes built on an in-
vention so simple that anyone could have dreamed it up, but only her
grandfather had. By the time I arrived, the apartment was crowded,
and my throat felt as if someone had gone over it with sandpaper. I
gave my coat to the maid who opened the door and started for the
living room. Frank Tucker intercepted me, held out a martini with
one hand, and cupped my behind with the other. I took the drink
and pushed his other hand away.

"If you don't want the merchandise touched," he said, "don't put
it on display."

There was something wrong with his logic, but the room was too
crowded and I felt too awful to sort it out. I took a hefty swallow of
the drink and, balancing it carefully, threaded my way through the
crowd to Charlie. I could feel the gin beginning to work as I did,
soothing my throat, putting out the fire behind my eyes, kneading
the aches in my body. I joined Charlie and his group, pasted a look
on my face that said I was following every word of the conversation,
finished my drink, and snared another from a passing tray. A poet
was telling a story I'd heard before—it occurred to me that I'd heard
a lot of the stories before—about two men at another party who
were complaining about their former wives, only to discover that
their former wives were the same woman. It was a good story, but I
suspected it was apocryphal. People tended to keep track of the marriages and even the affairs of their former spouses.

Within twenty minutes I was drunk. That's why I blame myself
for what happened. Not, as I said, that anything did happen. No

marriage splintered, no friendship came undone, no drink or punch was thrown, all of which had been known to occur, more than once, at Gideon's parties.

Halfway through my third martini, I decided that a nap upstairs in one of the guest rooms was the best course of action. I did not pass out. I even remembered to slip off my shoes before I stretched out on the bedspread. The room swam for a moment. I closed my eyes. The world went quiet.

At first I didn't know what had awakened me. Gradually, I realized someone was talking. I couldn't make out the words. I couldn't even recognize the voice, though it seemed vaguely familiar. Slowly the words began to filter through. Something about my mouth. The voice was whispering that I should put something in my mouth.

Dreamily, my lips began to part. I swam up from sleep and opened my eyes.

Frank Tucker was standing beside the bed, holding his penis in his hand. It dangled over my face, red, reptilian, and menacing.

"Open your mouth," he whispered.

I did as I was told and let out a scream. He dropped his penis and clamped his hand over my mouth. It was clammy with sweat and smelled sour.

"For Christ's sake, Nell."

I pried his hand off my mouth and rolled away from him.

He stood looking down at me for a moment. Then he put his penis back in his trousers, zipped his fly, and rearranged his face in a smirk.

"Ain't it something? One look at my cock, and you gals start howling with delight."

He laughed at his wit and was gone.

I sat up and swung my feet over the side of the bed. The worst part of it was that I had screamed. A simple no would have done the trick. I went on sitting on the side of the bed, trying to sort it out. The more I thought about it, the more foolish I appeared. Frank

Tucker had only been behaving according to type. I had clearly over-reacted.

"You disappeared."

I looked up. Charlie was standing in the doorway.

He took a step into the room. "Are you okay?"

No, I am not okay. Your good friend Frank Tucker just tried to stick his cock in my mouth.

The words would leave him no choice. You couldn't let another man, even a friend—especially a friend—go around forcing your wife into fellatio. You had to call him on it, one way or another. And that would be only the beginning. Word would spread. The story would get better with each telling. I had lured Frank up here, then changed my mind. I hadn't changed my mind, but someone had walked in, so I had pretended he was forcing himself on me. If things got really out of hand, someone might use the word *rape,* though the idea of being raped by a friend in a Park Avenue duplex was stretch-ing it. My imagination spun out the stories, but, even drunk, I knew one thing for sure. Whatever happened, it would not only cause a rift between Charlie and Frank and their various friends, who would have to take sides; it would also end up being my fault. What's all the fuss about? people would snicker. Everyone makes passes. That's what these parties are about. Why else does Gideon say to bring a pretty girl? And the pretty girls say either thanks, I'd like to, or no thanks, I'm not interested. Any schoolgirl knows the drill.

Charlie was still standing there waiting for me to answer the question.

"It's just this damn cold," I said. "Can we go home?"

I SWORE I was not going to tell Charlie about the incident, and I never did, but it must have weighed on my conscience, because I found myself constantly bringing up the subject of infidelity with him. I'd start discussing a new book and end up speculating whether the gossip about the author's hectic sex life was true. I began describing an art opening Sonia, the secretary, had persuaded me to attend with her, and got sidetracked into an anecdote about how she had gone home from it with an artist, whom she'd assumed was separated—how else could he invite her back to his apartment?—only to find that his wife was in the hospital delivering their first child. I confessed that an assistant editor in my office had asked me to say we'd had lunch together when we hadn't. Everywhere I turned, illicit sex was on the rampage. Once, I asked Charlie if he felt he was missing something.

"What makes you think I am?"

"Very funny," I said and let it go. If I pressed him, he'd only keep teasing me.

Another night, he put on an old Artie Shaw record after dinner and held out his arms, and I stood and stepped into them. We did that sometimes, went dancing in our small living room. He guided me around the floor, avoiding the furniture, turning one way, swirling the other. He spun me out and brought me back against him.

"Come here often?" I vamped in his ear.

"Only when I can get away from the little woman," he said and dipped me so low my head spun.

But despite his teasing and the world we inhabited, I trusted him. I'm not suggesting he wasn't human. I was willing to bet that when Sonia leaned over his desk, his body responded. He'd told me about what he called the Sonia effect. All she had to do was look up at a man and he checked his fly. But if Charlie's body reacted, I was pretty sure his mind resisted. Not because of me, but because of him.

Some men thrive on worrying about lipstick on their collars, explaining wet hair from an ill-timed shower, and playing footsie with a woman across the table while a wife sits nearby. Some enjoy the flirtation with disaster as much as the flirtation. But Charlie was not one of them. He wanted no more chaos in his life.

Sex was too close to death for him to play around with it. I'm not talking about Freud's eros and thanatos. I'm talking about something more personal. Before the war, when he was younger, sex had been simple. But since the war, and since he had found out about that large family he had never known and now never would, sex was all mixed up with mortality and survival and guilt, always guilt. Not before or during the act—then the physical impulses took over and the mind bowed out—but after. His body spent, his defenses down, he was easy prey for all those dead relatives. They swarmed around us as we lay in our sex-rumpled bed, not blaming him exactly, merely reminding him that he was here, and they were not, and the business of living might be fragile and meaningless, but it was not trivial. And it was not unrelated to honor.

I don't know how I knew that about Charlie, but I did. It was one thing I did not turn out to be wrong about.

Four

GIDEON ABEL HAD grown up on the Lower East Side of Manhattan, the son of Jewish immigrants from somewhere in that uneasy stretch of Eastern Europe that was always passing from Russia to Poland and back again. Nonetheless, or perhaps because of it, he had social as well as intellectual ambitions. He wanted to be not only a brilliant publisher but a gentleman publisher. To that end, he was an intentionally terrible businessman. It wasn't merely that *Compass* lost money every year. All little magazines lose money. That was what the Drinkwater Foundation was for, to make up the shortfall. But Gideon did not believe in contracts. Surely a handshake after lunch or a slap on the shoulder at a party was sufficient. Surely gentlemen, and the occasional lady, could be counted on to honor agreements. Some said the stance was an affectation, others that it was a holdover from the tribal allegiances of the Lower East Side, which his social conscience and success hadn't managed to stamp out completely. Whatever the origins, the repercussions could be dicey. The individuals who shook hands after those alcohol-fueled lunches and parties often remembered the matter they were shaking hands on differently. Lawsuits were not unusual. Gideon called them the cost of putting out a great magazine. Elliot McClellan, who ran the Drinkwater Foundation, called them irresponsible.

One day after lunch, Gideon sauntered into Charlie's office, sank into a chair, draped one gray flannel leg over the arm, and told Charlie he had just come from our friend McClellan. Our friend McClellan was the way Gideon always referred to him. Most publishers in Gideon's position would have been grateful for not having to worry about money, but Gideon could not muster gratitude because he had never worried about money.

He chatted about articles they had assigned, pieces they might assign, various writers, and a play he had seen the night before. Then he unwound himself from the chair, stood, and when he reached the door turned back to Charlie.

"Our friend McClellan says we have to start signing contracts. I know I can count on you to take care of it." He sauntered out as casually as he had sauntered in.

"Is that a promotion?" I asked Charlie when he told me about the incident that night.

"Surely you jest. My office just happens to be the first one he passes on his way back from lunch."

It was a nice try, but I was pretty sure it wasn't true—I don't mean the geography—and I knew Charlie didn't think so either. I suppose that was why he tried to sound cavalier when he came home several weeks later and mentioned that Elliot McClellan had called to invite him to lunch. That was something else I knew about Charlie. He wasn't superstitious. He knew the evil eye was a primitive concept. But that didn't stop him from trying to elude its gaze.

THIS IS WHAT Charlie told me about his lunch with Elliot McClellan as we sat in La Cave Henri IV, where we went to celebrate that night. I'm not suggesting that my memory is infallible. All you have to do is listen to two people recount the same incident to know that no one's is. But I'm not forgetting part of the story. I know now that Charlie never told it to me.

They met at McClellan's club in midtown.

"I couldn't get in the door." Charlie took a sip of his martini and grinned. He could not stop grinning that night. His smile lit up the shadowy corner banquette. We were possessive of the restaurant and that corner of it. I had turned twenty-three, twenty-four, and twenty-five there; Charlie twenty-six, twenty-seven, and twenty-eight; and we had celebrated all three anniversaries over the flickering candles on the red-and-white-checked tablecloth. The waiters always welcomed us like prodigal children and on the birthdays and anniversaries put a thin colored candle in the bread pudding, Charlie's favorite dessert.

"I mean that literally," he went on. "The building has double front doors. Any other place in town, any other place in the country, you see a pair of double doors, you open the right one, right? At this place, only the left side opens. So even before I was inside, I was feeling a bit, shall we say unwelcome, standing there rattling the knob and trying to push it open with my shoulder. Then someone came past and sailed through the door on the left."

I laughed, though I knew that no matter how he told the story, it wasn't a joke to him. And it could only have gotten worse after he went through the recalcitrant door into that imposing Italian Renaissance building. I had never been inside—women were not permitted—but I passed it often. His standing as an outsider in the old boys' club, a Jew in a Gentile world, would have hit him like a punch to the gut.

But there was another side to my sweet ambivalent Charlie, and I knew that too. Where else in the world, he would have been thinking, could someone like him walk into a club like that, even through the wrong door?

McClellan was waiting for him in the lobby. I had met Elliot McClellan a few times at Gideon's parties, and I could picture him standing in that sea of gray flannel, blue serge, and muted tweed. There would not have been a pair of high heels or nylons in sight, and that was the way the members wanted it. McClellan had the compact body of an athlete, blue eyes the color of a well-washed work shirt—a garment I was sure he had never worn—and a habit of continually pushing back the shock of light brown hair that kept falling over his forehead. The gesture would have been effeminate if he hadn't used the heel of his hand to do it. His features were regular, perhaps too regular. Whenever I saw him, I found myself searching for quirks and flaws. He wasn't tall, and that probably bothered him, but women didn't seem to mind. It wasn't just the regular features that came together handsomely, it was the inaudible hum he gave off, like an insect's mating call that is perceptible only to females of the species. My mother, with her determination to let no cliché go unspoken, would have said about him that still waters run deep. I didn't know how deep they ran, but I did know that the erotic undercurrent in McClellan's quiet gravitas was more disarming than all Frank Tucker's sexual blitzes. That, however, was a woman's point of view, and I had a feeling that McClellan considered himself a man's man. During the war, he had parachuted into France several times, though when anybody mentioned it, he always insisted he'd never been in any real danger. I couldn't decide whether he was an inveterate cynic or a true believer. Of course, you have to believe in something to be sufficiently disillusioned to become a cynic.

According to Charlie, they went up a flight of stairs to a dark paneled room with a fire going at one end and more Hudson River School paintings than he had ever seen outside a museum, as well as a Winslow Homer.

"It was hanging right over McClellan's head, and I couldn't take my eyes off it the whole time we were having drinks." He shook his head and grinned again.

I asked him what they talked about while they swilled martinis and he stared at a Winslow Homer.

"Me."

"A topic of infinite variety and interest."

"It was the damnedest thing. He kept asking me questions, but I couldn't get over the feeling that he already knew the answers. He had it all on wires, my year at City College before the war, the stint at Columbia after. He said my commanding officer was a friend of his father's."

"What's so strange about that? They're both part of the old boys' club."

"Sure, but I hadn't mentioned the ship I was on."

"So even before he popped the question you knew what was coming from all the homework he'd done."

"Pretty much. He knew about my parents leaving Budapest and what happened to the rest of the family. He even knew about the one cousin who's still there, though as he put it, he might as well not be, because living under Uncle Joe Stalin's boot is as good as being dead."

He stopped for a moment, and the grin slid from his face. I knew what he was thinking. McClellan had no right to invoke the memory of grandparents, aunts, uncles, and cousins whom Charlie himself had never known, any more than Charlie had a right to be sitting there, safe as houses, eating steak, drinking merlot, and going on with the charmed life he was sure he did not deserve.

Then, as the waiter took away their empty plates and brought coffee, McClellan got to the point. Gideon Abel was leaving the magazine.

"I still can't believe it," I said.

"Exactly. Gideon *is* the magazine. You know his joke about retiring. On the last day of his life, he plans to edit one long piece, then slump forward over his desk gracefully, red pencil in hand."

"Is the foundation forcing him out?"

"That was my first thought, but McClellan says no. According to him, Gideon wants to leave. He says the foundation has turned *Compass* into a business, and he might as well be manufacturing widgets. He hates having to keep books. He thinks contracts are an insult to everyone involved. McClellan says he actually misses the lawsuits."

I didn't doubt it. Gideon thrived on drama.

"McClellan thinks he wants to start another magazine. A quarterly where he can say anything he wants, and it won't matter because only twelve people in the country will read it, was the way he put it."

"And you stood up for Gideon and insisted he was a great man who had founded one of the most influential magazines of his time."

"You know me like a book."

"What did McClellan say to that?"

"That the foundation wanted the magazine to go on being influential. That was why they were asking me to take over."

Something was bothering me, but I was having trouble putting my finger on it through the haze of euphoria, gin, and wine. Then it came into focus.

"There's only one thing," I said.

"What's that?"

"McClellan's line about Gideon's wanting to be able to publish anything he wants. Does that mean the foundation has been censoring him? More to the point, that it plans to dictate what you can and can't publish?"

"I told you. They already know every left-wing organization I ever joined, every angry letter to the editor I ever wrote, every May Day parade I ever marched in."

"I thought there was only one."

"You know what I mean. According to him, that's the point. He says the woods are full of right-wing journals howling about the red menace. What the country needs, what the foundation wants to back, is an intelligent liberal—emphasis on *liberal*—anti-Soviet take on issues. Or to put it another way, who better to fight communists than former communists and the fellow travelers who marched along with them?"

"What if you want to run something critical of the government?"

I wasn't trying to ruin his evening. I wasn't even playing devil's advocate. I just didn't want this to come back and bite him somewhere down the road.

"I can publish excerpts from *Das Kapital,* assuming I want to cut the subscription base in my first few months on the job. The foundation money comes with no strings attached." He leaned back against the banquette and shook his head at me. "You're so busy worrying about my editorial integrity that you haven't asked the big question."

"Which is?"

"How much filthy lucre they're going to shower on me."

"How much?"

"Twelve thousand smackers a year." He was grinning again.

I smiled back at him through the candlelight. "And that evening at dinner in Montauk you told me we'd never be rich."

I CAN'T BE sure. It could have happened the night before, or the Saturday morning after, because those were heady times, but I used to like to think that the night of the celebratory dinner at La Cave Henri IV, in the wake of Charlie's lunch with Elliot McClellan, under a sliver of moon like the sickle on the Soviet flag swinging above our glass ceiling, we made Abby. Now the timing doesn't strike me as so fortuitous.

Five

AT FIRST WE told no one, not even Charlie's parents. We didn't want them to be disappointed if something went wrong during the first three months. We certainly didn't tell my mother. She'd had a hard enough time admitting to having a daughter. She'd never own up to a grandchild. Besides, our secret was too exquisitely private to share.

There was something else I didn't tell anyone, not even Charlie. Suddenly a mother, I no longer felt motherless.

The knowledge of the baby floating inside me arched over my life like a sunlit blue sky. I continued to go to the office—I was working at *Compass* now—and see friends, to go to the theater and movies and parties and do mundane things around the apartment, but even when I wasn't thinking about the baby, I was aware of it.

Sometimes I felt sorry for Charlie. He knew the secret, but he didn't carry it within him. Heaven knows he tried. At night, he lay in bed with his hand on my still flat stomach. Once he placed his head there and carried on a whispered conversation with the baby. I couldn't hear what he was saying, and I didn't ask.

I had a disgracefully easy pregnancy. No morning sickness, no backaches, no cravings for one food or sudden aversions to another. Then, suddenly, the delicious privacy of the secret was gone. The change was not merely that we told people. It was that I became public property. Worse than that, I became a public affront. No one used the word *unseemly,* but I knew that was what people were thinking. I was an eyesore and, strangely enough, the only one in sight. Occasionally I glimpsed another pregnant woman as I passed a neighborhood playground or went to the supermarket, but hard as I looked, I could not find one out in the real world.

As I waddled to the subway in the morning in ungainly tent tops over skirts with openings to accommodate my ever-expanding stomach, as I wove through the disreputable crowds on Broadway, as I wandered through a show at the Metropolitan Museum or MoMA, men stared at me, but with distaste rather than interest. Even the ones who stood up to give me a seat on the subway seemed more eager to get away from my presence than concerned for my comfort or welfare.

Women had a different reaction. In the pharmacy around the corner from the apartment, a strange girl put her hand on my stomach as if I were a Buddha to be rubbed for good luck. In Scribner's bookstore on Fifth Avenue, an older woman did the same thing. In the beginning, I had hoarded my secret like a miser. Now I couldn't wait for the baby to arrive.

At eleven twenty on a steaming Thursday in August, while the air conditioner in the window of the magazine office wheezed its protest and I edited the last paragraph of a book review, I felt the first contractions. Abby came hurtling into the world a scant six and a half hours later. She was in a rush.

She had ten minuscule fingers and ten minuscule toes, all of them beautiful. I counted them as soon as they put her in my arms. Later, when they wheeled me to the room and Charlie came in, he sat on the side of the bed, and I unwrapped the bundle, and we counted again. This was what perfection looked like.

A little while later, after Charlie's parents had staggered out into the hot night, stunned by the wonder of this child crying into the void left by so many, Elliot McClellan turned up. He was carrying a dozen roses. I was surprised, not by the flowers but by his appearance at the hospital. He and Charlie had grown friendly since Charlie had taken over the magazine, but not that friendly. I could tell from Charlie's excessive cordiality that the visit made him uncomfortable too.

Elliot said he could stay for only a moment, but he'd come with a purpose.

"Sonia said you'd both gone straight from the office to the hospital, so I assumed you didn't have one of these with you." He took a Polaroid camera from his briefcase.

I propped myself up in bed and moved Abby so her wizened red face was turned toward the camera.

"You too," Elliot said to Charlie. "We need the proud papa in the picture."

Charlie leaned over the bed, reached one arm around my shoulders, and put his other hand on the blanket. His long fingers palmed the baby like a basketball.

Elliot took a step back, focused, and snapped the shutter. The shiny white paper began inching out of the camera. He stood staring at his watch as the second hand swept around the dial, then tore off the paper, peeled the coating, glanced at the picture, and handed it to me.

My face had a glazed moronic expression. Charlie's smile made him look witless. We were slaphappy with love. Only later would I regret that Elliot hadn't brought a regular camera. In those days, no one knew how quickly Polaroid photographs would fade.

WHEN I LOOK back at that time, I don't recognize myself, or rather I do, and I am embarrassed by the woman I became. I was either besotted or unhinged, in thrall to my daughter or terrified of my inadequacy as a mother. I lived at polar ends, but of a severely circumscribed world.

The plan was that I would continue to contribute to the magazine from home. We had left our greenhouse in the sky for a sturdier nest on the twelfth floor of a fifteen-floor apartment building, with a real bedroom rather than a glassed-in aviary for us, another for Abby, and a small maid's room I could use as a study. I would work while Abby napped. But there was always so much to do while she slept, and I couldn't concentrate because I was listening for the whimper that indicated she was awake, and, I am ashamed to admit, I simply did not care as much as I used to about injustice and malfeasance and the rest of the world's evils.

My universe had shrunk to infant size and swelled each day with my daughter's burgeoning awareness. Her giddy perceptions of light and color, sound and touch made everything new and wondrous. When she pulled herself to a standing position in her crib, I saw prehistoric man begin to walk upright on the plains of Africa. When she crawled across the living room floor, I thought of Columbus, Magellan, and Lewis and Clark. I said I was unhinged. Her giggle lit up the room. She had an infectious giggle, my daughter. I know all mothers say that, but Abby's really was.

She also had a cry that was a fingernail down the blackboard of my soul. One night Charlie came home and found her screaming in her crib and me sobbing at the kitchen table. He picked her up, cradled her to him, and walked her around the apartment, patting and bouncing and crooning into her ear. She stopped howling, the little quisling. Charlie preened. I bristled with shame, and love.

Only two people understood. Nancy, who lived on the same floor, and Linda, who was four floors below. At first I had been wary of the two women. This was New York City, after all, not the suburbs. In the city, people did not make friends on the basis of proximity. But I kept bumping into them—literally, since the elevator did not accommodate two or three carriages easily—and I would have had to have been made of sterner stuff to resist their smiles and sympathies and shared dilemmas.

We sat in one another's apartments with mugs of coffee or tea, keeping an eye on the crawling babies while we confessed, and comforted, and secretly and guiltily compared. Sometimes when I remember how absent I was from the world in those days, I think I can't blame Charlie entirely for what happened. Then I remember the timing and know I can't let him off the hook so easily.

I managed to go through the motions of being my old self. I kept up with the news. I continued to see people, when I could find a babysitter I trusted. I even gave dinner parties. I remember a particular one on a night in late January when sleet pelted the windows, cars skidded and spun below us on Central Park West, and the snow shushed the noises of the city to a murmur. Despite the weather, everyone turned up. The people we knew missed deadlines but never a party.

We had rounded up the usual suspects, two editors, a writer, their wives and girlfriends, Frank Tucker, and Sonia Bingham. Sonia had mastered proper usage of the uppercase and gone on to sell several book and art reviews to *Compass* and a few other little magazines, although *sell* is perhaps too extravagant a word for the fees they paid. Fortunately Sonia had a small trust fund.

I was still a little wary of her. It wasn't only the pinup appearance; it was her eagerness to get her hands on my life. She was always offering to babysit, though the one time I tried to take her up on the offer, she was busy. I'm not faulting her. I called at the last minute. But like a lot of childless women, she was more in thrall to the idea of a child than to the reality. Sometimes in the late afternoon, after work or her appointment with her psychiatrist, she would telephone to ask if she could stop by. She liked to sit with a martini or highball at the kitchen table while I fed Abby, or on the closed toilet in the bathroom while I bathed her, recounting tales of her complicated love life and asking my advice, which, to my knowledge, she never took. I didn't blame her for that either. You could fit what I knew about balancing numerous love affairs on the head of a pin and still have plenty of room for angels. Mostly, I remained silent and hid my discomfort when I felt her studying me as if I were a blueprint and looking at Charlie as if he were breakfast. On second thought, maybe my wariness of her boiled down to nothing more than that. Charlie.

Halfway through the marinated London broil that January night at the dinner party, the conversation turned to two Harvard professors whom Senator McCarthy had hauled before an investigative committee a few days earlier. I was surprised that the group had taken so long to get around to the subject. One of the editors suggested the two professors should have taken the Fifth rather than answer the noxious and by now familiar question, "Are you now or have you ever been a member of the Communist Party?"

"They obviously didn't want to end up blacklisted," the other editor's wife pointed out.

"But now that they've answered one question, they either have to answer the rest by naming names or face contempt of Congress charges," the writer said.

"Anyone who names names is a traitor and a stoolie." That was Frank Tucker. "It must be wonderful," I'd said to him once, "to see the world so clearly in black and white."

"You ought to know, babe," he'd answered.

"You never know what you'll do until you're sitting in the hot glare of the press lights or, even worse, in the shadows of some obscure government office," Charlie reasoned.

"I know what I'd do," Tucker insisted.

I sat listening to the familiar arguments, noticing the wine stains I'd have to put in the sink to soak before I went to bed, trying to ignore Frank Tucker blowing his nose in my linen dinner napkin. Mouths moved, food went in, opinions came out. Sonia put a hand on Charlie's arm to make a point, then left it there for a moment or two. The conversation grew more heated. It was a miracle I even heard Abby's whimpers through all the noise.

I didn't bother to excuse myself. No one would notice I was gone. I made my way quietly down the hall to Abby's room, closed the door behind me, and lifted her out of the crib. Her arms closed around my neck in a baby-powder-and-spit-up-scented choke hold.

I checked her diaper, but I knew before I felt the cloth that it was dry and clean.

I carried her to the rocking chair and sat. My feet started us in motion; my hand patting her back kept rhythm with the movement. I began to sing about the cotton being high, her daddy rich, and her mama good-looking. The cries subsided to whimpers, then went quiet, but I kept rocking and singing. I was having too good a time to stop. I moved from *Porgy and Bess* to "Of Thee I Sing." It was a Gershwin night. Down the hall, the argument continued to rage. The words *snitch* and *betrayal* and *blacklist* hammered on the closed door. I heard Charlie's voice, though I couldn't make out the words— he wasn't shouting; he never shouted—then Sonia's laugh, rising and falling like an electric fountain. I kept rocking and patting and singing.

"Who cares if the sky cares to fall in the sea? So long as I care for you and you care for me," I sang softly into Abby's velvet ear. I knew I had the lyrics out of order, but that was okay. The sentiment was on the mark.

The sentiment, it occurs to me now, was my anthem at the time. Each morning, when I padded to the front door to take in the news-papers, I found myself staring into the fleshy smirking face of Sena-tor Joe McCarthy. Every time I turned on the radio, he was warning of communists in the State Department, the Army, government of-fices, schools, libraries, and every woodpile in the nation, though he could never decide on the actual number. One day it was 205, then 57, then 81, then 10. He would have been ludicrous had he not been so dangerous. But he could not have done what he did without help. Reporters blared his every accusation, no matter how far-fetched or loony; editors plastered his leering photograph across front pages. The junior senator from Wisconsin sold newspapers and made ca-reers, and newspapers and reporters made the junior senator in return. It was a sweetheart deal if ever there was one. But it had nothing to do with Abby and me.

HOW LONG DID I live in that cocoon, six months, eight? Abby was born in August 1953, and the Army-McCarthy hearings began in April 1954. Years later, I would watch the Watergate hearings with Abby and, after that, the Clarence Thomas–Anita Hill hearings while babysitting her daughter Elizabeth, but the Army-McCarthy hearings were the first nationally televised congressional inquiry, and for thirty-six days, 188 hours—I didn't keep track, I wasn't that bad, but the statistics were all over the papers—I was chained to the ABC or DuMont network. CBS and NBC preferred the revenue from their soap operas. I moved Abby's playpen into the bedroom to keep an eye on her or held her on my lap and turned the pages of *Goodnight Moon* or *The Velveteen Rabbit* while I watched Senator McCarthy drone and bully. His chief counsel, Roy Cohn, lurked at his side, looking, with his smudged heavy-lidded eyes and pouty mouth, like a sullen mean-spirited boy, the kind who ends up on the front page of a tabloid for murdering his parents and setting fire to the house to destroy the evidence.

The longer the hearings went on, the more convoluted the drama grew. The Army accused McCarthy and Cohn of trying to get special treatment for a staff member named Schine, who had been inducted into the service. McCarthy countered that the Army was holding Schine hostage to prevent McCarthy's committee from exposing a veritable coven of communists in the military. The proceedings featured monitored phone conversations, doctored photographs, fabricated memoranda, and other assorted skulduggery.

McCarthy and Cohn were repellent, but, though the hearings made me sick, I could not turn them off. I shouted at the television. Once I made Abby cry. I also fought with Charlie about them.

My first idea was that Charlie should write an editorial. He said it would be premature. The hearings were barely under way.

"But if we wait, it may be too late," I argued.

"McCarthy isn't going anywhere. More's the pity."

"Exactly my point. That's why we have to speak out against him."

But Charlie was adamant. I stopped arguing and started writing my own article. I even paid Orchid, who came down from Harlem to care for Abby, to take her to the park for a few extra afternoons so I could work without interruption. I spent my days watching the hearings, reading about them, and outlining the article. The bulletin board over my desk was covered with notes, clippings, and charts of names and dates. I kept waiting for Charlie to wander into my study and ask what I was working on. He didn't.

The article went more quickly than I expected. That was because I spent every moment I wasn't actually writing the piece thinking about it. One night, a week or so before the end of the hearings, I handed Charlie the article as he walked in the door. I didn't even let him put down his briefcase or loosen his tie.

"What's this?" he asked.

"A piece I've been working on."

He put the papers on the hall table. "Do you mind if I have a drink first?"

He started for the living room, loosening his tie and taking off his jacket as he went.

I picked up the pages and followed him.

He made two drinks and gave me one. I took it and handed the article back to him.

He looked down at the title. "Senator McCarthy's Points of Disorder," he read.

"I'll take out the pun. It was a bad idea."

He looked up at me. "I thought we agreed to wait on this."

"We didn't agree. You said you wanted to wait for an editorial."

"In politics, like just about everything else in life, timing is everything."

"Exactly. That's why we have to strike while the iron is hot."

"I hope the piece isn't written in clichés like that."

I was stung. He could be a tough editor, but he had never ridiculed me.

"Why don't you read it and find out?" I said and went back to the kitchen.

He followed me a few moments later, his drink in one hand, the article in the other.

"It's good," he said.

"Not too many clichés?"

"I'm sorry. I didn't mean that. It's just that I've had it up to here with McCarthy. I spend half my life in the office debating what to say, when to say it, whether to say it, and around and around."

"I don't see what there is to debate. The man is dangerous, and it's up to people like us to speak out."

"And the consequences be damned?"

"Isn't that the point of *Compass*?"

"Did it ever occur to you that this could mean the end of *Compass*?"

"You mean the end of the foundation's backing?"

"No, I mean the end of the magazine and of me. McCarthy, in case you haven't noticed, doesn't play nice or even fair."

"If we don't stand up to him, who will?"

"I'm not saying we won't stand up to him. I'm just suggesting we should wait for the outcome of the hearings."

"When it will be too late."

We went on like that for a while. I accused him of being too cautious, but I never used the word *craven*. I didn't have to. He knew what I thought of his behavior.

I REMAINED GLUED to the hearings. Then on an overcast Wednesday in June, I discovered why. I was waiting for good to triumph over evil. Charlie was right. I was a political naïf.

It started with Joseph Welch, the lawyer who had been hired by the Army as its special counsel. He was a wiry man with a kind face and a wardrobe of bow ties that were always a little askew. Occasionally, he let his wit show.

On that June afternoon while the city went about its business twelve floors below, I sat spellbound before a television screen as McCarthy began to accuse a young lawyer in Welch's firm of working for the Communist Party. The charge was not unusual. McCarthy was good at the fancy footwork of character assassination. If one line of attack seemed to be going nowhere or if the spotlight drifted off him for a moment, he danced on to another. In this case, he was circling a junior attorney called Fisher.

Welch tried to stop him, but McCarthy kept going. He was smirking and joking and making hash of another life. That was when Welch blew up. I say blew up, but his explosion was all the more powerful for being so controlled. Overnight, his words became a national slogan.

"Have you no sense of decency, sir, at long last? Have you left no sense of decency?"

On television, the hearing room went silent. At my feet, Abby sang good night to the stars and the air and noises everywhere. The silence went on for another few seconds. Even Abby looked up from her book. Then the crowded smoky hearing room erupted in applause. It was hard to tell, because McCarthy was looking down at his desk, but he seemed stunned. The next day, I read in the paper that he had turned to Cohn and asked what had happened.

What had happened was that the restrained eloquence of one man with a conscience had brought down a demagogue who had none. Six months later the Senate would vote to censure McCarthy. Within three years, he would be dead of drink. And Charlie ran my piece on McCarthy as the lead article in the next issue.

Six

No one was sure where the term *Cold War* came from. Some ascribed it to George Orwell, others to the columnist Walter Lippmann. But one fact was undisputed. It was heating up. Every issue of the magazine carried at least one article about an intellectual or academic confrontation between the Soviets and the West in some out-of-the-way country that many couldn't locate on a map. Though most of us could locate Guatemala on a map, few of us knew much about the country. But a reporter named Sydney Gruson did. That was why it was so odd that *The New York Times* pulled him off the story.

Sydney Gruson was a flamboyant newsman who had started off as a bellboy in a Toronto hotel at twelve and worked his way up to covering cataclysmic, often dangerous events around the world. Charlie knew him better than I did, because when Charlie had been at a meeting in Mexico City a year or two earlier, Sydney had put him up at his sprawling house—dripping with bougainvillea, Charlie said—and taken him to the racetrack to see Sydney's three Thoroughbreds run. But despite the high life, Gruson was a serious reporter with an uncanny ability to get to the bottom of murky, complicated stories. That was why he was so incensed when the *Times* told him to stay in Mexico rather than return to Guatemala to cover the coup brewing there. The coup was supposed to be indigenous, but anyone who could read between the lines in a newspaper knew it was CIA inspired and backed.

"Obviously someone at the CIA got to someone at the *Times,*" I told Charlie when we heard that Sydney had been pulled off the story.

"That's what Sydney thinks." Charlie had spoken to him that day.

The next morning I called Sydney in Mexico City. By the time Charlie got home that evening, I had made up my mind. I was going to write a piece on the simmering coup and the American press coverage of it.

A few days later, Charlie called to ask if he could bring Elliot home for dinner. He always called, I always said yes, and then each of us felt we had done the right thing. Twenty minutes later, he called again and said that since Elliot was coming to dinner, he might as well bring Sonia as well. She was at loose ends.

"Sonia alone of an evening. Now there's an unlikely scenario."

"I thought you two were friends."

"That's what friendship is, Ace, accepting each other's weaknesses, or in this case strengths."

The friendship had begun with her evening visits and blossomed since I'd gone back to working at the magazine three afternoons a week. We were two women navigating a man's world, not as equals, never that, but not as mere appendages either. We were in cahoots as well as competition, bound by having voices that were, in meetings, somehow out of the range of male hearing, and by the ability to make coffee, and the dubious honor of being the objects of innuendo-laced compliments. She got more of those than I did. That was because I was married, she insisted, and had nothing to do with her appearance. You see, she really was a friend.

The night Charlie brought her and Elliot home for dinner, they turned up at the apartment a little after seven. Sonia was wearing a knit dress that showed a lot of cleavage. I was in trousers and a shirt. It wasn't her fault. I could have changed, if I'd thought of it, but I hadn't until I saw her.

We went into the living room. Across the park, the windows of the Fifth Avenue buildings flamed crimson in the setting sun. Charlie headed for the bar to mix gin and tonics. Elliot sat beside Sonia on the sofa. She took a cigarette from the silver box on the coffee table. As he leaned toward her to light it, she put her hand on the back of his. She had once told me that Elliot was too buttoned-up to interest her romantically, but now I wondered if she had suddenly picked up the hum he gave off, the one audible only to females of the species. Or perhaps the gesture was simply a reflex on her part. She was ho-motropic.

When the flaming windows across the park began to darken, I excused myself and went into the kitchen to check on dinner. A moment later, Elliot followed. He stood leaning against the counter with a drink in one hand and a cigarette in the other, watching me as I took the pork roast out of the oven. I found myself standing up a little straighter. A man in the kitchen tends to do that to a woman, even if he's not the man she wants in the kitchen.

"Charlie says you're working on a piece about the coup in Guatemala and the press coverage of it."

"Or lack thereof," I said distractedly. At the moment I was more concerned about the meat thermometer, which had a history of un-reliability.

"I wish you wouldn't."

"You wish I wouldn't what?"

"Write the piece."

Now I was paying attention. I slid the pork roast back in the oven, closed the door, and turned to him. "Why not?"

"Because it's irresponsible."

"Overthrowing a duly elected government is irresponsible. Not reporting the facts is irresponsible. Reporting the irresponsibility is responsible."

"You have no proof that the coup is not being accurately reported."

"Why would the *Times* pull one of its best foreign correspondents off the story?"

"They didn't pull him off the story. They told him to stay in Mexico City to cover the spillover there."

I stood looking at him. "How did you know that?"

He shrugged. "I have friends at the paper."

"And I spoke to Sydney. He says there isn't going to be any spillover in Mexico City."

"So Gruson is your main source?"

"One of them."

I didn't like his smile.

"Nell, how many reporters do you know who think their editors are justified in pulling them off stories?"

"I trust Gruson."

"I trust Gruson's ego. A man who collects racehorses and lives the way he does isn't likely to take a slight gracefully."

"Am I interrupting something?" Charlie stood in the doorway with the empty ice bucket.

"We were discussing Sydney Gruson's character." I took the bucket from him.

"You're wasting your time on a wild-goose chase. There's no story there," Elliot said as he started down the hall toward the living room.

I thought Charlie would follow him, but he stepped into the kitchen and stood leaning against the counter and watching me as Elliot had. I began emptying the ice trays into the bucket.

"The trouble with Elliot," I whispered beneath the rattle of ice, "is that he thinks discretion is the better part of valor."

Charlie didn't say anything to that, but the linoleum of the kitchen floor squeaked under his shoes, and I sensed him behind me. He reached his arms around my waist and put his hands on my breasts. The move was classic. All over America, all over the world probably, husbands spy their wives at some domestic task and cannot resist encircling them that way.

"Don't let him get to you, Red."

"Sydney was pulled off the story because he knows what's really going on down there."

His only answer was his mouth on the back of my neck where my hair had separated as I leaned forward and his thumbs against my nipples. Standing there, pressed against me in the kitchen, he turned us into conspirators, bound together against the world.

THE PIECE ON the coup never ran. It wasn't Elliot's machinations or Charlie's fault. I had no one to blame but myself, though at first I was suspicious.

"You're sure that's the only reason you're killing it?" I asked Charlie when he told me I was too late.

"Why else?"

"Elliot."

His mouth hardened into a thin line. "Elliot has nothing to do with this. I wouldn't be able to run it for two months, and by then it will be yesterday's news and people will have moved on."

"I'm sorry it took me so long."

We were in his office. I was perched on his desk, he was sitting behind it. Now he stood, crossed to the door, closed it, came back, and put his arms around me.

"You were late because Abby had a fever, and you were up half the night three nights running. I happen to think that's more important than a piece on a correspondent who was pulled off a story."

"Apples and oranges," I said, but I was grateful, in a way. Though

I thought I was doing a herculean job balancing my two worlds, no one except Charlie seemed to notice. Nonetheless, I didn't like the implication that my primary purpose in life was rocking a crying baby rather than mounting a cogent argument. Poor Charlie. Life with me was not easy.

JOSEPH WELCH'S COMMENT in the Army-McCarthy hearings that June morning was, as I said, the death knell for McCarthy. Unfortunately, America turned out to be full of McCarthys, people who couldn't tell the difference between a genuine communist menace halfway around the world and a garden-variety liberal next door. The months after McCarthy's humiliation were the high summer of the great fear.

One night in July, Charlie called to say he was going to be late.

"What's wrong?" I was still at the stage when I thought I could tell from the tone of his voice if he was keeping something from me.

"Everything is fine," Charlie said. "I'm just going for a drink with Elliot."

There was nothing unusual in that. They often had lunch or a drink to talk about the magazine. Other interests bound them as well. They had discovered a shared passion for Conrad and, more surprisingly, A. E. Housman, whom most of the people we knew, including me, regarded as soppily Edwardian. After that, the friendship flowered. Elliot took Charlie sailing, and he came home with blisters on his hands and a gleam in his eye that indicated he'd heard the call of the sea. Charlie reciprocated with a bird-watching hike through Central Park during the fall migration. Despite Charlie's unbridled faith in America, his sensibilities were European; he had been raised by two Hungarians. Elliot was Anglo-Saxon American to the bone. His upper lip was perpetually stiff. He liked to say that he had no patience with people who treated their own minds as terra incognita. Nonetheless, Charlie persuaded him to read Freud, whom he had always resisted. So after my initial fear that something was amiss, I decided that, in this case, a drink was just a drink.

I was in the bedroom watching the early news when I heard Charlie's key in the lock, then the sound of the front door opening and closing and the thud of his briefcase hitting the floor. He started down the hall. Sometimes, when he was especially glad to be home, when he was eager to see Abby and me, his shoes tap-danced on the parquet. Tonight he was dragging his feet.

He stood in the doorway, his jacket rumpled, his tie loosened.

"Has it been on the news?"

"Has what been on the news?"

He stepped into the room and handed me a copy of the *World-Telegram and Sun* open to an inside page. The headline jumped up at me.

RED WRITER INDICTED

I skimmed the rest of the article. It wasn't long. Frank Tucker had been found in contempt of Congress for refusing to give the investigating committee the names of people with whom he had attended certain meetings in the past.

I sat staring at the newspaper. The moral equation was out of whack. How could a man who had tried to put his penis in the mouth of his good friend's sleeping wife risk going to prison for refusing to name names? I was still young enough to believe individuals were of a piece. But for the first time since I'd met Frank Tucker, I respected him.

TUCKER WAS NOT the only one being hauled on the rug. All across the country, writers, professors, movie stars, lawyers, civil servants, trade unionists, and most of the people we knew were worrying about youthful indiscretions, old love affairs, and friends they hadn't seen in years. Some people tried to save their skin by turning in others. Most waited in dread for a letter from one or another of the committees set up to investigate the loyalty of American citizens or a knock on the door by two men with hard blank expressions on their faces and FBI identifications in their hands.

We belonged to the second group.

Seven

THE LETTER LAY on the coffee table between us. It was chilling in its brevity, only three lines, if you didn't count the date, salutation, and signature. It gave away nothing. I picked it up and read it again, although I had already committed it to memory. I kept looking for something I'd missed.

This is to inform you that you are to report to the Office of Security on Wednesday, September 15, 1954, at 10:00 A.M.

An address ran below, and that was it.

"What's the Office of Security?"

Charlie shrugged.

"And who is this William Atkins who signed it?"

He shrugged again.

"There's something you're not telling me."

He stood, walked to the armoire we used as a bar, refilled his drink, and carried it back to the chair across from me.

"You know as much as I do." He held up his right hand. "Scout's honor."

Odd that I didn't believe him when he was telling the truth but that I fell for his lies. No, not lies, evasions and omissions.

"You're sure you're not trying to protect me?"

"If I were trying to protect you, I wouldn't have shown you the letter. I would have told you I was going to Washington on some other business."

He was right. I would have believed him. I looked down at the letter again. "Couldn't you refuse to go? It's not a subpoena."

"It will be if I don't show up. Besides, Elliot thinks it's a good idea to go and get it over with."

"What does Elliot have to do with it?"

"I mentioned it to him because he knows a lot of people in Washington. I thought he might be able to help."

"Can he?"

"He says if he gets involved, it will only make things worse. These people don't like interference."

"Who are 'these people'?"

He shrugged again. "Who knows. HUAC? The Senate Internal Subcommittee? The Senate Permanent Investigative Subcommittee? The FBI, which is working with all of them? It's worse than a Byzantine court."

"Or Stalin's show trials."

"Not quite. They murder people. We just blacklist or jail them."

I looked down at the menacing three lines again. "It's ridiculous. They don't tell you who they are. They don't say what they want to talk to you about. They don't give you any information at all."

He reached over, took the piece of paper from the table, folded it, and put it in his pocket. "You're going to wring as much information from that thing as you would casting chicken bones on the living room floor. Let it go."

I HAD NOT planned to say anything to Elliot, but when Charlie brought him home for a drink the following evening and then went in to say good night to Abby, the opportunity seemed too good to waste.

"About the letter from Washington," I began. I wasn't whispering. Charlie could hear me if he was listening. "Isn't there anything you can do?"

He shook his head. "I already told Charlie. When you start trying to pull strings, you only make matters worse. The best course of action is for him to go in, answer their questions, and get it over with. He'll clear himself, and it will all be forgotten in a few weeks."

"Tell that to Frank Tucker."

He sat looking at me for a moment. "I'm not the one who wanted Charlie to run a story on the Guatemala coup."

"It never ran."

"Other pieces did. Look, I'm not blaming you—"

"Of course you are."

He shrugged. "All the same, it's not the worst thing that could happen. Charlie will clear himself. And in the long run, it will be good for *Compass*."

"How do you figure that?"

"Maybe once they clear him, they'll stop going over every issue with a fine-tooth comb."

"Do they go over every issue with a fine-tooth comb?"

"Are you saying that comes as a surprise to you?"

It didn't, but something struck me as not quite right. I didn't figure out what it was until the following morning, just before dawn, when the sliver of bedroom window visible beneath the lowered blinds began fading from black to gray. Charlie was lying on his side with his back to me, but I knew he was awake. In sleep, his breathing was as steady as a metronome. Now the room was so quiet he might have been holding his breath. The predawn terrors were gathering force around us. I told myself they would be gone by the time the sun came up. They always were. The unpaid bill that heralds financial ruin turns out to require only a small late fee. The ache that must surely be the final stages of cancer has stopped hurting by the time the alarm goes off. But I knew these threats would not fade with the light, because I knew suddenly what had struck me as off-key about Elliot. The line about their going over every issue with a fine-tooth comb had given him away. Elliot had refused to help because he was the one who had turned Charlie in. That was the way the world worked these days. The only way for Elliot to clear himself of his association with *Compass* was to serve up someone else on the magazine. And who better than the man in charge?

I turned on my side and wound myself around Charlie. He hooked a leg back over mine and held my hand to his mouth.

"It'll be okay," he murmured into my palm.

"I know," I lied. Then I went on, though I had sworn I wouldn't. "Just one thing."

He waited.

"Don't trust Elliot too much."

"You were the one who wanted me to ask him to help."

"I changed my mind."

"Why?"

I put my lips against the back of his neck, smooth from the haircut he'd gotten that afternoon to go down to Washington.

"Because we're the only ones we can trust."

"HOW MANY SHIRTS?" I called from our room to Abby's, where Charlie was putting her to bed.

"Better put in four, just to be safe," his voice came back.

I took four shirts from his drawer, two white, two blue, stood staring at them for a moment, put the two blues back, took out two more whites, hesitated again, exchanged one of the whites for a blue, and carried all of them to the suitcase on the bed. As if the colors of his shirts would implicate or clear him.

I went to the closet, chose four ties, laid them across the shirts, fastened the inside straps to keep them in place, and closed the suitcase. The brass fittings snapped smartly.

When he came into the bedroom a few minutes later, he was al-

ready wearing his coat and carrying his hat. He lifted the suitcase in
one hand and picked up his briefcase with the other, which was
holding his hat. I followed him down the hallway to the front door.

He turned and bent to kiss me goodbye. I still wasn't accustomed
to his mouth without the mustache. He had shaved it off when he'd
gotten the summons to Washington. He joked that he was trying to
look all-American, but it wasn't entirely a joke.

He started down the hall. I stood in the open doorway while he
waited for the elevator. Only after he stepped into it and the doors
closed did I realize he hadn't put down his bag or his briefcase to kiss
me goodbye. He had already left me behind.

He called when he got to his hotel that night, as I had asked him
to, and every night for the next three that he was away. Each time, I
sat on the side of the bed, imagining him sitting on the side of an
unfamiliar bed in a strange hotel room, while I listened to his account of what had gone on that day. His voice throbbed with anger;
his words echoed humiliation. He was a spurned lover, jilted by the
country that had won his heart.

After we got off the phone each night, I wrote down everything
he had told me, or as much as I could remember. I'm not sure why.
Perhaps I thought it would come in handy if we had to see a lawyer.
Possibly I thought someday, when it was all over, I would write about
it. Or maybe I was just trying to hold on to a shred of sanity in a
world turned upside down. Whatever the reason, I'm glad I did.
Now that I'm trying to rewrite the story of my life, I need all the
original sources I can get my hands on, even if they're not entirely
reliable.

This is the way Charlie told the story.

His appointment the first morning was for ten o'clock. He got
there at nine forty-five. The waiting room was small, overheated,
and empty, except for four straight-back chairs against one wall, another chair behind a desk, and a secretary. Her voice was nasal, with

a trace of a southern accent. Her mouth looked as if she had sucked a lemon for breakfast.

He took off his coat, put it and his hat on one of the chairs, and sat in the one beside it. The secretary went on typing. He took *The Washington Post* he had bought from the pocket of his coat. He had a feeling he was in for a long wait.

At ten after eleven, a buzzer went off on the secretary's desk. Without looking up from her typing, she told him he could go in and tilted her head toward a door to an inner office.

It was as bare as the outer one: a scarred wooden table, a metal desk with a stenographic machine, a few chairs, and three men, two standing behind the table, one sitting at the desk with the stenographic machine.

The men behind the table introduced themselves. One was called Rider, the other Wilson. They did not give their first names, and they did not hold out their hands. Rider was half a head taller than Wilson and fleshier, but the god-awful uncanniness of it, Charlie said, was that they still managed to look like twins.

"Same cropped brown hair, same cheap shiny suits, same stony expressions, or lack thereof. Someone must have called central casting to find them."

Rider and Wilson sat on one side of the table. Rider gestured Charlie to the chair on the other. That was when he noticed the folder. It was a good three inches thick. He hadn't thought his life was that full. Then again, in government offices, paperwork had a way of begetting paperwork. He remembered that from the Navy.

Rider splayed a big hand on top of the folder. Wilson opened his mouth to speak. Their timing was perfect, born, Charlie suspected, of practice. They were a vaudeville team that performed daily.

"This is an investigation into your character, reputation, and loyalty," Wilson began.

"Under whose auspices?" Charlie asked.

"We'll ask the questions," Rider said. He lifted his hand a fraction of an inch and lowered it again on the file. "We have spoken to your friends and associates, both present and past."

"They have given us information that we would like you to verify," Wilson went on.

"If I can remember."

They stared at him for a long moment, then began.

They were thorough. He had to give them that. They had interviewed people he hadn't thought of in years. They knew every club he had joined at City College, every activity he had pursued at Columbia, whom he had been friendly with in the Navy, even the references he had given for jobs. They cast a wide net, but they were interested in only a few of the fish they'd swept into it. Tucker, as he had expected, though he could not understand why they should care, since Tucker was already in prison. A librarian named Gloria Evans, whom he'd known when he first came home from the war. A professor whose trinity of crimes consisted of serving as a dollar-a-year man in the Roosevelt administration, sitting on the board of a cultural committee that Wilson assured Charlie was a communist front, and writing him a recommendation for the job at *Compass*. One of them would go off on a tangent about someone else from his past, then the other would circle back to those three. When had he met them? How had he met them? How often had he seen them? What had they talked about? Who were their other friends? What were their interests? Had he slept with Gloria Evans?

"You told them you did, right?"

"Come on, Red, this is serious."

If he paused to frame an answer, they fired another question at him. By two o'clock he was sweating as if he'd been digging ditches in the hot sun, but he'd be damned if he'd give them the satisfaction of taking off his jacket or even loosening his tie. By four o'clock his stomach was rumbling. At seven Rider said they'd call it a day.

"I thought I was home free," he said. "Then Wilson told me to be back tomorrow morning at nine."

"Did they say why?"

"Why?" he snapped. "I'm sorry," he went on. "The two Kafkas have gotten to me. I don't know why. I don't think they do either. It's a fishing expedition."

The next morning, Rider started the questioning. He asked Charlie what he had done the night before. His tone was almost pleasant, as if he were making polite conversation, until they got down to the business at hand.

Charlie told him he'd had dinner at the hotel and worked.

"Didn't go out?" Wilson asked.

"Nope."

"Married man on his own in a strange city," Rider began.

"You'd think he'd want a good time," Wilson finished.

"What did you say?" I asked Charlie.

"Nothing."

They circled aimlessly for a while, going back to various names they'd asked him about the day before, then Rider got up, walked the length of the room, came back, and stood over Charlie's chair.

"Are you a homosexual?"

"What!" I said.

"That was my reaction," Charlie answered.

"Did you tell him about Abby and me?"

"They know about Abby and you. They probably know more about you than I do. They had a picture of you in front of the Republic Theatre, picketing the revival of *Birth of a Nation,* among other bits of information. Anyway, I told them I wasn't a homosexual, but Wilson asked again.

"Now I was getting angry. I asked what made them think I was. Instead of answering, they began asking me about Elliot."

"What about Elliot?"

"How long I've known him. How I met him. What I know about his life, his friends. I swear we were on the verge of his hopes, dreams, and aspirations. Then they went back to Tucker."

After a while they switched gears and started on the people at *Compass*. How long had he known Wally Dryer? What did he know about Gus Kagin's wife? Was he having an affair with Sonia Bingham?

"What did you say to that?" I asked.

"What do you think I said? I told them no, I was not having an affair with Sonia. Jesus, Nell, this is serious," he repeated.

"Sorry. The Kafkas are getting to me too. What made them think you were having an affair with Sonia?"

"That's what I asked them. They said I claimed I wasn't a pansy. In their extremely limited minds, those are my options. I have to be a homosexual or screwing a girl in my office. Then Wilson stood—it was his turn—walked the length of the room, came back, stood over my chair, and said, no, shouted, 'Drop your pants.'"

"What!" I screamed again.

"That's what I said," Charlie answered again.

"He said drop your pants," Rider repeated.

Charlie asked what that would prove. Neither of them answered.

"Can you tell a homosexual by looking?" I was far from an authority on the subject.

"If you can, it's news to me. But they wouldn't let it go. Finally I told them I'd drop my pants if they dropped theirs. That made them back down. They find sex a lot less sexy than communist leanings."

I was glad he could still joke about it.

The questioning went on that way for the rest of the afternoon. At seven thirty, they told him to be back the next morning at nine.

At six thirty on the third day, they told him he was free to go. He would not have to return the following morning.

"Then I'm cleared?" He fought to keep his voice even. Too much euphoria would make them suspect that he thought he was getting away with something.

"That will be determined," Rider said.

"You'll get a letter," Wilson added.

"When?" Charlie asked.

"When your case is closed," Rider said.

CHARLIE HAD NICKNAMED them the two Kafkas, and for the next eleven weeks, we lived inside a Kafka novel. Nonetheless, I kept trying to make sense of it. Charlie was wiser. He didn't even try. Or perhaps he knew more than I did and wasn't saying.

"It's insane," I argued. "How can you clear yourself when you don't know the charges?"

"We just have to wait," he insisted.

"You don't even know where their information comes from. The Sixth Amendment gives you the right to confront your accuser."

"That's only in criminal cases."

"When this is over, you have to write a piece on it."

"When this is over," he agreed.

And then it was. The letter exonerating him was as brief as the one telling him he was under investigation.

> Your case has been considered, and a favorable decision reached under the provisions of Executive Order 10450.

We did not have to look up Executive Order 10450. It had made headlines a little more than a year earlier, when Eisenhower had signed it. Until then, only affiliation with a suspect organization or a clear demonstration of disloyalty made an individual a security risk. Now the criteria were character, morality, and behavior. In other words, the government could destroy your life and put you in prison for drinking, gossiping, and screwing around, favorite pastimes of just about everyone we knew.

Eight

CHARLIE DID NOT write a piece on his interrogation. For all I knew it had never occurred. He could have been holed up somewhere here in town. He paid the bills, so I had no way of knowing if there really were long-distance telephone charges. I know I sound unhinged, but that's what happens when you begin to doubt. Catch him in one lie, and from then on everything he says is propaganda. Actually, I never did catch him.

But first came the exuberant years. There were conferences in Paris and Venice, symposia in Warsaw and Morocco, goodwill tours to India and South America. The Soviets wooed us with vodka and caviar, at least when we were abroad. I didn't see a grain of caviar in Russia, though the vodka flowed freely. Our government proselytized with whiskey and steak. *Expenses* was the magic word. Writers, artists, musicians, academics, and intellectuals who couldn't afford the bus fare to Philadelphia were suddenly flying first class around the globe. We should have known it was too good to be trusted, but success rarely breeds self-doubt. *People appreciate my work because of its excellence. Arts organizations want to fly me to exotic places because I have important things to say.* Even when I recognized ulterior motives, I dismissed the dangers. As long as I could write what I wanted, I would not be co-opted.

Charlie went on most of the jaunts alone. I was reluctant to leave

Abby. But occasionally his parents moved into the apartment, and Orchid came to help, and I accompanied him.

Sometimes I take out the photographs of those trips and try to remember them as they were rather than as I see them now. In one snapshot, we're in Istanbul, standing in front of the Hagia Sophia with a minor cultural attaché and several local writers, none of whose names I can recall. Charlie has a stern look on his face, because we're as green as just-minted money, and he's trying to hide the sheer giddiness of our good fortune.

In another picture, we're sitting side by side in straight-back chairs on a dusty square of earth, watching a group of women in vivid African print dresses dance, and smiling stiffly in a futile attempt to persuade the world, and ourselves, that we're card-carrying liberals, not imperialist swine reviewing the colonials.

In a third photo, we're gathered around a small table cluttered with glasses, cups and saucers, and ashtrays in a sun-dappled Roman piazza with Frank Tucker, two Italian writers, and a beautiful French girl Frank had acquired. "Discussing the future of freedom" is scrawled on the back of the picture in my handwriting, with no apparent irony.

Sometimes the trips did not go as planned. In Buenos Aires, a noted American poet threw away his medications, replaced them with double martinis, stripped naked, mounted an equestrian statue in one of the city's main squares, and delivered a speech in praise of Hitler. Charlie had to help the poet's minder wrestle him into a straitjacket and get him to the hospital. Most drunken binges, impolitic outbursts, and naked high jinks were less public.

The only travel photos I never looked at in later years were the ones from Leningrad.

In the fall of 1955, we learned that the touring company of *Porgy and Bess* would be the first American theatrical group to visit the USSR. When Elliot heard they were looking for someone to cover the trip, he recommended me. I was surprised. I knew he thought I was a loose cannon, and the Soviet Union was no place to send one of those. When I asked him about it, he said he admired my work and thought I could do a good job. Of course, I didn't believe him. I was also wary of the auspices of the trip. For years we had been hearing rumors that the CIA was pouring funds into cultural institutions and artistic endeavors to further American interests abroad. Traveling orchestras proved that the United States was not the cultural wasteland sophisticated Europeans believed. Jazz bands showcased an indigenous art form that demonstrated how much Americans loved negroes, as long as they had rhythm. Touring art shows made the argument that American abstract expressionism was to the twentieth century what French impressionism had been to the nineteenth. That was a real coup. Gossip said the CIA, with the help of the Museum of Modern Art and certain critics, had made popular the new school of painting, which they saw as the opposite of dull, prescribed Soviet realism. Here was the spirit of American individualism, vibrating in living color on larger-than-life canvases. The Agency's darling was said to be Jackson Pollock. Instead of an effete European-influenced artist, our national painter was a hard-drinking, hard-driving, all-American who wore cowboy boots and painted from the hip.

Some people insisted there was nothing wrong with CIA backing. Didn't we want the government to support the arts? Others of us answered that what was wrong was that this wasn't open and official government backing, it was clandestine support. And it was bound to come with strings. If the *Porgy and Bess* tour was propaganda to whitewash the country's despicable racial record, I wanted no part of it. But when I asked around, I found that the producer had actually had difficulty raising money for the tour. The CIA, which was usually generous with arts funding, and even the State Department, deemed the story of a bunch of impoverished negroes singing, dancing, and fornicating in a backwater southern bayou too subversive a picture of America to send behind the Iron Curtain.

Charlie didn't want me to go. He warned of subzero temperatures, endless snow, and eighteen hours of darkness a day. The trip was scheduled for late December. He said the trains and hotels, even the first-class ones, were reputed to be punishingly primitive. I told him those were discomforts, not deterrents.

He pointed out that he would worry about me the entire time I was away.

I asked, not in a kindly way I'm afraid, how well he thought I'd slept when he had gone to Accra.

He didn't want me to go, but he did not try to stop me. Most husbands would have.

Charlie was not the only one opposed to the trip. My old roommate, Natalie, whom I met for lunch every few months, said I was asking for trouble.

"The Russians invited us. It's a goodwill tour, not an espionage mission."

"I'm not talking about trouble with the Russians. I'm talking about Charlie."

"Charlie wants me to go," I lied.

"That's exactly my point. While the cat's away . . ."

"Charlie doesn't need me out of the country for that. He doesn't even need me out of town. Not in the world we live in."

Nancy and Linda, whom I no longer whiled away entire mornings or afternoons with, though Orchid sometimes took Abby to play with their children, were scandalized when they found out about the trip. What kind of mother leaves a two-and-a-half-year-old child to go halfway around the world to cavort with a bunch of commies, their faces said. Then Nancy picked up her little boy and blew wet kisses into his neck while he giggled deliriously.

My enlightened socialist mother-in-law agreed to stay in the apartment with Abby and Charlie, but I could tell she didn't think I ought to go either. Even my mother objected. Mourning had awakened her maternal instincts.

Eighteen months earlier, Mr. Richardson had collapsed on the squash court of the New York Athletic Club. He had left her nothing in his will—he did not want to hurt his wife, the letter his lawyer gave her explained—only ten crisp one-hundred-dollar bills tucked in the envelope along with the letter. When she amortized the gift over the time she had spent with him, it came, she told me, to sixty-one dollars and twenty-four cents a year. Her voice held a touch of irony rather than her usual self-pity, and I almost liked her for it. Then she told me I had no right to leave Abby to go gallivanting around the world. I didn't tell her that you could abandon a child by staying right at home.

Only Sonia encouraged me. "Why on earth wouldn't you go?" she asked.

"Abby and Charlie."

"What do you think is going to happen to them in two weeks? You'd better grab this, because if you don't, I'll go after it, and you'll be green with envy."

ON A CLEAR December night, I crossed the tarmac of Idlewild Airport under a black pincushion of a sky studded with metallic stars, boarded a plane, and flew to West Berlin with two other members of the group. The tour consisted of fifty-eight actors, seven stagehands, two conductors, several wives and clerks, six children, one teacher, two dogs, and one psychiatrist, all of whom, except the cast, were, predictably, white. However, only three of us were on the flight. Mrs. Ira Gershwin was in first class; a woman called Faith Anderson, who was the director's secretary, and I were not.

"Let's hope the Ruskies are saving their rubles to do it up brown once we're there," Miss Anderson said, as she wrestled her boxy cosmetics case into the overhead bin. The gesture made her breasts stand up and salute. She reminded me of the ads showing women dressed to the nines in hats, gloves, and elaborate skirts wearing only a bra on top. *I dreamed I traveled to the USSR in my Maidenform bra.* The cantilevered breasts gave her an aura of impregnability, but the turquoise harlequin glasses lent her a kittenish air.

She asked if I preferred the window or the aisle. I said it didn't matter to me. She stood aside to let me slip into the window seat, and as we buckled ourselves in, she ticked off a list of last-minute crises.

The visas had not yet arrived. "They swear they'll be waiting at the hotel in Berlin," she said.

The Soviets were upset, because they had just discovered that Paul Robeson was not in the cast. "I told them we couldn't have every negro actor in the country in the show," she said and didn't add that the last thing the U.S. government wanted was Robeson, an unrepentant communist, touring the USSR as a goodwill ambassador.

The psychiatrist had been dropped from the roster. "I'm not sure whether that's because someone higher up decided the trip won't be so nerve-racking after all, or because the Soviets think psychoanalysis is an antistate ideology that's the product of decaying capitalism. We substituted an NAACP legal adviser."

After the stewardess took away our dinner trays, Faith said she was exhausted from getting the show on the road, traded her harlequin glasses for a black eye mask with heavily lashed pink eyes embroidered on it, pulled a blanket over her enviable breasts, and went to sleep.

I tried closing my eyes, but I was too keyed up. I opened a book on Soviet Ukrainian writers, but the droning of the propellers made concentration difficult. Finally, I closed the book, took out a sheet of airmail stationery that I had brought and a pen, and began to write.

Years later, when I was cleaning out Charlie's dresser, I found the letter I wrote him that night in a small leather box in his top drawer.

It lay beneath three or four widowed cuff links, a couple of Navy medals that he insisted were given out in Cracker Jack boxes, and a Phi Beta Kappa key. As I opened it, the paper began to tear along the folds. I wondered if that was from age or from being repeatedly taken out and read.

But the real surprise all those years later was the letter itself. It sounded like a document to be opened after my death, which was funny, because I had not been afraid that night, only contemplative, and perhaps a little guilty after all for leaving him and Abby. I would not admit it to other people, but I could to myself. Soaring over the Atlantic, with no view but my own reflection in the darkened window, with no company except a sleeping stranger beside me, I felt like a bird, or a god, looking down on my life. I suppose by that I mean I had perspective, which, it occurs to me now, is another word for vision impaired by distance. Misperceptions, after all, often masquerade as profound insights. Whichever they were, that night I wrote to Charlie of my love for him and Abby, my great joy in my life with them, and how lucky I had been to find him, when I hadn't even known I was looking. He was the touchstone, I told him, of my existence.

To this day, I'm not sorry I wrote the letter. I would rather be gulled than do the gulling. Charlie always said I went for the moral high ground.

THE NEXT MORNING, a representative from the embassy was waiting for us at Tempelhof Airport in Berlin. Mrs. Gershwin, a small woman swathed in mink and weighed down by a variety of large diamonds, had descended the steps first and was standing on the tarmac. We were supposed to be on a goodwill tour, but I couldn't help thinking that her diamonds and furs were not likely to create much goodwill in a proletarian society that was suffering from a shortage of just about everything.

The representative shepherded us through customs, then drove us to the Kempinski Hotel.

"This is where first class begins," Faith said as we checked in. All that coping with crises seemed only to ramp up her capacity for optimism.

When I came back down to the lobby an hour later to leave for the orientation meeting, she was standing with a girl whose white fur coat with its attached scarf made her look as if she were being strangled from behind by a polar bear. The coat was too short for warmth but perfect for revealing the long fine legs of a Thoroughbred racehorse. Faith introduced her as Vera Bailey and said she had been traveling with the chorus for four years. As the hotel doorman ferried us to the cab under the shelter of his huge umbrella, Vera confided to me that she had seen the world.

"But what I want to know," she went on when the three of us were settled in the backseat, "is what I'm supposed to tell the Russians when they ask what it's like to be a negro in America."

"Tell them the truth," I said. "You're treated like a second-class citizen."

She looked dubious.

"Why don't you ask the officials at the briefing what you should say?" Faith suggested.

I closed my mouth and turned to look out the window. I was supposed to be an observer, not a troublemaker.

Beyond the rain-sluiced glass, the Kurfürstendamm, once Berlin's most fashionable street, lay gray, bleak, and, to my mind and despite our new status as staunch allies with Germany, hostile. If I squinted I could see flames leaping from pyres of books; shop windows shattering as thugs rampaged through the streets; and men, women, and children being herded to train stations, lugging suitcases and bundles they would never get to keep, while overhead swastikas swooped and snapped in the wind.

That was when it came to me, the real reason Charlie had not wanted me to go on the trip. We were to spend tonight in West Berlin. Tomorrow buses would transport us to East Berlin, where we would board the Blue Express to take us across Germany to Warsaw, then on through Moscow to Leningrad. As far as Charlie was concerned, the first leg of the itinerary was a tour of hell. He would not set foot in Germany, not for a night, not for an hour. The charnel house of the Jews, he called it.

I turned back to the other women. "Tell them the truth," I repeated to Vera.

The taxi let us out in front of a sooty old beaux arts building with patches of bright new limestone where it had been rebuilt since the war. Inside, folding chairs were set up at one end of a long mirrored hall. Faith said the cast would rehearse here after the meeting. The seats that weren't occupied were piled with heavy coats, scarves, hats, and gloves. A man I had been introduced to as Bob, who handled publicity for the tour, was lifting his trouser leg to show off red long underwear to another man named Bob, who was the assistant to the director. I threaded my way through the crowd to an empty seat toward the rear where I could observe the troupe.

The director of the show called the meeting to order and introduced a young man in a dark blue suit and wintry complexion as Mr. Forest, who had flown in from the American embassy in Moscow to brief us. The man stepped forward looking too ill at ease for a diplomat, even a young diplomat, and it occurred to me that he was not comfortable in front of a group of theater people, especially negro theater people.

He began by congratulating the entire troupe on its success. Someone in the audience called out that they weren't a success yet. Forest said that everything that happened in the Soviet Union was carefully planned, then seemed to realize the implication of his words and added that the Soviet people were enormously excited about the tour. After that, he opened the meeting to questions.

Hands went up. Would the milk for the children be pasteurized? Yes, he assured them. Could we drink the water? Absolutely. How cold was it likely to get? It could go down to thirty-two below zero. In that case, would the hotel rooms be warm enough? Probably overheated.

A man in the first row raised his hand. "How should we address the Russians we meet?"

"I wouldn't call them Comrade," Mr. Forest answered. "Mr., Mrs., and Miss are fine."

A woman asked about wiretaps and bugs in the rooms. Mr. Forest explained that no one knew for sure, but wiretaps and bugs were not uncommon. "I always assume I'm being monitored. I assume we're being monitored right now."

A hush fell over the room. Several people looked around. Clearly, no one else had made the same assumption, but it made sense. The Soviets would not wait until we were on their territory to begin keeping tabs on us.

"What about hidden cameras in the rooms?" someone else asked.

Mr. Forest assumed them too.

"That's indecent," a woman in the back cried.

Mr. Forest explained that the Soviet Union was an extremely puritanical country. "Couples can be arrested for kissing on the street."

One man called across the room to another that he'd better watch his step.

"Will we be tailed?"

"Everywhere you go you will be followed. Americans are a great novelty in the Soviet Union. The Russians will want to know all about you, though most of them will be too aware of government surveillance to approach you. Soviet citizens can get in trouble merely for speaking to a foreigner. But you can expect a lot of stares, though not necessarily a lot of smiles. The Russians can be warm, but they are frugal with their smiles. You will also probably have official followers," he added quietly.

A muscular man a few rows in front of me stood. "Let's stop pussyfooting around. We all know there's one big question, and it ain't about water or wiretaps or what to call folks. What are we supposed to say when they ask us what it's like to be a negro in America?"

Silence fell over the room. Mr. Forest looked as if he wanted to bolt. "You don't have to say anything, any more than they will talk to you about their political system."

"But they're going to ask us," the muscular man insisted. "They did last year in Yugoslavia."

"In that case tell them the truth."

"White truth or black truth?" someone shouted.

"Just remember," Mr. Forest went on, "any interviews you give are likely to be picked up by the American press and printed at home. We don't want this first tour to be the last. You are representatives of your country. Singing and dancing goodwill ambassadors. As Americans, we want to put our country's best foot forward."

"Tell it to Emmett Till," a man behind me grumbled.

"Don't you go making trouble," the woman beside him whispered.

An arm went up in the second row. The gesture, or rather the head and shoulders of the man who made it, ambushed me. I knew it was only a familiar psychological phenomenon. People often mistake strangers walking toward them on the street or sitting a few rows in front in the theater for people they knew in the past. My mother-in-law sometimes saw her dead sister walking in Prospect Park.

The diplomat looked like a drowning man who has spotted a lifeline being thrown to him. He nodded and the man stood and made his way to the front of the group. This was not a common psychological phenomenon. This was a snake-hipped walk from my past.

He turned to face the group. That was when I saw the mustache.

How odd that while Charlie had shaved his mustache, Woody had grown one. Otherwise, he had not changed. His hair was cropped a little closer, but that made him look only more boyish. The finely arched eyebrows that gave him a faintly Faustian air were the same, and, beneath the mustache, the full soft mouth was too.

His eyes swept over us and came to rest on me for a moment before they moved on. He did not look surprised. I hadn't known he would be on the trip, because he had replaced the psychiatrist at the last minute, but he would have seen a roster. I wondered why he hadn't contacted me before we'd left New York. There was no reason for him to, but there was no reason for him not to. Whatever had happened between us had been a long time ago.

"I'm Woodruff Jordan," he began, "but everyone calls me Woody." I had never noticed how practiced his smile was, or had it not been so practiced in those days? Then his face went sharp and serious as an ax. "Let's not kid ourselves. The Soviets know about race relations in America. They know about Emmett Till and the Scottsboro Boys and all the others. The more bigotry there is, the more violence, the better informed they are. Their government makes sure of that. I've seen the headlines."

"You read Russian, man?" someone called out.

Again, the practiced smile. He was smooth as silk.

"I know people who can translate Russian. What I'm trying to say is it's no good whitewashing the situation. We can't pretend the lynchings and cross burnings and rigged justice don't happen."

Mr. Forest looked as if he'd just realized that the lifeline he'd been hanging on to was a scrap of frayed rope.

"They know all about it," Woody went on. "What they don't know about is last year's *Brown v. Board of Education* ruling; and what a woman named Rosa Parks did on a bus in Montgomery, Alabama, two weeks ago; and what it means that we'll all be there in the USSR, which is more than they can say about their being in the U.S.A. So don't try to paint a rosy glow on the situation. Admit

America is rough on negroes. Admit we've got a long way to go. But tell them we're fighting back. Tell them the days when we"—he hung his head and shuffled his feet and mumbled yassuh, nosuh—"are gone. Tell them these days we're talking back, and maybe, just maybe, America is beginning, just beginning, to listen."

Mr. Forest began to step forward, but Woody wasn't finished.

"You're mad about the way we're treated back home, I'm mad, we're all mad. But save your anger until you get back to the U.S. I'm not handing you the old line about being patient, change will come, you can't rush it. What I am saying is, when you get home, march, picket, protest every which way from the sun. Parlay your anger into equality. But don't waste your effort here, where it won't do any good."

A murmur of approval ran through the audience as Woody started back to his seat. Mr. Forest stepped forward. He didn't look happy, but he did seem relieved.

As soon as the meeting broke up, a crowd gathered around Woody. Faith and I shared a taxi back to the hotel.

I SPENT THE afternoon walking the city. There was still a lot of rubble, but on every block, new buildings were pushing up, amnesia masquerading as optimism. The rain was still coming down, and I got drenched, went into a café to dry off, came out, and got drenched again. The more I walked, the stronger the feeling I'd had driving down the Kurfürstendamm that morning grew. The city struck me as haunted, by too many tears and not enough shame.

It was dark by the time I got back to the Kempinski. The floor of the lobby was a swamp of black water, and the squeak of my galoshes as I crossed it sounded as mournful as a child crying. The clerk behind the desk watched me approach with gloomy resignation. Gloomy resignation seemed to be the operative temperament of West Berlin. He handed me my key. As I turned to head for the bank of elevators, I saw Woody coming through the door from the street. His hat and trench coat were soaked through. As he crossed to me, his shoes made the same sad sounds on the marble. When he reached me, he took my hand and started to lean forward. I shied back. My reaction was ungraceful but effective. He straightened and asked how I was. I said fine and asked how he was.

We stood for a moment looking at each other. The experience was disconcerting, like tumbling down a rabbit hole. The world was different now, and we were different people, but the history still existed, even if it seemed, at this moment, out of focus.

Had he called me when he got back from Philadelphia that weekend or had I telephoned him? All I could remember was sitting in the sour-smelling dormitory phone booth, the receiver slippery in my sweaty hands, staring at the names of couples carved together for life on the scarred wooden table and the snatches of Emily Dickinson and Edna St. Vincent Millay scribbled on the walls. I could see that, but I couldn't recall the words I'd used. "I'm not pregnant." "It was a false alarm." Or something more spiteful? "You won't have to go into debt to your brother." And then I made a melodramatic little speech that I must have read in a novel or seen in a movie, something about the course of life being altered by a single incident. Things could never be the same between us, I said. Not after this. I'd thought I meant the pregnancy scare, but I'd really been talking about Charlie.

I reclaimed my hand, which he was still holding.

"Some weather," he said.

I was relieved. We had nothing left to talk about but the weather. I told him I wanted to get out of my wet things and started for the elevator. As I stepped into the cage and turned back, I saw him standing there watching me. The smile still struck me as practiced, but it was not unwinning.

When I got to my room, I found a package wrapped in plain brown paper. My name was written on the front in a small tight hand, but nothing indicated who had sent it. I tore off the paper to find a dozen or so pamphlets beneath a single piece of stationery. *BEWARE* was written in large letters. Beneath it were the words *Truth Institute* and an address.

I began riffling through the booklets. They appeared to be case histories, written in almost unintelligible English, of various inhabitants of West Berlin who had disappeared into the East, never to be heard from again. The propaganda was heavy-handed, but that did not make it any less frightening. I wondered if others in the group had received similar parcels. I couldn't make up my mind whether to ask. If they had, it would be reassuring. If they hadn't, the fact that I had would mark me in some way.

I was still wondering what to do when a knock sounded on the door. I opened it to find Faith holding a bottle of scotch.

"The Soviets!" She walked past me into the room, turned back to face me, and held up the bottle. "I don't believe in drinking alone."

By the time I came back from the bathroom with two glasses, she had put down the bottle and was standing beside the dresser staring at the pamphlets. "What are these?"

"That's what I was trying to figure out. You didn't get a package?"

She shook her head, then picked one up and began reading aloud. "'Fraulein von Mokte was seen to no one again. The witnessing of many eyes spoke of the mystery of her disappearing.'" She put the pamphlet back with the others. "They told us to be ready for some peculiar approaches. The West Germans aren't too happy about this tour. But if they're trying to scare us off, you'd think they'd get a decent translator."

"So much for legendary German efficiency."

"Don't talk to me about efficiency," she said as she poured scotch into the two glasses. "The Russians have raised its absence to an art form. Our visas were supposed to be waiting at the hotel. Not only are there no visas, but they're holding our passports. Then there's the train. We were promised four first-class sleeping cars. Now it turns out all they have are three second-class sleeping cars and two baggage cars, and the scenery and props will take up one of those."

"I guess that means we'll have to double up."

"Double up? Ha!" She slumped into the chair in front of the window like a rag doll. Only her Maidenform breasts remained at attention. Behind her, rain continued to streak down the darkened window. "Try four to a compartment. They swear there are four berths in each compartment. Of course, they swore our visas would be waiting here too." She lifted her glass to me. "*Na zdorovje!* I've been studying a Russian phrase book, but that's about as far as I've gotten."

I raised my glass to her. "*Na zdorovje.*"

"I spent the entire afternoon trying to straighten out the sleeping arrangements. Between people demanding to share compartments and people threatening to quit if they have to share compartments— you have no idea how many feuds people can work up to in four years on the road—the situation is hopeless. There's also the sex problem."

"I don't think that's your responsibility."

"I mean because of the uneven number of girls and men. I'm going to have to put the sexes together. Apparently, that's the way the Russians do it."

"Maybe they're not so puritanical after all."

She took a swallow of her drink. "I figure with four in a room, everybody will behave."

"Either that or have an orgy."

"Oh, god, I hadn't thought of that. Half the group will end up in Russian jails." She took another swig of her drink. "I put you in with the Delaneys—they're a sister and brother in the cast—and the man from the NAACP. What's his name? Jordan. After what you said in the taxi this morning and what he said at the meeting, I thought you'd get along. At least he said you would."

"He said we would?"

"I was wailing about the sleeping arrangements just now, and he told me you were old friends from college and wouldn't mind sharing the compartment. With the other two as chaperones, of course. I'm assuming you brought a warm flannel nightie and not some sheer satin number intended to drive the Ruskies wild with desire."

"I can't share a room with those three!"

She sat for a moment staring at me, then straightened. "Oh, lordy, what was I thinking? Putting a white woman in with three negroes. These last-minute arrangements really have sent me off my rocker. I'll put one of the chorus girls who isn't feuding with the Delaneys in your place, move Stella the wardrobe lady, and you can bunk with the two Bobs and me. They're safe as houses and, more to the point, so lily-white they could pass for Hitler Youth."

I told her I'd bunk with Woody and the Delaneys.

"Are you sure?"

"I'm sure."

She pulled herself up out of the chair, reclaimed her bottle, and headed for the door. "You're a sport," she said on her way out.

After she left, I wrapped the pamphlets back in the brown paper and put them in a bottom drawer. I would have liked to take them with me, but I knew I couldn't risk trying to get them past the Russian border guards. Then I opened the case of my portable typewriter and started a letter to Charlie. If the rumors were true, this was the last uncensored communication I'd be able to send him. I told him about the city and the aura that hung over it, the troupe, and the discussion of what to tell the Soviets when they asked what it was like to be a negro in America. I gave an account of Woody's answer, though I didn't identify Woody as the old boyfriend he'd heard a little, but not all, about. I didn't mention the sleeping arrangements either. I saw no point in worrying him.

Nine

B Y THE TIME the buses came to collect us the next evening, the rain had turned to a heavy mist. We climbed aboard, noisy and excited as schoolchildren on an outing. I took a seat next to the window in front of Vera Bailey and a German journalist who had taken one look at her and fallen hard, or so he said. Certainly the giggling, sighing, and silences behind me indicated that something was going on. A moment later, Woody dropped down beside me.

The caravan of three buses threaded its way along the streets of West Berlin. Beyond the windows, hunched figures hurried through the night, their faces turned down against the weather, their worn shoes scuffling over the wet pavement. The word *martinis*, written in neon, flashed in a window, a mark of American optimism that sent a current of homesickness through me. I glanced at my watch. It was a little after two in New York. Abby would be going down for her nap. Charlie would be on his way back from lunch, cutting through the crowd of holiday shoppers, sidestepping the Salvation Army saviors and the sidewalk Santas. It was another world, bright, polished, and somehow innocent, and for a moment I wondered what I was doing in this bleak wounded country, traveling through the night beside a part of my past I had no desire to remember.

The Brandenburg Gate came lumbering toward us, a dark behemoth crowned by bronze statues. Woody leaned across me to get a better view, and I drew back in my seat so our faces didn't touch.

"Abandon all hope, ye who enter here," he said.

Ahead of us, the streets were even darker than behind. Uninterrupted night lay like a shroud over the broken buildings and jagged stones.

Gradually I made out a group of guards standing in the road. The treaty that had divided the city specified open access between sectors, but I'd heard that the East Germans frequently stopped vehicles to check for papers, currency violations, and dubious characters. We had been warned that three busloads of Americans might arouse their suspicions, or at least their curiosity, despite our invitation from the Soviets.

"Bloody hell! The bloody Volpos are doing their bloody checks again," Vera's journalist said, and I wanted to tell him he was overdoing the British vernacular. "This is where I get off, sweetheart. The East is too dangerous for me." I turned in time to see him kiss Vera goodbye, stand, and begin hurrying down the aisle. He said something in German to the driver, the driver stopped and opened the door, and a gust of frigid air blew through the bus as the journalist disappeared into the darkness.

The driver closed the door, started up again, passed through the gate, and came to a halt on the other side. When he opened the door, I felt another blast of icy wind. Two guards stepped aboard. After they checked the driver's papers and the forms Faith handed them, one remained in front while the other walked slowly up the aisle, looking back and forth from one side to the other, studying the passengers. His expressionless face belonged in a wax museum. He stopped beside Woody and me.

"Der Reisepass."

Faith came hurrying down the aisle with the interpreter in tow. She explained to the interpreter, who explained to the guard, that our passports were in the hands of the Soviets waiting for visas. She had been told both would be delivered to the train.

The guard's face did not crack, but I saw his eyes dart to the front

of the bus where his colleague stood. He would have to get himself
out of this without losing face.

"I have a driver's license," I said to Faith.

Woody must have had the same idea, because he had already
taken his wallet from his breast pocket and was extracting his license. I took mine out of my handbag, and we forked them over.

The guard studied them for a long time. Finally, he handed them
back. It wasn't until three days later, when we reached Leningrad,
that we realized we were walking around with each other's licenses.
We had been too nervous to look at them when he handed them
back.

The guards got off the bus and waved us through. The driver
must have been nervous too, because he shifted gears too abruptly,
and the bus bucked like a bronco.

We drove through mile after mile of crumbling church steeples,
buildings with gaping holes where windows and doors used to be,
steps leading to nowhere, and apartments torn open and bared to
the world. Here and there, shadows moved about the exposed rooms
in the light of a single candle or small fire.

"It's like living on a stage set," Woody said.

"The perfect metaphor for a society where everyone is under surveillance."

"Don't forget to put that in one of your articles," he said, and I
couldn't tell if he was teasing me or being serious.

The station was bedlam. People found their luggage, misplaced
it, found it again; called to one another about sleeping arrangements; looked for places to buy cigarettes, gum, and candy.

As we made our way onto the platform, collective sighs of relief
rose like echoes into the damp night. The Blue Express was a series
of sleek green cars. Second class would not be a hardship.

"Why do they call it the Blue Express when the cars are green?" a
girl in the chorus said to no one in particular.

Faith came running up, shouting about another crisis. "The dining car won't be hooked on until we cross the border. That's thirty hours from now. I've got the Bobs and some of the cast combing the shops and delicatessens. So much for caviar and vodka," she called over her shoulder, as she kept going. "We'll be lucky to have bread and water."

Officials in Persian lamb hats and flaring coats stood beside the entrance to each car, as impassive and unhelpful as the guards at Buckingham Palace. Woody took my suitcase from me, heaved it up the steps to the train, and lifted his own after it. I climbed aboard, he followed, and we made our way down the aisle searching for our compartment.

It was in the middle of the car and looked much like the *wagons-lits* compartments of the trains Charlie and I had ridden in Western Europe. Two plush seats ran along the sides with closed berths above them and a table with a small silk-shaded lamp between. A man and girl sat on one side of the table. She was painting her nails; he was shuffling cards with the exaggerated finesse of a magician or a card-sharp. When they looked up, I read the surprise on their faces. Clearly, like Faith, they hadn't expected a lone white woman in their compartment.

As Woody stowed my suitcase, Miss Delaney's eyes darted to my left hand, and it occurred to me that she was trying to figure out if Woody and I were married. She looked curious but not disapprov-ing, and I was relieved. I still remembered the unforgiving stares I had gotten the few times we had strayed north of Columbia into Harlem. Of course, they were nothing compared to some of the looks Woody had received when we were together on campus.

He must have noticed her glance too. "Just old friends," he said. "From our misspent youth."

A small radio loudspeaker in the wall was playing martial music. "Do you mind if I turn that off?" I asked.

"It doesn't go off," she answered.

"The light doesn't neither." Mr. Delaney pointed to a single blue bulb in the ceiling.

"Do you suppose the radio's a bug and the lightbulb's a camera?" Miss Delaney whispered.

"In that case, we'll have to get up to some high jinks," Woody said and winked at me. He never used to wink. I know because men who wink make me nervous. They always seem to be about to play some joke I'm not in on.

Through the compartment window I saw Faith, several men, and a few porters coming down the platform at a brisk clip, carrying boxes and bags.

"Salvation," she cried, and they began handing the supplies up to the train. When they finished, they climbed aboard, leaving the three porters standing on the platform eyeing us morosely.

Woody reached into his pocket, took out a handful of coins, and began rolling down the window.

"You're not supposed to tip," I said. "They call it a capitalist insult."

As he leaned from the window, passing out the money, he glanced back over his shoulder at me. "They sure do look insulted."

The porters were bowing, and smiling, and thanking him.

I took a handful of change from my handbag and leaned out the window beside him.

"Welcome to the real world, Slim."

I had forgotten. Before Red, for a brief few months there was Slim.

From a loudspeaker somewhere in the distance, martial music blared, then a whistle blew, the train lurched forward, and the station began moving past the windows, inching at first, then picking up speed, until the brightly lit platform dropped behind us, and the world outside the windows turned black. One of the prop boys came by the compartment and announced they were setting up a canteen in the next car. "Compartment three for martinis, manhattans, and scotch. Four for cold cuts, potato salad, and anything else we could get our hands on."

"Come on, Slim, I'll buy you a drink," Woody said.

I wanted to ask him to stop calling me Slim, but the act of asking him not to call me something struck me as more intimate than the nickname.

THE TRIP FROM East Berlin to Leningrad by way of Warsaw and Moscow took three days and three nights. I did not sleep well on those nights. How do you sleep well when your husband is thousands of miles away and an old lover is tossing and turning in the berth above you? Apparently, Woody was not sleeping well either.

When I did doze off, my dreams ambushed me. In my debauched unconscious, Charlie and Woody slipped in and out of each other's skin with unsettling ease, leaving me sweaty, miserable, and unreasonably guilty the next morning. I could barely face Woody when he came back from the men's washroom, freshly shaved and smelling of the American soap he had borrowed from me. Both the borrowed soap and the close shave demonstrated his knack for survival. Neither the men's nor the women's washrooms had hot water, but he had bribed the samovar man to give him a glassful.

I learned something about intimacy on that trip, not the polite forced intimacy of four strangers living cheek by jowl, but the intense intimacy of my shared life back in New York. The lesson was instructive, if not particularly pretty. At home, I feared the unlikely bugging of the apartment because I dreaded hearing the pettiness in my voice when I was annoyed at Charlie. But if I had listened to the wiretaps of me in that railroad compartment, I would have heard nothing but affability. Even when Woody woke me in the morning banging around the compartment, looking for his shaving kit, I didn't allow myself to appear annoyed. If it had been Charlie, I would have asked, my voice as chilly as the water in the washroom, why it never occurred to him to take it out the night before. But I loved and trusted Charlie. I was too wary of Woody to let down my guard.

BY THE EVENING of the second day, we were aching from confinement and on edge with one another. Except for a brief moment in Brest Litovsk, we had not been permitted off the train. One of the stagehands, who had climbed down at another stop, was brought back by two guards with fixed bayonets. Then on the afternoon of the third day, when the sky behind us had turned a red so intense it seemed to vibrate, and darkness was rushing toward us from the east, word ran through the cars that we would be in Leningrad in an hour.

We began putting away books and crossword puzzles and decks of cards. The men yanked their ties into place and buttoned their jackets. The women took out their compacts, powdered their faces, and ran tubes of lipstick over their mouths. Half an hour later, we started bundling up. By the time we pulled into the station, we were sweating.

A crowd was waiting on the platform. They stared at us through the windows, curious, unsmiling, badly dressed, and, judging from their gaunt faces and gray skin, ill-nourished. A few of the cast members waved. Two of the girls blew kisses, as if they were onstage. The crowd went on staring.

The train slowed, then jerked to a halt. All along the platform, doors began opening. Wearing our best goodwill smiles, we stepped out of the cars and began making our way through the crowd. It parted for us like biblical waters, but the only sound was the occasional murmur of *"Amerikansky."* The effect of the hush was uncanny. Little by little, we dropped our voices and let our sentences die unfinished, until we, too, were mute.

Buses took us to the Hotel Astoria. One of the translators from the Department of Culture assured us it was the best in Leningrad, but the lobby had the look of a once great beauty trying to compensate for her fading looks by piling on more and more makeup. Every inch was crowded with chipped gilt tables, shredding satin-upholstered chairs and sofas, elaborate lamps that gave off little light, worn Oriental rugs, and swags of threadbare velvet. At one end, behind a low balustrade, a dozen Intourist workers sat at desks facing the lobby, the better to keep an eye on our comings and goings. Several Chinese men and a handful of Russians dressed in high-booted Cossack outfits navigated the labyrinth of furniture.

At the front desk, confusion reigned. Whoever had assigned the rooms, and Faith was busy assuring everyone that she was not responsible, had gotten things upside down. The stagehands and costume people had landed better accommodations—in some cases suites—than the director and stars.

"The proletarian state in action," one of the fortunate stagehands said, but no one laughed.

Various members of the cast were arguing with the desk clerk, Faith was trying to calm everyone, and Mrs. Gershwin was assuring people that she would take any old room that was available when Woody cut through the crowd to the front desk. I couldn't hear what he said, but within minutes the clerk began passing out keys.

"Nicely done," I said a little later, as we stood side by side in the elevator, staring at the operator's back. Two angry-looking boils on his neck made him look as if he had eyes in the back of his head.

He shrugged. "That's one of the things I'm here for."

"To assign rooms?"

"To look out for the cast. Keep them out of trouble. Save them from themselves as well as from the Soviets."

The elevator operator pulled open the door of the metal cage, and I stepped off. Woody followed.

"I'm not tailing you," he said and dangled his key.

I looked at the number. He had the room next to mine. I wondered if he had arranged that, but decided not to ask. If he hadn't thought of it, I didn't want him to know I had.

I said good night, went into the room, and locked the door behind me.

Before I unpacked, I did a search for bugs and cameras, though I doubted I would recognize one if I stumbled over it. Certainly, if I found anything, I wouldn't try to dismantle it. That would only put me under suspicion. I was merely curious. And if there was a camera, I wanted to stay out of its range while dressing and undressing.

After I put my things away in a musty armoire decorated with gilt cherubs, I bundled up again. Beyond the windows, the city was black, but I could not wait until morning for my first glimpse of it. The ride from the station on the bus did not count.

At the end of the corridor, a large woman with a dark mustache had her meaty thighs tucked beneath a ludicrously delicate desk. I had been so busy worrying about the juxtaposition of Woody's room and mine that I hadn't noticed her when we'd gotten off the elevator. I nodded. She went on scowling. I pressed the button for the elevator.

"Nyet," she barked.

I remembered that only Americans took elevators down; the rest of the world used them solely to go up. I started for the stairs.

"Nyet," she barked again and said something in Russian. I shook my head and shrugged my shoulders to indicate that I didn't speak Russian. She repeated whatever she had said. Woody came up as we were trying to sort it out.

"She wants your key," he explained.

"I was going to leave it at the desk."

"Who knows what you could do with it between here and the desk." He took the key from me and handed it to her. She hung it on a small board on the wall beside the desk, then bent over a ledger and began writing. I couldn't make out the Cyrillic alphabet, but I understood the numerals. She was writing down the time.

"Just like signing in and out of the dorm," Woody said. He winked again. I wished he would stop doing that.

Near the front desk in the lobby, Faith was directing a Russian in overalls, who was putting up a bulletin board.

"The pulsing heart of the operation," she said and pointed to the lists of rehearsal times, government-sponsored excursions to the ballet, opera, and museums, and the dining room schedule.

She turned and looked us over. "Are you two going out?"

The question made me realize that, in the past few days, Woody and I had become a couple in the eyes of the troupe.

"I was just going for a walk," I said.

"You'd better go along," she told Woody.

"I was planning to."

"I'm not going far," I insisted. "I just want to take a look at the square and St. Isaac's Cathedral."

"Exactly what I had in mind," he said.

"I can take care of myself." I heard the impatience in my voice.

"This is going to come as a shock to you," he said, "but you're not on the Upper West Side of New York now. You're in the Soviet Union, where strange things have been known to happen to unsuspecting people."

"Stop being melodramatic."

He started to answer, then stopped, took my arm, and steered me across the lobby. The only people within hearing were two Chinese men in shiny Western suits.

"This isn't personal. Maybe some of the rest of it is. I admit I have some pretty good memories. And you must too, or you wouldn't be so skittish around me."

"I'm not skittish. Besides, I'm married."

"Right, I forgot. Married people never stray. Especially if they're thousands of miles from home." He held up his hand before I could speak. "Okay, forget that. Look at it another way. Which do you think your husband would prefer, your going out into the streets of Leningrad at night alone, or your going with me? Assuming he knows about me."

I wasn't sure what to say to that. If I told him Charlie knew about him, it meant he was important enough for me to talk about. If Charlie didn't, he was too important for me to talk about.

"Come on, Slim." He took my arm and started toward the door.

"Would you do me a favor?" I said as I let him. "Stop calling me Slim."

He turned to look at me, and his mouth curled into a smile. It wasn't practiced. It was pure glee.

Outside the hotel, the cold cut my face like shards of broken glass and made my sinuses sting and my teeth ache. I could barely see through the swirls of snow. The sidewalks, if there were sidewalks beneath the drifts, were icy hurtles into the darkness. I took one step and slid. He grabbed my arm.

"I'm fine," I said.

He didn't let go.

"Really," I insisted.

He let go.

I lost my balance again, propellered my arms like a cartoon character, and regained it.

"You're as stubborn as ever."

The statement surprised me. I thought I'd been entirely too pliable with him.

We made our way around the square to the cathedral. Far above us, the gold dome glowed in the night like a candle. I was so transfixed that I didn't hear the sound of shoes crunching on snow until it was directly behind us. I jerked around so suddenly I lost my balance again. Woody reached out to steady me.

The stranger who had made me jump said something I couldn't understand, but his manner suggested it was an apology for frightening me. Beneath a moth-eaten fur hat, his face was not unkind, but slanted amber eyes gave it an exotic cast. He tipped the moth-eaten hat and moved on.

"A little jittery?" Woody said.

"He startled me."

"Apparently. Take my advice, Slim. Sorry. Take my advice, Nell. Don't go into intelligence work.

"Incidentally," he continued on our way back through the snow-shrouded square, "I think that was our tail."

"But he was so polite."

"The better to eat you with, Little Red Riding Hood." At least this time he didn't wink.

WHEN I CAME downstairs the next morning, the desk clerk handed me a letter. The address was in Charlie's handwriting.

I took it to a corner of the lobby, sat in one of the upholstery-sprung chairs, and tore it open. It was dated two days before I'd left. That didn't surprise me, but the tone of it did. It was so much like the letter I had written him from the plane. He even used the same word I had. Touchstone.

> Dear Red,
>
> I'm writing this in the office, though I know you and Abby are waiting for me at home. Tonight is my turn to read her a story. I'm writing now because I miss you like nobody's business, and you haven't even left. And because if I wait, I doubt this will reach you, and I want to be with you in Leningrad, even if I'm not.
>
> I'm feeling a little shabby about trying to discourage you from going. It was foolish of me, and selfish. Whenever I had a chance for a junket somewhere, you were packing my bag before I even said yes. All I can plead in self-defense is that I was

worried about you. Uncle Joe is dead, but life under the Soviets, as I understand it, is still no walk in the park. And you aren't just an ordinary American tourist, if there are ordinary American tourists in Russia these days. You have a certain visibility at home that will make you more visible over there.

At first, I thought he was flattering me. I had published a few pieces. That didn't exactly make me a household name. Then I remembered the package of pamphlets I had found in my room in West Berlin. When I'd asked around, I'd learned that no one else had received anything. Faith's explanation about the West Germans being opposed to the tour made sense, but it didn't explain why I was the only one they were trying to scare, unless they cared less about the tour itself than about the publicity it generated back home.

But I'm glad you're going. It is, as you and Sonia keep saying, the chance of a lifetime. If I didn't encourage you to grab it, if I tried to clip your wings, it would be not only unfair to you, but a betrayal of us.

You and I don't have an ordinary marriage, Red. We're too connected. I don't mean we live in each other's pockets, like couples who don't trust enough to let each other out of sight. I mean a more essential bond—emotional, intellectual, spiritual, moral—you can call it what you want, but you can't deny it exists. And I can't imagine my life without it, any more than I can imagine it without you. Or rather I can, and it scares the living daylights out of me.

This isn't much of a love letter, but you once said that you didn't trust smooth-tongued Lotharios. Lucky for me. But you are my love. And my conscience. And my touchstone. You keep me honest, or as honest as I can be. Remember that.

Watch yourself with the Ruskies. I won't say any more, because I'm sure this will be opened and read. Wring every drop from the trip. And remember that Abby and I are waiting at home for you.

All my love,
Charlie

I kept the letter for a long time, just as Charlie kept the one I wrote him on the plane. For a while, I'd take it out and read it for solace. For a while after that, it reminded me of a reversible coat I had owned around that time. If I wore it on one side, it looked a certain way. If I turned it inside out, it was an entirely different animal.

That morning, I put it in my bag, went to the desk, and told the clerk I wanted to make arrangements for a call to the States. We had been told that telephoning was possible, but preparations had to be made well in advance. After I filled out the papers and paid for the call, I sent Charlie a wire saying I had scheduled a call for six P.M. Leningrad time on Sunday, which would be ten A.M. in New York.

When I came out of the hotel, the man with the slanted amber eyes and moth-eaten hat was lingering across the street, a sad, seedy shadow in the white landscape. Later that morning, I stopped on the Nevsky Prospekt to look in a shop window and noticed him standing in front of what passed for a display several stores away. A few hours after that, when the falling darkness was beginning to camouflage the open wounds of the old buildings and soften the brutal lines of the new, I lost my footing in a snowbank. He held out his hand to help me up. He even insisted on brushing the snow from my coat before he pretended to go off in another direction.

That evening over dinner at the hotel, we compared our shadows. Woody had a big brute he said he wouldn't want to meet in a dark alley. Faith said she wouldn't mind meeting hers in a dark alley or anywhere else. He was a strapping fellow with a shock of straw-colored hair who looked as if he had just stepped down from one of those propaganda posters showing Russian youths cutting hay or building factories or running tractors, as they turned their sharp handsome profiles to the future. He was enough, she said, to make a girl think of defecting.

Being followed was the least of it. Every time we started to think that life under the Soviets wasn't so dire after all, an incident pulled us up short. When one of the actors took a picture of what looked like a perfectly ordinary building, a policeman confiscated his camera. A Russian reporter slipped one of the Bobs a note tucked inside a newspaper. "Please call my sister in New York and tell her I'm all right," it read, and had a phone number.

"We were sitting right here in the lobby," Bob said. "He was interviewing me about the show. Why did he have to slip me a note?"

A member of the cast spotted Vera's West Berlin journalist, who had insisted he could not risk entering East Berlin, outside the hotel one afternoon, but when she stopped to say hello, he pretended not to know her.

One evening I came back to my room to find that my drawers had been rifled. The underwear, stockings, and sweaters were a mess, but nothing was missing. The Soviets were honest, in their way.

They were also, on occasion, inefficient. On another night Woody and I came home late from the Mariinsky Theatre, which had been rechristened the Kirov. Just about everything in the Soviet Union, including the country, had been renamed, though the translators, desk clerks, and everyone else we spoke to kept forgetting and used the old designations, except for Leningrad. For some reason that had caught on. The Russians had taken some of the troupe to an interminable production of *Sleeping Beauty,* and it was after one by the time we got back to the hotel. When Woody and I got off the elevator on our floor, we found the matron slumped over her tiny desk, asleep.

"Do you think she'll get shot for that?" I whispered as we took our keys off the hooks.

"Just packed off to Siberia."

We started down the hall.

"But while the watchdog is asleep, the tourists can play. I have a bottle of very good Russian vodka in my room."

I told him I was too tired and kept walking past his door to my own. He followed me.

"I said good night, Woody."

"Just give me a minute."

The old Woody could turn a minute into an hour. It had been hard to tear myself away. I put the key in the lock and started to turn it. He put his hand on top of mine.

"Woody!"

"I just want to say something."

I took a step back from him and folded my arms across my chest. "All right, say whatever it is you suddenly have to say, and let me go to bed."

We stood for a moment in the silent hall. The only sound was the occasional snore of the matron at the far end. Suddenly the light went out. We had turned on the timer when we'd stepped off the elevator, but we had lingered too long. Now he was nothing more than a shadow in the darkness.

"I just want to say I'm sorry."

I could have asked him for what, but that would have been coy. I could have told him he had not acted badly. He had not offered to marry me—thank heavens—but he had agreed to stand by me while I did whatever I decided to do. I could remind him that I was the one who said the moment had passed. I could have absolved him. But standing there, careful to keep a foot of darkness between us, I did not want to absolve him. Not now, in a strange ominous country, with him next door and Charlie halfway around the world. My disillusion with him was my armor.

Ten

W E WERE FOLLOWED and bugged and spied on, but as we grew more accustomed to Leningrad, and I suppose Leningrad grew more accustomed to us, the surveillance took on the aura of an opera buffa. My shadow behaved more like a bodyguard. When two girls in the chorus got lost, their tail helped them find their way back to the hotel. Little by little, the fear slipped away. The two Bobs got roaring drunk with the real proletariat at a place no tourist had ever set foot, or so they insisted. A man, who had struck up a conversation with us in the bar at the Kirov the night we went to the ballet, developed a fearsome crush on Faith and would not give up until she agreed to go with him to the glaringly lit restaurant off the hotel lobby for viscous Georgian champagne and lugubrious Russian jazz. The next morning, she reported that he loved her, but he also loved his wife.

"I thought the Soviets were supposed to be puritanical."

"He didn't lay a hand on me. At least I don't think he did. Georgian champagne packs a mean wallop."

We were seeing, we told ourselves, the real Russia, and if it wasn't harmless, it did not seem to intend any harm to a group of singing and dancing goodwill ambassadors and their hangers-on. True, there were occasional overtures to dirtier work. Woody got one. So did some members of the cast. The Soviets could not understand,

Woody explained when he told me about the incident, how a negro could feel any loyalty to a country that treated him so badly.

"They have a point," I said.

We were walking side by side down Nevsky Prospekt, and his eyes slid to me. "You think the Soviets would treat me any better?" He grinned, but there was a terrible fury behind his bared teeth. It wasn't directed at me, but it encompassed me, and I suddenly saw what I had been too naïve to see years before. I was the enemy too. His mind saw shades of gray, but his heart knew only black and white. Nothing I could do would change that, not principles, not good intentions, not sex. Or maybe the sex had been part of it, his way of evening the score. I should have been angry or hurt, but I felt a sudden wave of sorrow for this man who spent his life banking his rage.

AT FIRST IT didn't occur to me that I might be a likely candidate for recruitment too, but the more I thought about it, the more logical it seemed. When Charlie had been called down to Washington for questioning, he'd said the two Kafkas knew all about me. The Soviets had to be at least as good. They'd know about my past sympathies, and my current position as Charlie's wife could make me useful. That was why I couldn't get over the feeling that the meeting in the commission store was not a coincidence. It was the other side of the coin of the package of pamphlets delivered to my hotel room in Berlin.

I had wandered into the place, which was more a state-run pawnshop than a store, out of curiosity. It turned out to be a dispiriting jumble of tattered clothing, worn shoes, chipped china, broken toys, and cheap jewelry. As I prowled among the objects, wondering who had owned them and, more to the point, who would buy them, the door opened and a woman entered. She was well dressed, for a Russian, in a fox-collared cloth coat that was not too shabby, though it was a good two sizes too big for her and made her look like a fragile child. Her skin, pulled tightly over fine bones, was parchment white, and her large dark eyes reminded me of the martyred saints in the old master paintings in the Hermitage, only hers were not cast heavenward. I couldn't tell whether the crimson spots on her cheeks were fever or hard-to-get rouge, and I didn't want to stare.

We moved around the small area, tracked by the salesman's gaze, deferential to each other as we stepped back or squeezed past. I came upon a box of wedding bands. As I rifled through them, I wondered if they had been sold for survival or taken off the fingers of corpses. Some of them had inscriptions etched around the inside. I couldn't read the words, but I knew what they said. Hope is the same in any alphabet.

I looked up. The woman was standing across the table from me.

"Sad," she said.

"You speak English?"

"A little."

I had a feeling it was more than a little.

"You are with the Americans," she said. "The *Porgy and Bess* of Mr. Gershwin."

"How did you know?" As soon as the words were out, I realized the stupidity of the question. I had American written all over me, and how many of us were wandering Leningrad these days?

"But I think you are not an actress."

"You're right. I'm a journalist."

"A journalist. An American journalist."

She sighed the words, and I wanted to tell her it wasn't all it was cracked up to be, though from her side of the Curtain, I suppose it was.

She glanced over her shoulder at the salesman, and when she spoke again, her voice was softer. "I would like to know about America. I would be most grateful if you would tell me."

"What would you like to know?"

"Not here," she said and turned to look at the man behind the counter again. "There is a café around the corner. I will leave now. You follow in a few minutes. Will you do that?"

"I'll do it, but are you sure you want to? A man follows me. Officially, I mean."

Her smile revealed a missing tooth on the upper right side. "Of course, you have a follower. But since we are not leaving here together and not arriving there together, and since he will not come inside, he will not know that we talk."

Now I was sure I was being recruited. No ordinary Russian would take such a chance just to hear about America.

She left the shop, and I followed a few minutes later. It took me a while to find the café. No sign gave it away.

She was sitting in a corner, still bundled up in her oversize coat, her face a pale cameo nestled in the mangy fox collar. I sat across from her at the small table and kept my coat on too. There was no heat. She said her name was Darya Etinger. I told her mine was Cornelia Benjamin.

As we shook gloved hands across the table, a sullen-looking waitress in a stained apron approached. Darya spoke in Russian, then explained to me that she had ordered tea and cakes for us.

"Benjamin," Darya repeated when the waitress was out of earshot. "You are a Jew?"

"My husband is."

She seemed to think about that for a moment, but surely the information could not be a surprise to her. Or had they not bothered to brief her? Was she merely a conduit? Whichever it was, I found myself waiting for a reaction. Charlie's watchfulness had rubbed off on me, and my old roommate Natalie's warning had turned out to be apt. Since my marriage I had discovered what a large portion of the world thought of Jews.

"You do not recognize my name?" she asked.

"Should I?"

"I am a Jew too."

I was surprised that she was working in intelligence. Many of the old Bolsheviks had been Jews, but since then, the communist government had done a good job fanning the embers of the old imperial anti-Semitism. The tsars had had their pogroms; the Soviets had their Night of the Murdered Poets and their Doctors' Plot. I suddenly remembered that one of the men murdered in the Doctors' Plot, which many of us had sent letters and wires to protest, was named Etinger, though, for all I knew, the name was as common in Russia as Smith and Jones were in America, or as Cohen and Schwartz in this case.

Our tea and cakes came, and she poured for both of us before she went on.

"You were not afraid to marry a Jew? Or perhaps there is no prejudice in America?"

"Oh, there's prejudice." I started to tell her about it, but she had other questions on her mind.

Where in America did I live? Did I have children? How many people did we share our flat with? Did I have to know somebody high up in government to get my job? What kinds of things did I write? Could I publish anything I wanted or was there censorship?

I thought of my piece on how the CIA managed to keep a reporter from covering the coup in Guatemala, but that was too complicated and too controversial to try to explain.

"No censorship, only editorial judgment. That means that the person in charge may think something is not good enough to publish, or that too many other pieces on the subject have already run, or that readers have no interest in the topic. There are all sorts of reasons an editor might decide not to publish a story."

"This happens often?"

"Sometimes."

"But you, if you wrote about Russia, your editor would publish it?"

"I'm here to write about Russia."

"So if I told you stories, they would appear in America?"

Woody said they had approached him not for intelligence work but for a different kind of infiltration. He was supposed to rise in the ranks of the NAACP and bring it into line with communist policy.

"It depends on the stories. I won't write propaganda."

She put her hand over her mouth. Her fingers were long and tapering and would have been lovely if two of them on her right hand were not badly misshapen. They looked as if they'd been broken and never properly set. The fingers and the missing tooth spoke of mean times, and I wondered if she was a true believer or merely trying to survive.

She took her hand away from her mouth. "I do not speak propaganda. I speak truth."

I still had the feeling I was being softened up. She had started by asking about America, but she seemed on the way to peddling the Soviet Union. Even the sales pitch, however, would be worth writing about. I debated taking out my notebook, but I didn't want to scare her into silence. Before I could, she stood.

"You will meet me again tomorrow?" she asked. "Then I will tell you the truth about life in the Soviet Union."

I started to tell her that I was at the Hotel Astoria, though I was fairly sure she knew that too.

She cut me off. "I will meet you outside the Hermitage. At two o'clock."

"Where outside the Hermitage?"

"If you are there, I will find you."

It sounded a little too hugger-mugger for my taste, but I promised her I would be there.

THE NEXT DAY, Sunday, I opened the curtains to a Leningrad I had never seen. It was not snowing. An expanse of cobalt sky stretched over the city. Winter sunlight glinted off the snow and hurled blue shadows from the buildings.

I spent the morning at a desk in the lobby, writing up the previous day's meeting with Darya. Ordinarily, I would have stayed in my room to type the notes, but I wanted to soak up as much ambience as possible. The cheerless gazes of the Intourist representatives as they kept track of people coming and going, the hard-faced wariness of the Russian and Chinese businessmen as they tried to outsmart one another, and the feeling that watchers were everywhere were part of the story. My notes weren't exactly in cipher, merely a kind of shorthand. Perhaps I was overreacting, but I remembered my rifled drawers.

I took my notes in to lunch and was still working on them when Woody sat down across the table from me and asked what I was up to. I told him about my encounter with the Russian recruiter the previous afternoon.

"I'm meeting her today at the Hermitage."

"Are you crazy?"

"What do you mean?"

"The first time they're just sounding you out. If you say no, they'll leave you alone. But if you show any interest at all, they won't give up."

"Maybe she isn't even after me. Maybe she just likes talking to an *Amerikansky.*"

"And maybe I'm Nikita Khrushchev. If you're going, I'm going with you."

"Sorry, buster, but this is my party, and you're not invited."

I gathered up my notes and left him sitting there watching me go. It was not an unpleasant sensation.

The man with the amber eyes was waiting for me on the street. He pretended to be looking in a shop window while I got into one of the Intourist cars that were always parked in front of the hotel. The driver gave me a jovial hello and commented on the fine weather. I was surprised. All the drivers I'd had so far had scowled at me in silence. When I said I wanted to go to the Hermitage, he launched into a patriotic listing of the wonders I would see there. The capitalist world, he assured me, had nothing to rival it.

Beyond the windows, the city sparkled in the crystalline air, the buildings glowing like pastel candles on a child's birthday cake, the gold onion domes pulsating in the hard light. The frozen Neva was a silver ribbon flung across the landscape.

The car stopped at the embankment in front of the Winter Palace, and I climbed out. Across an expanse of blinding white snow, the buildings loomed like gargantuan cream-frosted cakes. As I stood there, a line of children marched past, two by two, giddy and giggling, their regulation red Pioneer scarves flaming in the brittle air.

I started to stroll, stopping periodically to take in the details of the buildings and consult my guidebook. I wanted to give her a chance to find me. Whatever she was after would lend a nice personal touch to the story. Every once in a while, I glanced around at the crowd. It must have been the weather, because everywhere I looked Russians were smiling. Even their clothes looked less drab. A young couple walked by, her yellow hair flying free from a crimson babushka, his body curved over hers in a question mark of desire.

Two girls, about eight or nine, began following me. Little by little, they grew braver and drew closer. They pointed at me, and giggled behind their hands, and pointed again.

"Amerikansky?" one asked.

"Amerikansky," I said, and they giggled some more.

I took a handful of hard candies from my handbag and held them out. Wrapped in cellophane, they glowed in the sunshine like rubies and emeralds. The girls looked at the candies warily. I inched my hand closer to them. The girl who had asked if I was *Amerikansky* took a red and a green, stared at them for a moment, then handed the green to the other girl. They unwrapped them, popped them in their mouths, and grinned at me.

"Goodbye," I said, *"do svidaniya."*

"*Do svidaniya,*" they responded still giggling, as I started back along the embankment toward the Winter Palace.

A ZiL limo, the regulation Soviet car, modeled, ironically, on the 1954 Cadillac, and always black, like Henry Ford's Model Ts, whizzed past. Another sped by a moment later. A third was coming slowly toward me from the other direction. The leisurely pace was odd. There was so little traffic that most of the automobiles raced down the streets and burned rubber on the turns as if beneath the shiny black suits of the party bureaucrats, which matched the shiny black cars, throbbed the hearts of teenage hot-rodders.

The sun beat down on the creeping car as it inched along, turning the hood to patent leather and the windows to mirrors. The sight was so eye-aching that I had to look away from it. That was when I saw her coming toward me, her oversize coat flapping around her ankles as she hurried, her face even whiter and her flushed cheeks brighter in the unforgiving light. She was walking so quickly that she was keeping pace with the car. It didn't occur to me that it might be keeping pace with her.

She looked up. I waved.

The speed of what happened next made it even more unreal. If I hadn't had another witness, I would not have been sure that any of it actually occurred.

The doors of the car flew open, and three men leapt out. Two sprinted around to the sidewalk. The third was already there. They were on her like a pack of dogs on a piece of raw meat. Arms lifted into the air and came down with sickening force. Legs swung back and forth like brutal metronomes. A spurt of red exploded into the icy air. Then it was over as suddenly as it had begun. They were gone. The black car was pulling away.

I started to run after it. It was not courage, merely instinct. A hand on my arm tugged me away from the car and began steering me toward the Winter Palace.

"Keep walking," Woody said. "Keep moving with the crowd."

All around us, people were picking up their pace and averting their eyes, but they were careful not to run, cautious not to see.

"Don't look back."

But I could not help myself. I turned to glance over my shoulder. The car was gone. There was no sign of Darya. The occurrence might have been a dream.

People were beginning to slow their pace again. A woman was herding the two girls I had given candy to across the square. The blonde in the red babushka was hanging on to her boyfriend's arm. The crowd strolled, enjoying the gift of the afternoon, basking in the slanting rays of a sun that was already inching down the western sky, pinning shadows to their heels. Only one thing betrayed the carefree holiday mood. The crowd was still giving the spot where they had taken Darya down a wide berth. I lifted my hand to shade my eyes to get a better look. A stain, red as the Soviet flag, lay on the snow.

Woody found an Intourist car and pushed me into it.

"You followed me," I said.

"You're damn lucky I did."

We were silent the rest of the way back to the hotel. When we got there, he said he still had that bottle of good Russian vodka in his room. It wasn't a come-on. We were both too shaken for that.

I thanked him but said I was going up to my room. I had made arrangements for a call to Charlie for six, Leningrad time. It was only a little after four, but this was the Soviet Union, and there was no telling when it might come through. I needed to talk to him. I knew I couldn't tell him what had happened. The connection would be cut. But I wanted to hear his voice. I was desperate to feel his presence, even attenuated through a telephone line.

I turned on a single lamp and lay down on the bed to wait. The hands of my travel clock carved a wedge out of the gloom. I willed them to move faster, but they refused. The big hand crept from ten to eleven to twelve, then continued on to one and two. At five twenty, I picked the clock up and wound it. At quarter to six, I started to repeat the gesture, then thought better of it and put the clock back on the night table. I did not want to break it.

I closed my eyes. On the backs of my lids, the doors of the car kept springing open, and the men kept jumping out, and Darya kept disappearing into the maw of flailing arms and legs.

At ten of six, the phone rang. I lunged for it. The woman on the other end had such a thick accent that I could barely make out what she was saying. Then miraculously, my mother-in-law's voice was coming over the wire, though the connection was bad, and I had almost as much trouble understanding her as I'd had the woman at the switchboard. I asked her to put Charlie on.

"He's not here." The words crackled over the wire.

"What?"

"He's not here." Now she was shouting.

"But I wired him I was going to call."

I couldn't make out the next sentence, but then the word *weekend* came through.

"Where did he go?" I shouted back.

I made out Elliot's name and Connecticut.

"Why didn't he wire me he wouldn't be home?" But even as I shouted the words into the phone, I knew my mother-in-law was not the one to ask.

We talked about Abby for a moment, then she put Abby on to say hello, and, as I listened to the static, I pictured my daughter sitting silent and recalcitrant as Sarah held the phone to her ear and begged her to say hello to Mommy. The operator came on and told me the call was terminated.

I hung up the receiver and lay down on the bed again. Charlie could not have forgotten the call. Only I could think of half a dozen reasons he might have. Another crisis had arisen at the magazine. One of Elliot's other weekend guests was a writer Charlie was cultivating or someone high up in the arts or government he wanted to interview.

I got up, paced the room a few times, went to the window, and stood looking out. A lone man hurried across the square, his shadow on the snow getting longer as he grew distant from one streetlight, shorter as he neared another. The only other sign of life was a skeletal dog limping along behind him, dragging his own mangy shadow in his wake.

Perhaps Charlie had wired me that he wouldn't be home, and I hadn't gotten the telegram. Perhaps he had never received my wire in the first place. I thought of going down to the lobby and trying to place another call, but the arrangements took hours to make, the actual connection days to happen. And I was in no condition to deal with Soviet bureaucracy.

I went back to the bed and stretched out again. The ceiling was cracked and peeling. In the maze of yellow lights that was the chandelier, a dull red pinprick glowed, the malevolent eye of the all-seeing camera I was sure they had trained on me. I was still shivering, despite the overheated room.

I sat up, slipped into my shoes again, and went out into the hall. The matron watched me coming. She was frowning, but then she was always frowning. Her expression did not change when I stopped in front of Woody's door and knocked. He didn't look surprised when he opened the door and found me there.

"I have to talk about it," I said. "I have to talk about her."

He poured me a drink and topped off his own. We had no ice. We omitted the *na zdorovje*s too. Then I started to talk. I didn't care if his room was bugged. The worst they could do was throw me out of the country, and at this point I would have welcomed that. I was like a shell-shocked victim trapped in a nightmare of repetition. The men exploding from the car. Darya going down. The black arms swinging, the black legs kicking. The entire scene suddenly disappearing as if it had never happened. "Did you see the blood on the snow?" I kept asking. "Did you see the blood on the snow?"

There was something else I kept asking him. "What do you think she wanted to tell me? What was so important they would go to that length to stop her?"

He shook his head. "It doesn't have to have been important. Her crime was talking to you in the first place."

But I needed more. If there was something concrete, perhaps I could make sense of what had happened. Only I knew I couldn't.

The travel clock on his night table went from eight to eleven to midnight. The level of vodka in the bottle inched down. I kept repeating myself. So did he. Then suddenly we stopped talking.

Perhaps what happened was inevitable. I have read that the prospect of death is a spur to sex. A woman still shaking from the echoes of the terrifying word *positive* on her biopsy report seeks solace in the arms of a husband or lover. A formerly faithful man leaves his wife's hospital room and hires a prostitute. The response may be pathetic or heartbreaking or immoral, depending on your point of view. It is certainly futile. But it is human.

He was shorter than Charlie and broader through the chest. My mind registered the difference dimly. My body adjusted itself to it automatically.

I cannot say we made love. We committed sex. Desperate sex. Lonely sex. Frightened sex. Solace-seeking sex. And afterward I was still wondering why Charlie hadn't been there when I needed him.

Eleven

THE NEXT MORNING I was sick to my stomach. I tried to throw up, but couldn't. I limped back to bed and pulled the covers over my head, but I could not hide from my self-disgust. If only Charlie had picked up the phone. If only I hadn't gone down the hall to Woody's room. If only when we found ourselves standing inches apart, I had turned and left the room. But the if-onlys of life are a childish conceit. The universe does not permit redos.

I got up, went to the window, and stood staring out, as I had the night before. Before. The word was charged.

In the east, the sky was going from black to soot-streaked gray. The snow was coming down again. Big wet flakes, driven by the wind, fell and rose and swirled in the arcs of illumination cast by the streetlights. I stood with my forehead against the cold glass trying to figure out how I would get through the day ahead, the four days in Moscow, the regret-tinged days that would pile up after my return home. The thought of the last made the nausea surge in my chest again. Charlie's face loomed out of the darkness. Abby's wide trusting eyes reproached me.

MOSCOW WAS UGLY, gray, brutal. Or was that only my guilt hanging over it? I managed to avoid Woody, and he let me. I felt as grimy and soulless as the city.

I HAD NOT been frightened on the flight over, despite the letter that sounded like a last testament to be opened after my death. I was terrified now. I envisioned the plane crashing into a mountain, going down in a fiery ball, disappearing into an icy sea. Surely there would be divine retribution. Only I knew there wouldn't be. I was my own punishment.

In the days after I got home, I swung through great arcs of emotion, affectionate and clingy one moment, withdrawn and brooding the next; rattling off funny stories about the tour, railing against the Soviet system. I snapped at Abby, then scooped her up in outbursts of apologetic love. The first time Charlie and I made love, I cried. He didn't ask what was wrong. He blamed it on Darya. I let him.

He said he had never received the telegram I'd sent telling him when I was going to call. If he had, he would have wired me to call him at Elliot's house. I asked him who had been there. He said no one I knew.

"No one?"

"Mostly just some locals in for dinner. And someone connected to the foundation. Elliot wanted me to put on my *Compass* dog-and-pony show."

"He's never asked you to do that before."

As Sonia, primed by her psychiatrist, might have said, it was a classic case of projection. Addled with guilt for my own actions, I was trying to find something to pin on Charlie.

"Are you suggesting I wasn't at Elliot's?"

"It just seems odd that you'd be at a house party with no one I knew."

"Nonetheless, I was. If you don't believe me, ask Elliot."

I didn't ask Elliot. Charlie knew I wouldn't. Trust isn't a cup of sugar you can borrow from a neighbor when the household supply runs out.

The hardest part was keeping my mouth shut. When I talked to Charlie about Darya's abduction, and I could not stop going over it, I kept saying *we*. I was dying for him to ask who the other half of the pronoun was. He never did.

Sometimes I tried to put my transgression in what I called perspective. I was making too much of a fleeting physical encounter. All I had to do was look around me to know that. Sonia's life was a revolving door of affairs. Mary McCarthy, whom I had seen long ago in the honeymoon suite at the Waldorf and met occasionally over the years, boasted that she'd once slept with three different men in a single day. Neither of them went around beating their breasts and shouting mea culpas. But they weren't married and in love with their husbands.

Little by little, we mended, or perhaps I should say I did. That summer I got pregnant again. It wasn't the old saw of having a baby to save the marriage. Abby was three, and we wanted another child.

CERTAIN EVENTS, SOME public, some personal, etch indelible marks on the steel plate of memory. The entire world can tell you where it was when it heard of President Kennedy's assassination. I cannot remember, though I've been told where I was. But I can pinpoint my position when I knew I'd lost the baby. I was in a taxi on my way to give a talk to the American Association of University Women. I can also tell you where I was when I had my second miscarriage, and my third. On my way to a party with Charlie the second time; in my study in the apartment the third. The doctor had warned I'd better take it easy. I did take it easy, but I still lost the baby.

I mourned my unborn babies. Sometimes at three in the morning, when the world was at its bleakest, I was sure they were divine retribution for my night with Woody, though usually by the time the sun rose, I was an unbeliever again.

Charlie took the miscarriages even harder than I did. I wanted another child. He had a world to repopulate. He could have blamed me. My body was the culprit. In certain societies and religions, he could have put me aside. The phrase is chilling, especially since on occasion I was sure I deserved it. Instead, he clung to me, to Abby, and to the life we were patching back together. Occasionally I felt even more guilty that he didn't know that was what we were doing.

Certainly, the polished surface of our lives showed no cracks. Charlie won a prestigious editorial award. The articles I wrote for *Compass* about my trip to Russia were such a success that a publisher brought them out as a book, a thin book, but a book nonetheless.

To my surprise and unabashedly egotistical glee, I got an honorary degree. It was from a tiny women's college I had never heard of, but from the way I swaggered across the stage to receive it, I might have been crossing Harvard Yard. In my speech to the graduates, I warned them against the widening schism between communism and what was called the free world. Bombs were not the solution, I told them. Fallout shelters would not save us. The only hope was the will to peace on both sides. The mosaic of innocent faces gazing up at me suggested they saw the future in more personal terms.

Compass was prospering. We had become part of a loose association designed to improve distribution abroad known as the world family of magazines. It included *Partisan Review, The Kenyon Review, The Sewanee Review,* and several others. We were in heady, if not particularly polite, company. Feuds raged. Sniping was endemic. Dueling reviews drew metaphorical blood. Each issue of the other magazines arrived in the office like a grenade with the pin already pulled.

Charlie bought first serial rights to publish an excerpt from a book by Richard Wright, and we decided to run an interview with him as a sidebar. At first Wright refused to see me. He relented only after I agreed to let him approve any quote I wanted to use. I learned why during the interview.

We had agreed to meet for lunch. At the time, I wondered if he was testing me. I'd heard a story that a few years earlier, his agent, worried about the reception a negro would get in a midtown restaurant, had ordered sandwiches, which they'd eaten in the agency office. I was determined to take Wright out for lunch. The only problem was where. Charlie suggested the Algonquin. A literary watering hole was likely to be more welcoming to a celebrated negro writer.

I arrived first. After the maître d' seated me, I told him I was waiting for Mr. Richard Wright. He smiled and bowed. Either he was broad-minded or he didn't read. A few minutes later when he showed Wright to the table he looked less sanguine. As Wright and I shook hands, I felt other diners glance at us curiously, then quickly look away.

As he settled into the chair, I made mental notes for my description of him. His face was strong with a high intelligent forehead and dark wary eyes beneath heavy, almost sleepy, lids. The somnolent lids were misleading. I had the feeling he didn't miss much.

He began by reminding me that I had agreed to let him check any quotes I might want to use. I said again that I had no problem with the arrangement.

"Did you see the piece in *Time* magazine?" he asked.

Time had published an article about the many negro artists living well in Paris these days. Wright was one of them.

"I never said any of those things about America's treatment of negroes," he told me. "They didn't even interview me."

I was skeptical. A misquote seemed likely, an entirely fabricated interview improbable. The doubt must have shown on my face. He took a telegram from the pocket of his tweed jacket.

"I sent two copies," he explained, as he handed it to me, "one to them and one to myself."

WORDS ASCRIBED TO ME IN YOUR ARTICLE ENTIRELY FABRI-
CATED STOP WAS NOT INTERVIEWED BY ANY TIME REPORTER

STOP A CLEAR LAPSE IN JOURNALISTIC ETHICS STOP YOU ARE
COPYING COMMUNIST TACTICS OF CHARACTER ASSASSINATION
STOP RICHARD WRIGHT

I looked from the telegram to him. "You didn't even talk to an interviewer?"

"They claim the photographer they sent to take my picture was also an interviewer." He took another slip of paper from his pocket. It was a statement by the photographer that she had been hired only to take his photograph.

"I plan to sue," he said, in case I hadn't gotten the message from the telegram. I had, but there was one thing I didn't understand. Why was he objecting to a series of statements that he might have made, and in fact had made in a variety of forms over the years? It was not one of the questions I'd prepared, but it was too good to pass up.

"Because," he explained, "I might think it, but I didn't say it to a reporter from *Time* magazine. It was a plant."

"A plant?"

"The CIA is trying to discredit me."

"I would think the CIA would be delighted with you." In the past, he had warned Western powers to keep their hands off their former colonies. In the excerpt we were running, he urged those same powers to offer financial and technical assistance to their former colonies, because if they didn't, the Soviet Union and Communist China would.

"They're delighted with me when I speak out against communism. They're less happy when I don't toe their line. Like the petition they wanted me to sign against the invasion of Hungary. I told them I'd sign it if it also protested French and British aggression in Egypt. In other words, I'm a troublemaker. Uppity." His smile was self-mocking, but the rage behind it reminded me of Woody's grin when he'd told me about being recruited in Leningrad. "This country can't make up its mind who it hates more, communists or colored people."

I was writing rapidly as he spoke. When he finished, I looked up from my notebook. "Can I use that?"

He thought for a moment, then laughed. "Sure."

I USED THE quote. I also told of his anger at the *Time* article. Charlie ran the interview. The letters to the editor were generally positive. Even Elliot rang in. He said he liked the way I let Wright hoist with his own petard.

"What do you mean?"

"The guy is obviously paranoid."

"Which just might be a logical state of mind for a negro in this country." I was sorry as soon as I spoke. I hadn't made up my mind whether Richard Wright was paranoid or on the mark.

ABBY STARTED KINDERGARTEN in a private school across the park. Charlie and I had agonized over the decision. Was it morally responsible to buy her a superior education? Was it fair to deprive her of one to assuage our consciences? On rainy or cold days, she and I took a taxi; in clement weather, we rode the bus; sometimes we walked. One morning shortly after she began first grade, when I was under the gun with a book review that Charlie wanted to run in the next issue, he said he would take her to school. That doesn't sound shocking now, but in those days it was.

He had offered to take her so I could get down to work, but after they left the apartment, I couldn't resist going into the living room to stand at the window waiting for them to come out of the building. They emerged from under the awning and started north. He was holding her hand, and she was looking up at him. Even at this distance, I could see that she was talking a mile a minute. Suddenly she stopped and pointed to her shoe. Charlie put his briefcase on the sidewalk, knelt on one knee, and tied the shoelace of her regulation brown oxford. As he did, she reached around him and made donkey ears behind his head. He finished tying her shoe, turned his head, caught her in the act, and held his fingers behind her head. She opened her mouth in what must have been a shriek and twisted away. I stood watching as they chased each other back and forth. Only when she got dangerously close to the street did he swoop her up. She threw her arms around his neck, clung to him, then lifted two fingers behind his head to make ears on him again.

Twelve

LOOKING BACK AT it now, I see the conference in Venice as the turning point, though marriage is rarely such an orderly proposition. In the four and a half years since Leningrad, we'd had good times. In the future, we would have bad times again. In the future, I would have a terrible time. But that summer week in Venice, I felt as if we were living inside a perfectly cut, multifaceted gem. Life was shot with light and depth and brilliance.

The occasion of the conference was the fiftieth anniversary of Tolstoy's death, and the organizers were pulling out all the stops for an international celebration on the island of San Giorgio. We had traveled first class before, but never like this. As soon as the bellboy closed the door of our hotel room I told Charlie I wouldn't be able to sleep there.

"What do you mean? It's a palace."

"That's my point. It's probably costing so much that I'm going to have to stay up all night to get the foundation's money's worth."

The conference was the first of two warring celebrations that year. The Soviets would hold a series of state events in Moscow in November. They were peddling Tolstoy as the precursor of the revolution, and passing off his religious concerns as bourgeois backsliding. The West was hailing him, Charlie said when he chaired a panel, as the disciple of St. Mark rather than St. Marx. He got a laugh at that.

The days were crowded with formal sessions, lunches, receptions, dinners, and late-night parties, but one afternoon Charlie and I sneaked away and took a vaporetto on our own. The sun, burning in a cloudless sky, hurled reflections of the pink and blue and green buildings into the Grand Canal, making twin Venices, one rising from the water, another floating on it.

We got off in Cannaregio. We might as well have stepped into a dream of the city. The streets baked silent and deserted in the midday heat. Two children chased each other around an empty square. Overhead, a woman sang while she hung red and yellow and blue and white laundry, gaudy as flags, on a line strung across an alley. We were the only tourists.

We wandered hand in hand, getting lost, finding our way, and getting lost again. Our shoes sounded like shots on the silent stones. The sun hammered our dark glasses and pressed down on our heads like helmets, and we ducked into shadows, came out again to thumb our noses at the heat, and escaped into a small stone church that had nothing to recommend it except air so cool it might have risen from another century. We stumbled into a cramped trattoria with rough wooden tables and a curtain-camouflaged kitchen as big as a closet, and swooned over sardines with raisins—until then I'd always thought I hated sardines—and crisp white wine that made us and the world glow like a sunset. On the way back to the hotel, we splurged on a gondola, and lay in it side by side, sweat-slicked, sun-addled, limp with pleasure.

Back in the hotel, the maid had closed the shutters, and the big high-ceilinged room lay in hushed shadows, musky with the bouquet of freshly laundered sheets, expensive soap, and the swampy humanity of the canals. Standing in the middle of the marble floor, we began to peel off our sweaty clothes. Charlie followed me into the bathroom, which was almost as big as the bedroom, a cool cave of red-veined marble with a tub the size of a small skiff. I turned on the taps. We stood side by side, watching the tub fill, grinning conspiratorially because we had read each other's minds. We churned up a small tempest and disturbed the hot Venetian peace with our noisy bliss.

Afterward, we lay side by side on the cool sheets, listening to water taxis purring along the canals, and waves slapping against stones, and gondoliers trying to lure tourists into postcard pleasures. The sounds reverberated through the vast room, echoing off the polished surfaces and fading into the soft fabrics. Charlie's breathing grew more even. I turned to look at him. He was asleep.

I got out of bed, put on a robe, and padded onto the balcony. The canal lay in shadows now, the water a shimmering mosaic of a dozen different blacks, the reflection of the pastel buildings dripping into it like melting ice cream. In the distance, a church balanced the descending sun on its steeple. I leaned against the balustrade, lulled by the enveloping heat and the hypnotizing shimmer of the water and sex. But gradually voices began to penetrate. They were coming from the balcony below, and speaking English with American accents. I didn't recognize them, but I could tell from the conversation that they were part of the conference.

"We invite sixteen Russian scholars, and what do we get? Four communist stooges. The commissars weren't about to let the real thing out of the country. They might spill the beans or, worse yet, defect," one of the voices complained.

"But here's the joke," another said. "This morning I was standing in line to get my per diem, and guess who was in front of me. That loathsome little party hack, Yermilov. Burn in communist hell, Yermilov, I wanted to tell him. You have taken CIA money." The laughter rose around me like the rotten breath of the back canals.

I went inside. Charlie was still asleep. I sat on the side of the bed and shook him. I had to wake him in a few minutes anyway or we'd be late for dinner.

"Who's paying for all this?" I gestured around the room in which I had, in fact, been sleeping very well.

He rubbed his eyes and grinned. "Hi, Red."

"Who's paying for all this?" I repeated.

"The foundation, of course."

"They're not usually so extravagant."

"Right. You'd be happier in some fleabag with roaches?"

"No, but I just overheard a conversation—"

"Where did you overhear a conversation? I doze off for a few minutes, and you're out on the town?"

"I'm serious. I was on the balcony, and I heard people talking on the one beneath us."

"Who?"

"I don't know. But they were American, and they were obviously with the conference, because they were talking about Yermilov burning in communist hell for taking CIA money."

He sat up. He was awake now.

"For Pete's sake, Red, you know as well as I do that someone is always trying to recruit someone else at these things. Of course, there are people here on CIA money. But if you're looking for honest-to-goodness spies, you're in for a big disappointment. More like a couple of second-rate academics whose only way of getting to Italy other than chaperoning a bunch of hormone-hopped kids on a student tour is fronting for the CIA. We, however, are here on the foundation's dime, and the only reason it's fifty cents this time is that this is where everyone else is staying. The whole point of these things is socialization, and I don't mean of the means of production."

Later I found out that the foundation really had paid our expenses.

WE GOT HOME in time for the July political conventions. Charlie and I sat in bed in our air-conditioned room watching perspiring delegates singing, cheering, and stomping around the convention floor; senators, congressmen, and governors strutting and posturing for the camera; and Chet Huntley explaining it all to us. I wrote a piece on the power of television to keep politicians if not honest then at least in line. I should have known better. People had said the same about radio, and look at what Huey Long, Father Coughlin, and Hitler had done with that.

In August Abby turned seven. On a steamy Saturday afternoon, ten six- and seven-year-old girls in beautifully ironed sundresses and polished Mary Janes giggled and whispered and finally ran rampant through the apartment. The next evening, her three adoring grandparents—my mother was making up for her shortcomings as a mother by overplaying her role as a grandmother—celebrated with us at a dinner with more gifts than any child should be permitted to open in a single sitting.

In September, we watched a tanned young man with a lock-up-your-daughters smile debate a gaunt Vice President with an unsightly five-o'clock shadow. The next morning I wrote a piece calling televised debates between candidates—this was the first ever broadcast—the hottest thing in electioneering since the campaign button. The writing was a little vivid for *Compass,* but the young man with the tan was infectious. We were all succumbing to the virus.

Four months later, on an icy day in January, after an eight-inch snowfall that softened the contours of the city and muffled its cacophony, we took the train to Washington and sat in the audience— the new administration had invited scores of writers, artists, and intellectuals to the inauguration—as the same young man, hatless, coatless, and heedless of the frigid weather that numbed the extremities and reddened the noses of the rest of us mortals, told Americans to ask not what their country could do for them, but what they could do for their country. I wrote about that too.

He called it the New Frontier, but his wife got closer to the public psyche when she christened it Camelot. Of course, that came later, after the optimism had darkened to the bloody stain of tragedy on her pink suit. But on that snowy inaugural day, the future thrummed with promise. In place of a stodgy old military man and a dowdy woman, who was rumored to drink too much and have White House staff flatten against the wall in an effort to make themselves invisible when she passed because she didn't like to have to see servants, we had a worldly first couple, who spoke German to the Germans, even if it was only a simple four-word sentence, and French to the French. In place of a ludicrous inauguration act in which a Hollywood cowboy lassoed the President, with the permission of the Secret Service, we had Robert Frost reading poetry. Instead of Lawrence Welk blaring his saccharine oompah music in the East Room, we had Pablo Casals playing Mendelssohn and Schumann. And we had people like us being invited to the White House. I never got to fly on Air Force One as Frank Tucker did, but I went through a receiving line, shook the President's hand, and heard that he had read something I'd written in *Compass* and found it interesting. For days afterward, Charlie teased me that he'd thought he was going to have to catch me as I swooned.

But behind all the dazzle and seduction were the ideas and the ideals. The bad old days of blacklists, witch hunts, and government skulduggery were over, though that did not mean the world had suddenly turned into a good and just place.

In May 1963, Americans sat in front of their television sets and watched film clips of children in Birmingham, Alabama, being rolled down streets by fire hoses and mauled by attack dogs. In June, a white fertilizer salesman, enraged by a presidential speech on civil rights, fired an Enfield rifle into the back of a negro civil rights worker as he made his way to a ranch house that looked like home to millions of Americans. In August, on a more promising note, Charlie and I, holding Abby's hands, stood with a quarter of a million other Americans in front of the Lincoln Memorial and listened to a negro minister sing out the words of an old spiritual. *"Free at last! Free at last! Thank God Almighty, we are free at last!"*

My life was whole again. I hadn't forgotten Leningrad, I still cringed with shame and regret when I thought of it, but I thought of it less often. The marriage was patched, made even stronger, I sometimes thought, by its testing. The magazine was successful. Abby, who turned ten that summer, was becoming a person. She had Charlie's sense of humor, and my tendency to moral indignation, and her own brand of compassion, not the compassion of a child for a stray kitten but that of a human being for her fellow man, or in this case woman.

I had just gotten off the phone with my mother, and was grumbling about something or other. I had been talking to myself, but Abby interrupted the conversation.

"I feel sorry for her."

The surprise must have shown on my face.

"I do," she insisted. "Grandma Sarah has Grandpa, and you have Daddy and me, but Grandma Claire is all alone."

Where had this child come from?

WHEN I LOOK back at that year, 1963, at the world before it turned rotten, another event stands out. In May, Charlie published a letter from the same minister who would lead the march on Washington that summer. He had written it in the margins of newspapers and on toilet paper in the cell of a Birmingham jail, because his jailers had denied him paper. Elliot didn't want Charlie to run it. I was there when they argued about washing the country's dirty linen in public. But Charlie stood firm. I was proud of him, if not of myself, but that had to do not with the letter but with the way Charlie had gotten his hands on a copy. When he came into the office to tell me about it, he said he'd had a call from a lawyer at the NAACP. "The one you were with in Leningrad," he added.

Thirteen

November 22, 1963

"Is this mrs. Benjamin?" the man on the other end of the phone was asking.

"Yes."

"Mrs. Charles Benjamin?"

"Who is this?" I asked.

"Dr. Schwartz. I'm calling from the emergency room at Roosevelt Hospital."

I saw Abby bouncing off a car fender, pinned under a truck, pursued by a pack of young thugs, cornered by a middle-aged pervert. I never should have let her go to school with Susannah, a feckless teenager leading a careless ten-year-old.

"There . . . has . . . been . . . an . . . accident."

He could not possibly have been speaking as slowly as I was hearing, but that was the way his words sounded, like a slow drip, drip, drip of fear.

"What happened to her?" I had not meant to shout.

"Your . . ." And now the wait between words was interminable. I looked at the clock on my desk. The minute hand had stopped. I tried to pull out my desk chair to sit, but my body was trapped as if in a dream, weighed down, glued, paralyzed.

". . . husband," he said.

The axis of fear shifted, not because of the balance of love, but because a built-in seismogram told me that a doctor would not call from an emergency room for a minor injury to a grown man.

"What happened?" Now I was whispering.

"I think you ought to come in, Mrs. Benjamin."

Whatever had happened was so bad that he could not tell me on the telephone.

I grabbed my coat and handbag. In the hall, the elevator refused to arrive. I leaned on the buzzer. There was no sound of gears grinding. I ran down the stairs. The doorman asked if I wanted a taxi. I raced past him onto Central Park West and flagged one down.

Red lights refused to turn green. Pedestrians shuffled across the street as if they had all the time in the world. While I pleaded with the driver to go faster, a cruel film kept looping around in my head. Charlie and I were standing at the front door of the apartment. He leaned down to kiss me goodbye; I turned my face away, again and again and again.

The emergency room was chaos. A woman moaned. Another shouted she needed help. A man sat on a chair bleeding onto the floor. The nurse, when I finally got through to her, directed me to a different area. At least they had gotten him out of that bedlam and into a room of his own.

I sprinted out of the emergency room, up flights of stairs, down halls. Another nurse asked me which Dr. Schwartz I was looking for. There were two. I told her I wanted the Dr. Schwartz who had called about my husband, Charles Benjamin.

She picked up a clipboard and began going through papers. It was the drawling doctor and the cab ride all over again. Finally she told me to wait there and started down the hall. She wasn't hurrying, but at least she wasn't strolling. She came back a few moments later with a man in a white coat and owlish glasses. He introduced himself as Dr. Schwartz, took me into a small office, and gestured to a chair. I went on standing. He asked me to sit down. I told him I wanted to see my husband. That was when he said it. He said he was sorry. Charlie was dead. This time I heard the words so fast they knocked me over.

Then I came up swinging. I told him there must be some mistake. He had the wrong man. The Charlie who had left the apartment a few hours earlier, my Charlie, could not be dead.

Again he said he was sorry. Then he added that someone had to identify the body.

I stood rooted in place.

I'm sorry, he said a third time and put his hand on my shoulder. "It will only take a minute," he added as if I were worried about the time. He began inching me to the door. I let him lead me down the hall. The sooner I pointed out their mistake, that this was not my Charlie, the better.

They had laid him out on a metal table. All I could think of was how cold that metal must be.

The rest is a blur. They took me to another office. A policeman came in. At first, I could not understand him. His words were thick and distant, like a foghorn echoing over water. Mugging. Gun. Close range. Instant. He said he wanted to ask me some questions, and I suppose I answered them, but all the time I was sitting there, another film loop was running in my head. In this one, I did not quarrel with Charlie. I did not turn my face away. And I did not let him walk through the park because it was such a beautiful day. I told him the park was dangerous and insisted he take a taxi or the subway. And he was still alive.

AT TWO O'CLOCK that afternoon, while Sonia was making her way to school to pick up Abby; Elliot was talking to two more policemen; my in-laws were sitting in the living room, dumb with the shock that this could happen even in America; and I was sleeping a deep unrestful sleep, thanks to the sedative the doctor had given me, another doctor pronounced another young man dead before his time by violent means. Now the whole country—the whole world—was in mourning.

I STARTED TO say the hardest part was telling Abby, but that wasn't true. Every word I spoke in those days hurt, every breath was painful. But her face, twisted with misery and confusion and fear, sharpened the sting.

She began asking me about heaven. I equivocated. Finally she came out with it. "Does this mean I'll never see Daddy again?" I had never wanted to believe in an afterlife so much.

I SHOULD HAVE found solace in the national grieving, but a population that stood on street corners crying, and sat glued to their flickering television screens watching the same images again and again, and had the nerve to mourn the loss of a total stranger gave me no comfort. They did not know what suffering was. They did not feel the emptiness left behind, the black nausea-inducing hole that suddenly opens up in a life. They were miming sorrow they had no right to, playacting at pain that left me stripped as raw as if my skin had been peeled away.

I became an expert in comparative bereavement. The world grieved when a newspaper ran a photo of rocking chairs being carried out of the White House. No one except me noticed the impression of Charlie's body in the empty black leather of the living room Eames chair. Men and women wept when a small blond girl in a sky blue coat laid her cheek against a flag-draped coffin. Nobody except me noticed that my adventurous daughter, who had pleaded to go to school without me, had developed a sudden inability to sleep in her own bed, and night after night crept into mine to curl up against me like a wounded kitten. The new President, who did not seem like a President at all, proclaimed a day of national mourning, and a line three miles long, four abreast, snaked through the streets of the capital to pay last respects, while the rest of the nation watched the spectacle on television, and long-distance calls reached a historic peak. No one wanted to be alone at this terrible time.

I was not alone. Abby stood beside me at her father's grave, her narrow shoulders hunched into the curve of my arm, her body slumped against mine, the wind whipping her coat around her bare legs. Charlie's parents stood on my other side. The crowd at the cemetery did not stretch for three miles, but it was heartening, if that kind of thing heartens you, especially in view of the fact that an hour earlier, on national television, a man had shot the man arrested for shooting the President. Elliot was there, and Sonia; writers, editors, colleagues, and friends; people I knew well, people I hadn't seen in years, and people I didn't know at all. The crowd did not make me feel any less alone.

I averted my eyes from the raw red wound in the earth and the plain pine box suspended above it, and forced myself to listen to the few words the rabbi spoke. It could not hurt, said Charlie's father, the former atheist who had found his foxhole in his son's death, and I agreed that it could not hurt. Nothing could hurt as much as this.

The rabbi stopped speaking. The machinery started to whir. The plain pine box began inching its way toward the hole in the earth. That was when the realization hit me. Charlie was inside the box. I heard the sob before I knew it came from me.

The coffin settled with a thud. I stood for a moment, stunned by the finality of the sound. Charlie's father stepped forward, picked up a shovel, dug it into the pile of earth beside the hole, and dumped the soil into the grave. The sound, as it struck the coffin, was like a spattering of heavy rain.

He held the shovel out to me. I took it, stepped forward to the grave, and stood looking down at the dirt-splashed box. I could not do it. I could not bury Charlie. I dropped the shovel and turned away.

BOOK TWO

1963–1968

Fourteen

I WAS STUPID WITH loss. The hole was too huge, the deficiency too cosmic to comprehend, but little things brought it home. As I sat at the kitchen table with the newspaper each morning, trying to make sense of events I no longer cared about, I felt Charlie's presence across from me and looked up to find an empty chair. A dozen times a day I thought I must tell Charlie this, what will Charlie make of that. Then I remembered. I would never tell Charlie anything again. I would never hear his voice or his laugh or even those long-suffering silences that had driven me crazy. Asleep, I reached out for him. My hand found cold sheets. I kept fighting the truth, but little by little, it won. Charlie was gone. I did not know what to do with the knowledge.

To make matters worse, as if anything could make matters worse, Christmas was upon us, and Abby was ten. I had to go through the motions of giving her a semblance of a holiday.

At her school pageant, I sat alone and averted my eyes when husbands and wives reached for each other's hands as a small angel or shepherd stumbled onstage. When Abby, decked out in my pinned-up silk bathrobe, appeared as a wise man, I sensed, despite my skepticism, Charlie looking down on her. Afterward, we went to Rumplemeyer's for hot chocolate and sat across the table admiring each other's whipped cream mustaches.

"Daddy used to make—" She stopped abruptly.

". . . the best whipped cream mustaches," I finished for her.

"I didn't want to make you sad."

"You don't make me sad, sweetie. I miss Daddy. We both do. That's why we shouldn't stop talking about him. Talking about him is a way of keeping him alive."

Abby was as close as I could come to solace. The rest of the world was an affront. The peace-on-earth-goodwill-toward-men bonhomie of the holiday crowds seemed to be jeering at me. When people on the street apologized for bumping into me or sideswiping me with their shopping bags, I did not smile and say it was all right. I scowled to keep from crying and elbowed my way on. Once, on Broadway, a woman shouted, "Scrooge," after me. "Fuck you," I threw back, then berated myself all the way home.

The fragrant walls of pines, firs, and spruces set out for sale on the streets made me as sick to my stomach as the stench of rotting garbage. The decorative red lights turned the world bloody. The thought of blood took me back to Charlie's last moments.

I hurried past sidewalk Santas with a snarl on my face, until I caught one with tobacco-stained whiskers and bleary eyes taking a nip from a bottle. A soul mate. I stuffed a dollar into his cardboard chimney.

I wanted no part of this foul celebration of life, hope, and prosperity, but I had to take Abby to the Park Avenue tree lighting. She had gone to her first tree-lighting ceremony in Charlie's arms, then on his shoulders, and finally, in the past few years, swinging between the two of us. We went every year, because the ritual had begun as a memorial to the men and women who had died in the war, and Charlie and I could list plenty of people we'd known in that group; and because it signaled the beginning of the holiday season; and because it had become our family tradition.

Abby and I bundled up in warm coats, scarves, hats, and gloves and headed across the park. The streets and sidewalks around the

Brick Church were already cordoned off to accommodate the crowd, and we had to get out of the taxi a few blocks away. All around us, people were flowing out of apartment buildings and townhouses: women in fur coats, men in Santa hats, and one in a full Santa suit. Toddlers rode their fathers' shoulders as Abby once had. Teenagers tried, unsuccessfully, to feign boredom. Here and there, dogs strained at leashes. They were families, complete, without a gaping hole at the center. Abby sensed it too. She slipped her mittened hand into my gloved one.

We kept burrowing through the crowd toward the church. Strangers wished us Merry Christmas. A man with a pitcher of eggnog in one hand and a stack of plastic cups in the other offered me a drink. These people laughing, drinking, and celebrating were the same ones who had stood on street corners crying, sat glued to their televisions watching hour after odious hour of public mourning, and claimed the world would never be the same.

Somehow Elliot found us in the crowd. His apartment overlooked the Brick Church, and he always had people up for supper after the lighting. On especially cold nights, some of his guests watched the ceremony from his windows, but we never had. Charlie was a purist. He insisted that watching the ceremony from indoors was unsporting, like shooting a lion from a Jeep.

On the church porch, the minister stepped forward. Adults fell quiet, and children and teenagers stopped horsing around. He announced a carol. A couple of thousand mouths opened to sing about a midnight clear. I looked down and saw Abby watching me. I began to squeeze out the words, like a miser paying a debt.

The crowd moved on to "God Rest Ye Merry, Gentlemen." Beside me, the ghost of Charlie laid down a jazzy beat while his fingers played the drums in the small of my back. At "We Three Kings" he turned operatic. For a dizzy moment there in the dark, he was with me again. Then he was gone. These days that was always happening.

Sonia turned up. She put her arm around Abby's shoulders, and together they belted out "Jingle Bells." I had never been so grateful to her.

The ceremony was winding down. I knew what was coming. I started to make an excuse to Elliot about being cold, but before I could finish, he told me that he and Sonia would take care of Abby and the housekeeper would let me in.

The doorman, who knew me, wished me a Merry Christmas. The elevator man did the same. The first note of a bugle sounded as the door slid closed. I was in luck. The sound did not penetrate the elevator shaft of a prewar Park Avenue building. I would not have to listen to taps, those mournful notes that can twist even a whole heart.

As the housekeeper opened the door for me, the last note sounded and a hush fell over the crowd. I crossed the living room to the windows facing the church and saw the minister raise his arms. "Let there be light" boomed through the loudspeaker out into the night, and a river of radiance poured down the islands in the middle of Park Avenue for two and a half miles, all the way to the brand-new eyesore that was the Pan Am Building.

"Corny," Charlie used to whisper each year, but standing in the half circle of his arm, I could feel the shiver go down his spine.

I turned my back on the street. A few minutes later, the other guests began drifting in.

For the next hour, I tried to make myself invisible, shrinking into corners, hovering on the outskirts of groups, nodding my head in inane agreement with anything that was said. After I made sure that Abby was settled with a dinner plate and two girls about her age on the floor in front of the fireplace, I skirted the buffet table and went roaming the apartment in search of a hiding place. The living room was full. In the study, a group of people sat around the coffee table with plates of food and glasses of wine. Someone invited me to join them. I said I just had to get some dinner and fled. My only hope was Elliot's bedroom. Surely no one would be eating in there.

The door was open. I started down the short hall that led from the main corridor to the bedroom. That was when I heard Elliot's voice. He was saying something about doing things for your country. I started to turn around, but it was too late. Wally Dryer had seen me. He looked embarrassed. With good reason, I thought. He had moved into Charlie's office at the magazine with unseemly speed.

"I'm sorry. I didn't mean to interrupt."

"Not at all," Elliot said. "We were just talking about JFK."

There it was again, the martyred President, the slain national hero, the only death that mattered.

"So I heard. Ask not what your country can do for you, et cetera, et cetera, et cetera." My voice was acid.

I told Elliot I'd come looking for him to say good night. I was prepared for an argument. It was too early. Abby hadn't had dessert. But he merely took the glass of wine I hadn't realized I was holding and said he hoped Abby had enjoyed herself. He was good at reading people. I felt a wave of gratitude to him for that.

In the taxi on the way home, Abby was silent. I asked if she'd had a good time. The lighted trees sped past as I waited for an answer.

"I hate Patty Warren," she said finally. Patty Warren was one of the girls she'd had dinner with in front of the fireplace.

I started to ask what Patty had done, then realized. When I'd gone back to the living room to tell Abby we were leaving, Patty had been sitting on her father's lap.

IN THE WEEKS after Charlie's death, Elliot began stopping by the apartment every week or so, just for a moment he always said as soon as he arrived. He knew I did not want to ask him to stay for dinner. Maybe he even knew that these days I rarely had dinner. As I said, he was an observant man. I sat at the table with Abby while she ate. After she went to bed, I drank.

He asked how we were getting along.

How in hell do you think we're getting along?

"We're fine."

He inquired if we needed anything.

Charlie. We need Charlie.

"Nothing."

He reported on the police investigation. He was keeping in touch with the detective in charge. They had a few leads. He was sure justice would be done. I could not keep it in any longer. I laughed. The sound was like glass shattering.

He told me not to worry about financial matters. The foundation would take care of things until I got back on my feet. I almost laughed at that too. I was down for the count and not likely to get up again. He mentioned something about a life insurance policy. The term struck me as grotesque. Charlie's death was proof that you could not ensure a life.

Nonetheless, I had to face practical matters. Abby had to eat, and have a roof over her head, and go to school. On New Year's Eve, after I tucked her in and wished her a happy 1964, a phrase that sounded like a taunt, though I hadn't intended it to, I poured myself a drink, carried it to the bedroom, and sat at the desk that used to be Charlie's, that would always be Charlie's. The green student's lamp cast a lozenge of illumination over the surface. I took a swallow of my drink and got down to work.

I was not a stranger to Charlie's desk. I had occasionally sat there to write checks for good causes or minor household expenses, but, except for that, I knew little about our finances, beyond Charlie's salary, which had increased as the magazine had flourished, and the modest amount we had in a savings account. I doubted there was much more to know. Charlie had never kept anything from me, as I heard other men did from their wives. My old roommate, Natalie, swore her husband, who was a lawyer, had money stashed in secret accounts all over town. "I wouldn't be surprised if he even has some under the floorboards," she'd told me once. I had no such suspicions of Charlie.

I spent the better part of an hour going through old checks, studying the small fake-leather-bound passbook of the savings account as if it were a code that had to be cracked, and adding and subtracting figures that I might as well have pulled out of a hat. I had no idea how much we needed to live. I had never drawn up a budget. I wasn't extravagant, I was even capable of saving, though I could be impulsive. But living by the numbers struck me as spirit-killing. Nonetheless, I would have to have a budget now. I would also have to look for another apartment. Wally Dryer, Charlie's old second in command, who had looked so embarrassed for moving into Charlie's office so quickly when I'd come upon him in Elliot's bedroom, said he wanted me to stay on as a contributing editor, but Abby and I could not go on living as we were on what *Compass* paid me. I remembered the soul-searching Charlie and I had done about sending her to private school. Now the lack of money trumped the moral issue. She would have to transfer to public school.

As I closed the top middle drawer and pulled open the deep one on the bottom left that served as a file cabinet, I thought of the widowed First Lady. She would not have to worry about keeping her children in school. I wasn't complaining. In the financial department, I was more fortunate than most. But I would have to become practical.

I bent to the file drawer. I wasn't a stranger to that either. Some of the folder labels were in my handwriting. Birth certificates. Diplomas. Military records. Abby: vaccinations, shots, illnesses. But when I'd taken out and put back those files, I had never paid much attention to the others in the drawer. Now I began walking my fingers through them. Apartment lease. Appliance warranties. Canceled checks. Charitable gifts. Expense accounts. Life insurance. My fingers stopped. I knew the policy existed, and not only from Elliot's mention of it. Shortly after Abby was born, Charlie had come home one evening and said he'd made an appointment with an insurance agent, a friend of Elliot's, to talk about a policy. The idea had struck me as peculiar—more than peculiar, quixotic. Nothing in my life had ever been insured. I didn't think it was possible. The idea had also been frightening. I did not like betting on Charlie's mortality. I had changed the subject.

I lifted the folder out of the drawer, put it on the desk, and sat staring at it. The papers inside, like the death certificate and the will, would be one more piece of tangible evidence, the mounting proofs that Charlie was gone.

The carpet runner muffled my steps down the hall to the living room. On the way back, ice rattled in my glass and whiskey sloshed over onto the rug.

The folder was still waiting for me on top of the desk. I sat, took a long swallow of my drink, and opened it. My eyes moved over a jumble of words. Insured. Charles David Benjamin. Beneficiary. Cornelia Reeves Benjamin. Dates, conditions, stipulations. Wrongful death. Accidental death. Suicide null and void. Variations on a theme, each worse than the last or just as bad. My eyes skimmed over the page, then snagged on a figure. At first I thought the number was a mistake, but the words following it, wrapped neatly in parentheses, spelled it out. $300,000. (Three hundred thousand dollars.)

I sat staring at the figure and the words. Charlie could not have taken out a policy for three hundred thousand dollars. He would not have thought in sums that fantastic. It was a rich man's number. A lottery pipe dream. Pie in the sky. Besides, he could not have afforded the premiums. I counted the zeros. I read the words again.

I tried to remember what he had told me when he'd bought the policy. I was sure he hadn't mentioned the amount. Even someone cavalier about money and suspicious of and superstitious about insurance policies would have heard the rustle of all those zeros.

I went on staring at the numerals and the words. It was a windfall. Abby could stay in school. We would not have to move. So why wasn't I relieved?

My eye moved down to the signature. Charles David Benjamin. The handwriting was familiar, but the man who had signed it was a stranger, or at least someone with a side I did not know.

I was about to close the folder when I noticed the signature beneath Charlie's over the line that said "Witness." Elliot J. McClellan. That explained it. Elliot had talked him into the policy. But I still didn't understand where Charlie had found the money to pay the premiums.

A FEW NIGHTS later, Elliot stopped in on the way home from his office. He had worked late, and Abby was already in bed. He said he was sorry he'd missed her. The statement was not mere politesse. Babies bored him, but budding minds and developing predilections intrigued him.

We went into the living room. I told him to make himself a drink. I had given up on graciousness. When we were settled at either end of the sofa, he asked how I'd gotten along during the New Year's holiday. That was when I brought up Charlie's life insurance policy.

"I had forgotten how much it was for," I said.

The explanation wasn't as implausible as it sounded. Once or twice Elliot had been around when Charlie had teased me about my indifference to money, until I crossed the threshold of Saks or Bergdorf's. Besides, lots of things had slipped my mind in the past weeks.

"I still can't imagine how we afforded the premiums."

"Charlie was good with money."

I remembered the night on Long Island when Charlie had told me we'd never be rich, but we wouldn't starve.

"Charlie wasn't that interested in money."

"You're not that interested in money. Charlie had a healthy respect for it. At least once Abby was born."

"That explains why he bought such a big policy. It doesn't explain how he paid for it."

I didn't know why I was pressing Elliot. I was the one who'd had joint checking and savings accounts with Charlie. But there was something here that didn't make sense, and he was the one who had witnessed Charlie's signature.

He pushed the hair back from his forehead with the heel of his hand and stared into his drink. "He didn't," he said finally.

"What do you mean he didn't?"

He looked up at me. "The foundation did."

"What?"

"The foundation bought the policy for him. It was his condition for staying at *Compass*."

This was getting worse and worse. I'd had no idea that Charlie had ever thought of leaving *Compass*.

"I assumed you knew."

He was lying. If he'd assumed I knew, he would not have been so skittish about telling me.

"He'd gotten an offer from *Fortune*."

"Charlie would never have gone to work at *Fortune*."

"He would have for you and Abby."

"Not for me. He knew I would have hated it."

"This was right after Abby was born. You'd barely have noticed."

The words lingered after Elliot left. I was back in the months of Abby's infancy, obsessed with her, oblivious to the world, careless of Charlie. He had told me about the policy and how much it was worth. He had even explained that the foundation was paying for it. But I had been too preoccupied to pay attention.

It was the face turned away from his kiss again. That, I was beginning to realize, was the dirty little secret of widowhood. Guilt, for the wrongs you can never make right, for the sins of omission and commission you can never undo, for the breaks of faith you can never mend. Like Leningrad. The story of my life with Charlie had gone to press. There would be no more rewrites.

ELLIOT WAS NOT the only one who came to the apartment. People arrived carrying concern like the casseroles they would have brought if we had lived a different kind of life. I wanted to be left alone, but the world was determined to keep me company.

Charlie's parents came looking for traces of him and found them in Abby, not only in her eyes and her hair but in her turns of phrase. I noticed that too. I hadn't been as aware when Charlie was alive, but now I realized they'd had a language of their own. I could speak it, but it didn't come as naturally to me as it did to her.

My mother suggested that she move in with us. She would take care of Abby while I worked. You never took care of me, I wanted to say, but didn't. I simply thanked her and told her there wasn't room for the three of us in the apartment.

People told me time would heal the wound. Even as they said it, I knew time was not the panacea it was cracked up to be, but I didn't suspect it was a thief. Instead of making life without Charlie easier, it found new ways to rob me of him.

After the first shock of his death wore off, I sought solace in the past. One day, I took the subway up to 116th Street. The students— few of the boys wore ties and jackets these days and many of the girls wore pants, which we never would have done—should have made me feel old, but instead I found myself wandering the campus in my twenty-year-old skin, vibrating like a tuning fork with the memory of our young besotted selves. I came across a photo of a greenhouse in a magazine, and for days afterward I lived in a dream of that glassed-in bedroom in the old fifth-floor walk-up, where we kissed and pawed and slammed our bodies together as snow swirled, and rain whispered, and planes streaked through the night like slow shooting stars on their way to an airport that was still called Idlewild, because JFK, like Charlie, was still alive. One night a plane fell into the Hudson, only it wasn't a plane, it really was a shooting star, or am I misremembering this? Sometimes Charlie felt so far away that I feared I was making up the whole story of us.

Little by little, he began to fade. No, not fade, atrophy. There were still moments, usually when I was not trying to think about him, that I caught a glimpse of him, as if out of the corner of my eye. But when I turned to follow it, he disappeared. Even the photographs on my desk and dresser, in Abby's room and on end tables no longer brought him back. I'd pick one up and stare at it hard, but Charlie refused to return the look.

I had his letters from the editor bound in a private edition. I did it mostly for Abby and me, but I gave copies to his parents, Elliot, Sonia, and a few other friends. I even sent one to Frank Tucker. I doubt he opened it, but he did write me a letter thanking me and reminiscing about some good times he'd had with Charlie. I was grateful for that. He had given me fresh memories, even if they were borrowed.

A few days later, he called and suggested we have dinner. I would not have minded so much if his voice hadn't sounded as viscous as an oil slick. The approach was typical of Frank, but these days I was getting similar reactions from other men. At first, I didn't notice the change. In those days I noticed little but Charlie's absence. But gradually I began to realize that just as my status had changed from wife to widow—how I hated that word, with the round o opened into a keen of mourning—so other people's perceptions of me had altered. Wives viewed me with gimlet eyes. Men saw me as an unexploited resource.

Around the time that Frank Tucker wrote and called, I got a condolence letter from Woody. I stood at my desk reading it. The sentiments were formal, proper, sincere-sounding, but the paper reeked so strongly of guilt—mine, not his—that it might have been perfumed. I dropped it in the wastebasket. Like scented stationery, it continued to foul the room. I carried the wastebasket down the hall to the incinerator and dumped it, but when I got back to my study, the odor still clung.

IN MID-JANUARY, THE police arrested a suspect in Charlie's murder. He was a negro, he was barely literate, his vision was severely impaired and uncorrected because he could not afford glasses, and he had been in half a dozen foster homes by the time he was twelve. He was everything I would have wanted to save, under other circumstances. That did not mean I was vindictive. I simply did not care. Nothing they did to Randall White would bring Charlie back. Locking him up would prevent future crimes against others, but I did not care about others. Randall White had mugged my social conscience along with Charlie.

The police, however, were jubilant. "We got the guy," the detective told me when he broke the news. "Open-and-shut."

"How can you be sure?"

"He had your husband's wallet."

Suddenly I did care. This man had shot Charlie, then walked around for weeks afterward with his wallet.

"Your husband's driver's license was still in it. That's how dumb the kid is."

"Did it have anything else?" I wanted to know how much of Charlie's life his murderer had stolen.

"No money, that's for sure. The kid probably shot himself up with whatever was there in twenty-four hours. Some other cards and papers, and a picture of you and I guess your daughter."

I had always been opposed to capital punishment, but Randall White deserved the electric chair.

"He denied it for a while," the detective went on, "but I knew he was lying. You can always tell when a nigger is lying. His knee begins to go up and down, like he's jiving to it."

To this day, I am ashamed that I said nothing to that, especially in view of what happened later.

"Anyway, the guy confessed. Finally. So it's an open-and-shut," he repeated.

EIGHT MONTHS LATER Randall White went on trial. I did not go to the courtroom. I could not bear to sit through detailed accounts of the last violent moments of Charlie's life. I did not want to hear lawyers bickering over the details of his death.

The trial was brief, the jurors' deliberations speedy. They found Randall White guilty in a matter of hours. I understood their hurry. They, and the entire nation, had another murder on their minds. The Warren Commission report was due out any day.

Sometimes I think I ought to start a club for wives, husbands, and children of the other people who died on November 22, 1963, not only for the relatives of celebrities like Aldous Huxley and C. S. Lewis, whose deaths on that day were barely noticed, but for all of us whose grief was crushed into insignificance by the steamroller of national mourning.

Fifteen

I HAD RAGED AGAINST the national mourning. Now I found a shameful comfort in the national disillusion. The exposés, confessions, and revisionist books about the late President were still several years in the future, but the gossip, jokes, and innuendo began almost immediately. There had been speculation while he was in office—witness Frank Tucker's comment about a gentlemen's agreement not to sully the presidential image. But now the gentlemen who had been party to the agreement, and some of the ladies, were beginning to talk.

"I heard it from a girl who roomed with a girl who slept with him when she was a White House intern," an editor I knew swore.

"A guy I ran into last week was at one of the White House pool orgies," a reporter insisted.

Tucker said the President had slipped away from the inaugural ball to tryst briefly with a Hollywood star.

The man for whom the entire country had gone into mourning was not what he had seemed. Even those of us who considered ourselves more worldly about these matters—no public figure is what he seems; no one is what he seems—were shocked. The disparity between the myth and the reality was too great. The doting father watching his mischievous children cavort in the Oval Office, the adoring husband who introduced himself as the man who accompanied Jackie Kennedy to Paris, the idealistic lad with the promissory note of a smile was a world-class philanderer. One line in particular was going around. I must have heard it in half a dozen iterations, and every time the teller of the story insisted he'd heard it directly from someone to whom the late President had said it. It was to the effect that if he didn't have sex with a strange/different/new girl at least once/twice/three times a day, he got a head-/stomach-/ backache. Maybe he really had delivered the line in a variety of ways to dozens of different listeners. Maybe those buttoned-up dour-looking men sitting around the Oval Office in newspaper photo-graphs weren't fretting about Khrushchev or Castro or a nuclear holocaust, but salivating over the President's salacious boasts. Cer-tainly that was what the men who repeated the stories were doing. Women tended to speculate about whether the First Lady had known. Once again Frank Tucker stepped in as the voice of author-ity. He said that when Jackie returned to the White House from a trip, she always had someone call ahead to make sure no stray girls were left littering the premises.

Some were heartbroken and insisted the stories couldn't be true. Others were enraged and suddenly saw weakness, deceit, and bun-gling where before they'd found strength, competence, and vision. Different people react differently to betrayal. I felt strangely vindi-cated. The man whose death had overshadowed Charlie's was being cut down to size.

DISILLUSION WAS THE national mood. A year after Charlie died, *The Nation* ran an article suggesting that the CIA was funding an Anglo-American literary and cultural journal called *Encounter*. The charge wasn't exactly news. For some time, people had whispered that the Agency was behind the magazine, though the editors denied it. Charlie and I used to joke about how slavishly it toed the govern-ment's foreign policy line. Once he had come home from a confer-ence in London with a story that substantiated the rumors. He'd had lunch at a club in Pall Mall with two editors from *Encounter*. The younger editor was late, and on his arrival announced that he'd changed taxis three times on the way to the club to make sure he wasn't being followed. The senior editor had laughed at the melodrama and said for Christ's sake, they were editors, not secret agents. Then he remembered that Charlie was not one of them, pulled a straight face, and changed the subject.

I was glad the word was finally out. It was time the world got wise. I only wished Charlie were here to know that his suspicions had been well founded. I only wished Charlie were here.

Sixteen

"I DON'T WANT TO upset you," Elliot began.

I swiveled my desk chair to face the single tall window. It was a bright March afternoon, and the wind was knocking the clouds around like bowling pins.

"Then don't start a conversation that way."

"It's about Randall White."

Six months earlier, Randall White had been sentenced to life in prison without possibility of parole. He could do no more damage to Abby and me. Nonetheless, I felt fear spread its raptor wings in my chest.

"What about Randall White?" I forced myself to ask.

"A reporter who covered the case for the *World-Telegram and Sun* has been trying to get it reopened. He says he's found evidence that proves White didn't do it."

"He was caught with Charlie's wallet."

After the trial, the police had returned the wallet. It lay now in the top drawer of Charlie's dresser, greasy and torn around the edges. I couldn't look at it, but I couldn't throw it away.

"And he confessed," I added.

"He says he found the wallet in a trash can and the police beat the confession out of him."

The detective's comment about being able to tell when a negro was lying came back to me.

"What's the new evidence?"

"White was picked up by the Philadelphia police that morning. For burglary. They let him go, but not until late that afternoon."

"Why didn't he say that at the time?"

"Apparently he did, but it didn't fit the detectives' story so they decided he was lying."

"Didn't they check with the Philadelphia police?"

"And risk losing the only suspect they had?"

The injustice would never stop unspooling. I swiveled back to my desk and sat staring at the photograph of Charlie pushing Abby in the swing. She was sailing through the sun-shot afternoon, and his grin was a slice of blinding white hope in the grainy photo. Now the world was paying us back for our willful innocence.

THIS TIME THE jury deliberated for two days. I could not understand what they found to argue about. They had the police blotter from Philadelphia. In the end, they found Randall White not guilty. The detectives were never charged with any wrongdoing, nor did they ever admit any. Randall White received no compensation for his imprisonment.

Elliot suggested I write a piece on the railroading of Randall White. I was surprised. He usually tried to tone me down, not fire me up. But I found the idea repellent. I told him I was in the middle of an article about the last days of Richard Wright. It was the one I'd been working on the day Charlie died. I hadn't been able to look at it for more than a year, but a few weeks earlier I'd gone back to it.

"This is more timely," Elliot said.

"I'd feel as if I were exploiting Charlie's death."

"Write it, Nell. Charlie would want you to."

He couldn't persuade me, but Charlie did.

It was the hardest article I had ever written. For weeks I lived with the violence of Charlie's last moments of life. Again and again, I saw his body, the body I knew so well, crumpling to the ground.

Once, I tore up the pages. The next day, I taped them back together and kept going.

Compass published the piece. Several newspapers ran articles about it. Elliot insisted it was the best thing I'd ever written.

"You only say that because it's not controversial. Who isn't opposed to police brutality and miscarriages of justice?"

"I say it because it's true, and because this one even did some good."

I told him I resented the implication that nothing else I'd written had, but he had a point. The wrongful imprisonment of Randall White turned out to be one of several cases around that time that led the U.S. Supreme Court to issue the Miranda Rights ruling, and New York State to abolish the death penalty, except in special cases.

ONE NIGHT A few weeks later, I walked into Abby's room, where she was supposed to be doing her homework, to find her reading the article. I was surprised. She was twelve, and, though she liked to see my byline, she never read what was beneath it. My impulse was to snatch it out of her hands. The world was rife with brutality and bloodshed. On the Pettus Bridge in Alabama, so-called law enforcement officers had used tear gas, whips, and clubs against unarmed marchers. Halfway around the world, in a place called Ia Drang Valley in Vietnam, Americans were killing and dying. It was bad enough that the ugly headlines spilled across the table as she ate her cereal in the morning, blared from the television on the evening news, and screamed up from the magazine covers that lay around the apartment. She knew Charlie had been shot. She did not have to read the details. But trying to stop her from reading it would only make her more determined to.

I stalled and asked if she had finished her homework. She said she had and went back to reading. I stood, no, hovered indecisively in the middle of the room.

"Mom!" She did not even bother to look up from the magazine.

I turned and left.

Half an hour later, I went back. She was just getting into bed. I sat on the side of it. I often sat for a moment to talk when I went in to say good night.

"Why did you suddenly decide to read that?"

She shrugged her bony shoulders.

"Did it upset you?"

"No." She hugged her knees to her. Through her pajamas, I could see the outline of her spine, fragile as an X-ray.

"It upset me writing it."

"I felt sorry for the man, Randall White. I felt bad that I used to hate him."

"That was only natural."

She shrugged again. Whatever was going on, she was not ready to tell me about it. Charlie had always known how to wait with her. I was learning.

A WEEK OR so later, she brought up the subject with Elliot. He was around a lot lately. I suspected he felt some obligation or loyalty to Charlie, though I wasn't sure why. I had never understood their friendship. It didn't make sense that two men who were so different could form such a bond. But I had never doubted the strength of it. I also think he genuinely enjoyed spending time with Abby and me. Perhaps he wanted an instant family that would provide the superficial pleasures without the messy intimacy. That was fine with me. Messy intimacy was the last thing I wanted. Elliot's careful handling, as if he knew I was broken, fit just fine.

The Sunday that Abby asked Elliot about Charlie's death, they had just come back from the Museum of Natural History. I was grateful to him. I loved taking her to the Met, MoMA, and other art museums, but the dusty exhibits of Indians sitting around campfires working with primitive tools and animals in their habitats depressed me. When they came back to the apartment that afternoon, they teased me about my limitations. Elliot called me naturephobic. Abby chimed in with Europhilic. I was glad. She needed someone with whom she could gang up on me.

I asked Elliot to stay for dinner. That was how I overheard their conversation. Elliot was teaching her to play chess, and they'd set up the board on a table in front of the window in the living room. The days were getting shorter, and beyond their heads the sky over the park had a bruised black-and-blue look. I was in the dining room setting the table. Actually, I had finished setting the table, but when I heard Abby's question, I lingered.

"Can I ask you something about how my dad died?"

In the moment of silence that followed, I sensed Elliot debating the answer.

"Sure," he said finally. "What do you want to know?"

"If that man, the one my mom wrote the article about, didn't kill him, who did? She says we'll probably never know."

"She's probably right."

"So it was just some stranger who came along and wanted his money?"

"Who else would it be?"

"I don't know." She hesitated. "Maybe it was like the President. Someone wanted to shoot him because of who he was."

"Nobody wanted to shoot your dad. Everyone liked him. He was just in the wrong place at the wrong time."

LATER THAT NIGHT, after Elliot left, when I went into Abby's room to say good night, I sat on the side of the bed.

"I heard you asking Uncle Elliot about who killed Daddy."

She sat staring at me for a moment. "Lauren says her dad says there was more to what happened in the park that day than meets the eye."

Now I knew where the questions were coming from. What I didn't understand was why Bill Dreyfus was stirring them up. He had barely known Charlie. The only connection was our daughters and some legal work he had done for *Compass,* thanks to the Drinkwater Foundation, a few years earlier. According to Charlie, he was a good lawyer but had a wacky streak. I agreed. Recently, he had buttonholed me at a school function with a lecture on the Warren Commission Report cover-up. Talking conspiracy theory to a sentient adult was annoying. Spreading it among children was unconscionable.

"Tell Lauren her dad is full of hot air."

"What?"

"Years ago he tried to sell Daddy shares in a hot-air balloon company."

Her eyes widened. "Really?"

"Daddy's reaction exactly. So you can tell Lauren there is not more there than meets the eye. Daddy was mugged. It was a senseless random crime. You can also tell her to tell her father to mind his own business."

Now her eyes were round and dark as Oreos. "Can I?"

"Maybe you'd better leave that to me."

I DID NOT tell Bill Dreyfus to mind his own business. If he said something again, I would, but I did not want to give his comment that much credence. Nonetheless, I could not help wondering what he meant. Charlie had decided to walk to work through the park that morning because it was a beautiful day. And because he wanted to walk off the anger I had directed at him. The knowledge continued to fester. If I hadn't made a scene, if I hadn't followed him to the door quarreling about Frank Tucker, he might have taken the subway or a cab, and . . . I was haunted by the contingency.

But Bill Dreyfus made it sound as if Charlie had done something to invite the mugging. It was an old ploy for warding off fear. Crimes don't happen to innocent people. Therefore they can't happen to me.

I WENT BACK to the piece on Richard Wright, though I was having difficulty making it work. The story had too many loose threads. At nine o'clock on the night Wright died, he rang for the nurse. When she arrived, he joked with her. Two hours later, he rang again. He was dead by the time she reached his room. His close friend, the cartoonist Ollie Harrington, had written me, in answer to questions I'd sent him, that every black man he knew believed Wright had been the object of foul play, but I wasn't sure how much credence to give his words. Harrington had fled America and requested political asylum in East Berlin. Nonetheless, I kept at the article, putting in paragraphs, taking them out, and putting them back.

The harder I worked, the easier it was to get through the days. I still hadn't found a way to get through the nights. Two years is a long time not to be held. My body ached for the casual affections of marriage, fingers brushing fingers while passing the salt, a hand trailed across a backside on the way to somewhere else, a cheek laid against a shoulder in sleep. My hair longed to be stroked. My skin hungered to be touched. I missed the pilfered glances while I dressed and undressed. I knew all that was too much to ask. I decided to settle for sex.

Occasionally I flirted with the idea of settling for sex with Elliot. Perhaps *settling* is the wrong word. Even when I'd been happy with Charlie, I'd noticed the hum he gave off to females of the species. But I was afraid of ruining the friendship, with me, and even more with Abby. A stranger would be safer.

At a party at Gideon Abel's to celebrate a book of poetry he'd published, I made up my mind to go home with an English writer whom I'd spent most of the evening talking to. He had a plummy accent, a quick wit, and a façade of kindness. I wasn't setting the bar high, but then I wasn't looking for love, only a connection. He suggested we go someplace for a nightcap. I was about to say yes when Sonia joined us and asked how his wife was.

"I didn't know if you'd care," she told me later, "but I thought you ought to know."

I did care. I wasn't looking for love, but I didn't want to sow mayhem.

The few other times I was tempted, something always intervened. Abby had persuaded me she didn't need a babysitter, so I wanted to get home early. I was on deadline and had to be up and working at the crack of dawn. Sonia said it had nothing to do with Abby or deadlines, only with fear. I wasn't sure she was wrong. My senses were withering from neglect, but my emotions were still raw. I had always been uncontrolled in sex. Now I could not trust my reactions. I did not want to break down sobbing in a strange bed at an inopportune moment. That was why I had flirted with the idea of Elliot. He already knew how broken I was.

I PUT ASIDE the piece on Richard Wright again and wrote an article opposing the bombing campaign against North Vietnam. Wally refused to publish it. The logical thing for me to do was to take it elsewhere, but I wanted it to run in what I still thought of as Charlie's magazine, because I knew Charlie would want it there. A memory loomed in my peripheral vision. Charlie was leaning over me in a smoky apartment crowded with students, talking about an anti-draft rally he had attended the day before. I looked up from the typewriter and tried to catch the vision, but he was gone.

I finally took the piece to *The New York Review of Books*. The *Review* was one of the few magazines that was publishing articles against the war in Vietnam.

The country was coming apart over the war. Elliot and I tried to stay off the subject, but when I refused an invitation to the White House that I had originally accepted, we got into an argument.

The problem started when Robert Lowell agreed to read at a White House arts festival, then changed his mind and refused. His letter to President Johnson made front-page news.

I waited for the act of conscience to become a literary dogfight.

Within twenty-four hours, Saul Bellow and John Hersey went on record to say they would read from their own works at the White House as planned, though they were quick to add that they, too, disapproved of the administration's foreign policy. The lines were drawn. Letters and telegrams poured into the White House. Friends fought with one another about whether they should attend the festival or boycott it.

"You can't refuse an invitation to the White House," Elliot said.

We were at his place in Connecticut, sitting on the wide porch that wrapped around the house like an embrace. Beyond the striped green awnings, the sun was a dim glow in an ashen sky, and the air was still and thick with an impending storm. Abby had gone inside to read.

"I've been to the White House," I said, and suddenly I was back in those halcyon days when Charlie and I had gone down the receiving line to a golden-boy President who said he had read an article I'd written. Perhaps the war was not the only reason I was boycotting the festival. The memory of that last time was so raw that I could not risk repeating it without Charlie, and without illusions.

"Your problem is that you confuse the dignity of the office with the policies of the man holding it."

"Your problem is that you refuse to recognize that the country is fighting an unjust imperialist war, and please, no speeches about the domino theory."

"It's disrespectful not to go."

"It's immoral to go," I said and wondered again how he and Charlie had gotten along so well.

We went on that way for some time. He infuriated me. But here's the odd thing. My anger did not drown out the hum.

A FEW WEEKS later, Elliot did something that surprised me. Perhaps this is vain, but I like to think it was due to my influence. It wasn't his fault that he got it wrong, or at least not completely right.

One night at a dinner party—I was not there; he told me the story later—he was seated next to the wife of a diplomat on the staff of the UN delegation from Chad. She mentioned that she, her husband, and their five-year-old son had driven up from Washington the week before. They'd stopped for lunch at a restaurant in Maryland. At least, they'd tried to stop for lunch. Three different restaurants turned them away. At the third, they asked for a glass of water for their son. The manager told them they did not serve coloreds.

"It's absurd," Elliot said. "We're spending millions of dollars to court these countries to keep them out of the communist camp. Then we turn around and insult their leaders."

He had decided to put foundation money behind an effort to ensure better treatment of diplomats from newly formed African nations.

"An admirable endeavor," I said.

"I detect a note of sarcasm."

"No, it is admirable. I just wonder about all the American negroes who don't have diplomatic immunity and can't get a glass of water on the road from Washington to New York."

He shook his head. "I can't win for losing."

SHORTLY AFTER OUR conversation about the African diplomats, I went to bed with a man named Nicholas Selden, whom I met at a party at Sonia's. He was an expat novelist living in Rome and in New York for a few days to see his publisher. I was fairly sure I wouldn't run into him again for some time, if ever, and Orchid was staying with Abby, because I had known I'd be late. I did not break down in sobs in Nicholas Selden's bed, which was really a bed in the apartment of the friend with whom he was staying. My body turned out to be still in working order. The next morning I was not sorry I had gone home with him, though I was glad that by then I was back in my own bed. He had wanted me to spend the night, but I'd told him I had left my daughter with a babysitter and

had to get home. I was ready for sex, but not for morning-after intimacies.

I lay in my own bed, feeling smug and satisfied. The tight spring
that my body had become had uncoiled, and Nicholas Selden's face
and body were already fading. I crossed my arms behind my head
and stretched. I had gone to bed with someone who was not Charlie
without betraying Charlie.

During the next few months, I repeated the experience with two
other men, though not as successfully. The second turned out to have
a penchant for shouting scatological words during the act and, what
was worse, begging me to shout them in return. That should have
turned me off casual sex, but I was afraid that if I stopped with him,
I'd never be able to start again, so I risked another encounter with
another man, but afterward, when I got up out of a strange bed, put
on my clothes, and went down to the late-night street to hail a cab—
no, I told him, no need to get up; I can take care of myself—I decided it was time to stop. I had proved I could function physically,
but I feared I was beginning to fray around the emotional edges.

The problem was that as soon as I stopped going to bed with
other men, the hum Elliot gave off grew louder. Sometimes it
screamed like the cicadas at nightfall at his house in the country.
That was why what happened with him happened, why things began
to go right, before they went so abysmally wrong.

Seventeen

THINGS BEGAN TO go right between Elliot and me the night of the antiwar march on Washington. We disagreed about that too. I did not understand how any right-thinking individual could refuse to go. He could not comprehend how I could risk—*risk* was his word, not mine—taking Abby.

"It's a Saturday, she doesn't have school, and she's dying to go."

"Of course, she's dying to go. She's your daughter. But she's also twelve years old. You're supposed to have more sense."

"Charlie and I took her to the civil rights march. You should hear her chant *Free at last, free at last.*"

He hesitated, and I guessed what he was thinking, but he knew better than to criticize Charlie or his judgment to me.

"I've heard her chant, thank you, and, while it's admirable, I think she should expand her repertory. Why don't I get two tickets to the matinee of *Man of La Mancha* and take her to that while you go to Washington to save the world?"

"That's a great idea. Let's all forget the unjust imperialist war and go to the theater." I started to hum "The Impossible Dream."

"It's better than spending the day shuffling around the capital with a bunch of hippies, who're smoking god knows what. You want to subject Abby to that?"

I started to laugh.

"What's so funny?"

"That you think a bunch of kids with long hair and ratty clothes, chanting about peace, are dangerous. In that case, come with us. We'll need all the protection we can get. And maybe you'll see the light of day."

Nonetheless, I did ask Abby if she'd prefer to go to the theater with Elliot. "No way," she said. "This'll be just like the civil rights march you and Daddy took me to."

Elliot did not go to Washington with us, but there were plenty of familiar faces on the train. Sonia was along with her television producer beau Miles, though they would not be returning with us. After the march they planned to lock themselves in a room at the Willard Hotel to celebrate their first anniversary as a couple. Wally Dryer wasn't there, but the rest of the staff of *Compass* was. Frank Tucker was on the train with a girl who bore an uncanny resemblance to the Tenniel illustrations of Alice in Wonderland, though that may have merely been the tangled mass of yellow hair. Under her parka, she wore a long dress of a thin flowered material and, it became evident when she took off the jacket, nothing else. An aura of high spirits, camaraderie, and self-righteous virtue floated in the air like the dust and soot of the old railroad cars.

As it turned out, little in the demonstration would have offended Elliot. A few young people, who carried an aroma stronger than their self-righteous virtue, brandished Viet Cong flags, but most of the signs were less abrasive.

STOP THE BOMBING

HONOR PEACE

WAR ERODES THE GREAT SOCIETY

Some were even polite. One little girl in a stroller carried a placard not much bigger than an oversize lollipop. PEACE IN VIETNAM,

PLEASE. The chants of "Hey, hey, LBJ, how many kids did you kill today?" were still in the future.

We milled around the White House, freshly laundered by an early-morning shower. We sat on the grass in front of the Washington Monument under a brassy November sun and listened to speeches. We trooped back to Union Station, bone tired and pleased as punch. We had spent ourselves for a good cause.

Abby slept on the way back to New York. When the train pulled into Penn Station, I had to shake her awake. We gathered our things and jostled our way up the stairs with the other hollow-eyed, exhausted, self-styled Good Samaritans.

At the top of the steps, the new concourse surprised me again. I still expected the old soaring steel-and-glass space. That station had made entering the city an occasion. This ugly, harshly lit building made arrival feel furtive and sleazy. I wondered how long the taxi queue was going to be. Then I saw him.

Elliot was standing a little away from the gate, an obstruction in the stream of rumpled humanity flowing out of the stairwell. His face had a smooth freshly shaved glow, and his tweed jacket and flannel trousers looked as if he'd just taken them off the hanger. Beneath my tired sweater and wrinkled jacket, I felt a pang of gratitude mixed with disappointment. If he could come to the station to meet us, why couldn't he march with us to stop the war? Charlie used to tease me that I was that classic left-wing cliché, a woman who loved mankind in the abstract but was impatient of her fellow man, and woman, in the flesh. Elliot was the opposite. He didn't seem to be incensed about people killing and dying halfway around the world, but he was concerned about how Abby and I would get uptown.

We were in front of him before he picked us out of the crowd.

"Taking down names for the CIA?" I asked.

"Only if they're carrying Viet Cong flags." He turned to Abby. "How was it?"

"Far out." She grinned. "You would have hated it."

"That's why I didn't go." He turned back to me. "I have a car waiting on Seventh Avenue."

"You're going to get your just rewards for this in heaven."

"I was hoping I wouldn't have to wait that long," he said as we started toward the exit. I was surprised. He was not usually flirtatious.

We had left that morning in a mild drizzle, but a new front had come through, and a cold wind worked us over as we came out of the station. Abby hugged herself. Elliot put his arm around her and rubbed her shoulders.

"This is no way to come home from a peace march," I said when I saw the driver sitting in the long black town car.

"On the contrary. If you have to go to a peace march, this is the only way to come home from it."

"Uncle Elliot's right, Mom. Lighten up." She looked up at him and grinned, and I was grateful again. I did not want her growing up as I had, in a stifling hothouse where two women, their roots tangled in the arid soil, gasped for the same meager supply of air and sun and water.

Abby dozed off again in the car. This time her head fell on Elliot's shoulder. When we reached our building, he shook her awake gently. Later, I would come to doubt almost everything about Elliot except his affection for Abby.

He got out of the car and walked us to the door of the building. Abby mumbled good night sleepily and started inside. I was exhausted, but it didn't seem right not to ask him up for a drink after he'd gone to the trouble of hiring a car and coming down to the station to meet us.

"Do you want to come up? I have just enough energy left for one drink."

"You could have fooled me. Get some sleep. I'll take a rain check."

On my way up in the elevator I told myself I was relieved. We had left the apartment before six that morning. It was after midnight. The last thing I wanted was to sit around making polite conversation. But I couldn't help thinking he should have wanted me to.

THE NEXT EVENING, Elliot called to ask if I'd like to have dinner that week. "Just the grown-ups," he added. I said I would.

On Wednesday evening, Abby wandered into my room while I was getting dressed. "So I guess this is a date."

"Of course it's not a date."

She leaned against the doorframe with her hands jammed in the back pockets of her jeans. "Sure looks like one from where I stand."

"Then maybe you ought to move to get a new perspective."

"Amanda has a stepdad."

"Amanda's parents are divorced."

"That's what I mean. It doesn't seem fair for her to have a dad and a stepdad when I don't have either. You're the one who's always talking about the redistribution of wealth."

"That's what I get for reading you *A Child's Guide to Karl Marx* in your crib."

She crossed the room and came up behind me. "Your tag's sticking out," she said as she tucked it in. Then she met my eyes in the mirror. "You look cool. Really."

ELLIOT HAD GIVEN me a choice of restaurants, Grenouille, "21," or an Italian spot that was still a couple of cuts above checked tablecloths and Chianti bottle candlesticks. I opted for the last. This was going to be awkward enough without swank. I kept thinking about the scatological shouter. What if the hum masked strange predilections or repellent tics? No matter how well you knew a man, or a woman for that matter, sex was uncharted territory, until you were lost in it, and then it was too late.

He was standing at the bar when I arrived, leaning on it with one elbow, his hand curled around a drink, a picture of composure until he saw me. The smile he pasted on his face was so thin I could see through it. He knew as well as I that this was a mistake.

He asked me if I wanted a drink there or at the table. Later I wondered if he would have broken the news at the bar if I'd said I wanted a drink there. I doubt it. He knew how I would react, and he wouldn't have wanted other people listening.

I followed the maître d' through the labyrinth of tables to one in the corner. I can't remember what we talked about while we waited for my drink. Nothing consequential, I'm sure. We were both too uneasy, though as it turned out for different reasons. The timing, we would agree later, was terrible.

"Remember the reporter who tracked down the police blotter that won Randall White a new trial?" he asked after the waiter had brought my drink and left.

I wasn't likely to forget him. I took a swallow of my drink and waited.

"I got a call just before I left the office. Apparently, he was working on another crime story and turned up some new evidence about Charlie's death."

I put down my drink, then picked it up again. I wanted no more investigations, no more trials, no more endless replays of those obscene events.

"What's the new evidence?" I forced myself to ask.

He shook his head, as if in apology. He did not want to tell this story any more than I wanted to hear it.

The police had arrested a drug dealer for the murder of a rival drug dealer. In hope of leniency, the suspect offered to give them the name of the killer in the Umpire Rock murder case.

I had been staring at the table as he talked. Now my eyes flew up to his face. "The what?"

"I'm sorry, I thought you knew. That's what the newspapers called it. They found the body near Umpire Rock."

I had stayed away from the news accounts. It had taken me weeks to be able to read the obituaries. I don't know why it upset me now. Charlie was dead, and the words they used about the fact made no difference, but the idea of Charlie being the body and this tragedy a catchy headline struck me as unconscionable.

"According to the drug dealer," Elliot went on, "a friend turned up flush with money the afternoon Charlie was killed. When the dealer asked where he'd got it, he told him about mugging a man in Central Park."

My head swiveled away from Elliot. It wasn't his fault that he was the bearer of news I did not want to hear, but I still couldn't look at him. I put down my glass, and stood.

"I'm sorry. I can't do this."

"I'll take you home."

But I was already on my way to the coat check, and he had to stop to pay the bill.

He caught up with me outside the restaurant and took my arm. I wrenched it away. He stepped to the curb and lifted his hand to hail a cab. A taxi swerved up. He opened the door.

"I'd rather walk." I started down the block.

He told the driver to go on and fell in step with me.

The rest of the night is a broken mirror, jagged fragments of untidy behavior. When we reached Central Park West, I crossed the street to the park and turned in to it. I had it in my mind that I would walk there. That was where Charlie was.

Elliot took my arm to stop me. I shook him off again.

"You can't go into the park," he said quietly. One of us, at least, would avoid histrionics.

I turned away from him and started down the sidewalk on the park side of the street. He caught up with me again. I told him I wanted to be alone. He stopped. I kept going. I couldn't hear his steps over the noise of the cars and buses, but I knew he was there, keeping pace behind me.

I'm not sure how long we walked that way, I with my shoulders hunched forward, burrowing into the darkness, Elliot, upright and watchful, I knew without turning to see him, shadowing my steps. Gradually, I became aware of the physical discomfort. I was wearing high heels. The situation was ludicrous. Twenty minutes, half an hour, however long ago, I had been unhinged enough to court disaster in the park. Now I was brought down by a blister.

I sat on a bench, worn out by the endless unraveling of misery and injustice. Charlie was dead. Why did they have to keep exhuming the horror of that morning? Why couldn't they let me grieve for him in peace?

"Do you mind if I sit with you?"

I shrugged. He sat. A rat darted out from beneath the bench into the park.

"I think I ought to walk you home," he said.

We got up from the bench. He was careful not to touch me but stood waiting until I began to walk, then fell in step beside me, keeping several inches of cold night air between us. If he noticed that I was limping, he didn't say anything. We reached a corner and stood waiting for the light to change.

"I'm sorry," I said.

The light turned. He did not take my arm as we crossed.

"I didn't see how I could keep it from you."

"You couldn't. It's not your fault." We walked on for a while. "I just needed someone to blame."

I saw his hand begin to go to my elbow. Then it returned to his coat pocket. The delicacy of the gesture touched me.

A FEW DAYS later, I told Abby about the new suspect. By then the police had been in touch with me about reopening the case. His name was Roberto Vega, and his life story was a translation into Spanish of Randall White's.

Abby took the news better than I had. I think she even found some comfort in it.

Eighteen

A FTER THE NIGHT I fled the restaurant, Elliot gave me time to calm down, then called and suggested dinner again. I chose the Friday night of a long holiday weekend. Abby was going skiing in Vermont with Lauren and her family.

At a little after six, she and I stood under the awning of our building in the chill February evening waiting for them. When a car swerved out of the line of traffic and pulled up to the curb, I stretched my mouth into a crescent of a smile, thanked Lauren's parents for inviting Abby, and hugged her. She felt as fragile as porcelain.

I remained under the canopy, waving, as my daughter disappeared into the ribbons of swerving lights streaming up and down Central Park West. When I could no longer make out the car, I turned and started back into the building.

Upstairs, in the silence of the empty apartment, my loneliness bumped against the high ceilings like an untethered helium balloon. I went down the hall to the bathroom, stripped off my clothes, and stepped into the shower. I would keep moving.

Elliot was waiting at the bar. The restaurant was not the one where he'd told me about Roberto Vega, but his stance was the same. He was not a heavy drinker, or at least no heavier than everyone else I knew, but he looked at home at a bar. Then again, he looked at home most places. Before he could ask if I wanted to go straight to the table, I slid onto the barstool beside him. Something about sitting high on a stool, legs crossed, one stiletto heel caught on the rung, a long-stemmed martini glass in hand, struck me as appropriate to the business at hand.

I had only a moment's pause about what I was up to. It came on the way out of the restaurant. As Elliot was helping me on with my coat, I suddenly thought of Frank Tucker. For years Frank had made passes at me, because he was conditioned to make passes at women. But he also liked the idea of screwing Charlie by screwing his wife. I don't mean to suggest that he disliked Charlie. On the contrary, I think he admired him enough to compete with him. Perhaps Elliot felt the same way. Perhaps the rotten underbelly of Elliot's loyalty to Charlie was a need for beyond-the-grave one-upmanship. My suspicions faded when we got into the taxi. He suggested we go to his apartment, though mine was empty. If he'd wanted to trounce Charlie, the best place to do it would have been in Charlie's bed.

My fears about fetishes or even quirkiness turned out to be unfounded. Nothing that happened with Elliot that night would make the pages of Krafft-Ebing's catalog of sexual pathology. Nor did I disgrace myself with untidy emotion. Perhaps because he'd been a bachelor for so long and had never grown accustomed to one woman, he was attuned to women. The sex was accomplished, not a word I usually associate with the act. I didn't think of Charlie more than half a dozen times.

The next morning we sat in his dining room overlooking the Park Avenue Brick Church, drinking coffee and trading sections of the papers and observations about the news. Nothing in my life had changed, except where I'd once felt a faint annoying itch, I now sensed a low murmur of well-being. Years ago, in love with Charlie, I would have thought that was the saddest statement in the world. I remembered sitting in Bickford's the morning after I went to his room for the first time, loopy with love, pitying everyone who was not us. One night together had stood the world on its head. Now I just wanted to keep it on an even keel. Elliot was an expert at that.

We fell into a kind of schedule. That was telling too. In the early days, Charlie and I had stalked each other around the campus, hoping for a chance meeting. Even after we married, the thrill of serendipitous encounters guided our steps. One evening, a year or so into our marriage, I came out of a supermarket on Broadway and found him loitering. "What's a nice boy like you doing in a place like this?" I asked, and we clung together, the brown paper bag of groceries between us, all the way home. But Charlie and I had been eager to put down stakes in each other's lives. Elliot and I were determined not to intrude. I cooked dinner for him and Abby. He got tickets for plays and concerts. Occasionally, we were invited to the same dinner party. Gradually, hostesses began to seat us apart. Word was getting out that we were together.

I found the situation comforting, or at least comfortable. I was tired of being the lone woman who skewed dinner table seating arrangements and was unwelcome in certain public places. The humiliation of that second discovery still stung. It happened a year or so after Charlie died. I was on my way home from a meeting at *Compass*. Maybe that was why I wanted to stop for a drink. I still couldn't bear to see Wally Dryer sitting behind Charlie's desk. As I walked up Broadway, I felt the hole within me as if the wind were going through it. I didn't want to visit that on Abby.

I passed a French restaurant with a little zinc bar that Charlie and I used to like, and the memory of being there with him reached out and grabbed me. I turned back and went in. For a moment I felt the ache of coming home. Charlie and the bartender used to talk about the Brooklyn Dodgers, though even then they were no longer in Brooklyn.

If the bartender recognized me, he gave no sign of it. He barely glanced at me when I slid onto the stool. He took a good three minutes to wander over to ask what I wanted. Only when a man came in, sat beside me, and tried to strike up a conversation, and I turned my back, did he become civil, and then only barely.

Sonia was the one who explained the situation to me. "A woman alone in a bar like that is either a pro looking for customers or an amateur looking for a pickup."

"How do you know something like that?"

"Just be glad you don't."

But now I did.

I don't mean to sound as if Elliot was nothing more than a solution to a social problem and a seductive sexual hum. He was extremely good company. He knew a great deal about a great deal and was articulate and often droll about all of it. And he ran, as I had imagined my mother's cliché putting it, deep. Every time I thought I had him pegged, he surprised me. In prep school he'd had his heart set on becoming a concert pianist and had been encouraged by the various teachers he studied with, but then he broke his hand in a football scrimmage and decided he'd always be second-rate. "At least the injury was a good excuse for being second-rate," he admitted when he told me the story, and I liked him for the confession. He was generous. A couple of bright kids from Harlem were going to Yale on his money. And he was infinitely discreet, in the large ways of keeping confidences, and in smaller ways as well. For a man who knew all sorts of important people, he never dropped a name. That may not sound like much, but it is more unusual, and to my mind more admirable, than most people think. Of course, the other side of the discretion was his reserve. Maybe I kept discovering new facets of Elliot because he kept the essential Elliot under lock and key. That was even more intriguing.

ABBY HAD ALREADY left for school that morning, and I was sitting at the table finishing a second mug of coffee and the front page of the *Times*. Outside the kitchen window, a mouse-gray sky spat desultory rain, though the weather forecast read fair.

I was skimming a piece about electronic spying by the CIA. Ac-

cording to the article, the latest devices were so powerful and inge-
nious that soon the world would be bereft of secrets. Even now, part
of President Johnson's bedtime reading of his daily intelligence reports included the latest sexual high jinks of other world leaders.

I was about to close the paper and get down to work when a
sentence toward the end caught my eye. It had nothing to do with
electronic spying.

"The CIA has also funded organizations of liberal intellectuals
such as the Congress for Cultural Freedom."

The Congress for Cultural Freedom, which Charlie and I had
both had dealings with over the years, sponsored artistic and intellectual programs and publications around the world, including *The
Thames Review,* a journal to which I had contributed several pieces.
Attending CCF-sponsored conferences when Drinkwater paid our
way was one thing; writing for a CIA-front magazine was another
story.

I went into my office, flipped through my Rolodex, found the
number for Hugh Baker, the publisher of *The Thames Review,* and
dialed it. The receptionist was cheerful as she told me Mr. Baker was
not in today. "I can take a message," she added. "He'll be calling in
later."

I asked her to have him phone me as soon as possible.

I spent the next hour paging through back issues of the magazine. It held no answers, and I couldn't decide whether I had been
willfully blind before or was unduly suspicious now. That was when
I remembered that Sonia had contributed several pieces of art criti-
cism to the review. I dialed her number.

"Am I interrupting something?" I asked, when she picked up the
phone.

"Only an orgy of pencil sharpening."

"You write on a typewriter."

"With which I have an even more fraught relationship."

I asked if she had seen the piece on electronic spying in the morning paper. She hadn't. I read her the line about the Congress for Cultural Freedom.

"The question is, does that mean *The Thames Review*?" I asked.

"Impossible. Hugh would have told us."

"That was my first reaction, but now I wonder. If you're taking money from a clandestine organization, you don't go around telling people about it."

"I can't believe it. Not Hugh."

That was when I remembered that she and Hugh Baker had had a brief affair. It wasn't the first time I wondered at the fact that a woman who was so smart about so many things could be so credulous of men.

"I don't want to believe it," I said. "I hate the idea that we were hoodwinked into contributing to a CIA rag."

"Last I heard you thought it was a good magazine. When did it become a rag?"

"All right, it's not a rag. It's just dishonest. Which makes us dishonest. We were shilling for the government and didn't even know it."

"I'm going to call Hugh."

"I already did. He's not in his office today. I left a message for him to call me back.

"I suppose there's a silver lining of sorts," I added as we were getting off the phone. "We're usually annoyed when magazines turn down our work. It's kind of refreshing to be angry because they publish it."

A few hours later, Hugh Baker called.

"Don't you think I would have told you if you were working for the CIA?" he asked.

"I don't know. Would you?"

He laughed. "Okay, then let me put it another way. Maybe you'll believe this. I'm glad the CIA never offered me money, because to tell the truth, I don't know what I would have done. We've gone through some pretty lean times."

The denial was a little too clever to be entirely persuasive.

THAT NIGHT I asked Elliot what he knew about Hugh Baker. We had met at the Metropolitan Museum for the preview of a show on American craftsmanship in silver to which he'd lent two family pieces. I sprang the question on him as soon as he came up to me in the great hall. I should have known better. The place was too crowded for serious talk. Well-dressed men and women jostled one another. Before Elliot could answer, a man, whose name was often followed by the word *philanthropist,* accompanied by a woman in a Norman Norell dress my more acquisitive side would have killed for, joined us. It went on that way for some time. The galleries were even more packed than the entrance hall. Elliot didn't get a chance to answer my question until we had gotten our coats and were standing outside the museum. A damp April wind barreled up Fifth Avenue, whipping discarded newspapers, cigarette butts, and the occasional beer or soda can into whirlpools of detritus. The city seemed to be getting dirtier and more dangerous by the day.

"What do you want to know about him?" he asked.

I told him about the article. He had seen it.

"It didn't mention Hugh Baker or *The Thames Review,*" he said.

"It mentioned the Congress for Cultural Freedom."

"So you're wondering if Hugh took money that came to the congress from the CIA."

"He says he didn't, but I'm not sure I believe him."

"You can believe him," Elliot said. "Hugh Baker wouldn't take money from the CIA."

"How well do you know him?"

"Well enough to know that."

"But what if he didn't know where the money was coming from?"

"That's not the way it works. Someone at the magazine would have to be informed, and he's the publisher."

"How do you know something like that?"

He took my arm as we started down the wide steps. "I run a nonprofit foundation. It's my job to know things like that."

THE ISSUE CONTINUED to simmer. Speculation raged, fingers pointed, denials flew. Then, a week after the article ran, Elliot showed up with more news. Abby was in her room doing her homework. The smell of roasting chicken hung like bunting in the apartment. He put his coat in the closet and went into the living room to make himself a drink. I went back to the kitchen. A moment later he joined me there. It occurred to me as he stood leaning against the counter, watching me baste, that he'd been doing that for a long time, in one capacity or another.

"I have good news," he said. "You don't have to worry about *The Thames Review* or even the Congress for Cultural Freedom for that matter."

I turned from the stove to him.

"Why not?"

"I had lunch at the club today. Everyone is still talking about the piece. And someone said there's going to be a letter to the editor in tomorrow's *Times* attesting to the independence of the congress."

"I didn't expect them to come out and admit it."

"The letter is signed by Arthur Schlesinger, John Kenneth Galbraith, George Kennan, and Robert Oppenheimer. You didn't believe Hugh Baker and you weren't sure about me—"

"That's not true."

He smiled. "You're a lousy actress. But those four are the gold standard of rectitude and gravitas, though I admit there have been some pretty ugly attempts to dirty Oppenheimer's skirts. The point is, you can go back to writing for the review with a clear conscience."

Nineteen

THREE WEEKS LATER, on a clement day in May when the city was doused in spring sunshine, Roberto Vega went on trial. Once again, I stayed away.

I had expected the proceedings to drag on, but they did not last much longer than the previous trials, though the jury did deliberate for two days before acquitting Vega. According to Elliot, they did not find the sworn testimony of a confessed drug dealer and murderer persuasive.

"So we still don't know who killed Daddy," Abby said.

THAT JULY, CHARLIE'S parents took Abby to the New Jersey shore for a week. When my mother lamented her inability to give her granddaughter a holiday, I sent the two of them for another week to Montauk, the town on the eastern tip of Long Island where Charlie had told me over a lobster dinner that we'd never be rich, but we wouldn't starve.

I had more time to myself that summer but saw less of Elliot. I sensed there were problems at the foundation, though he didn't say as much. All I knew was that he was taking the train or the new Eastern Air Lines Shuttle to Washington more often. But in August, he and I spent the week that Abby and my mother were away at his house in Connecticut. Except for the night Sonia and Miles stopped in on their way home from Tanglewood, we were alone the entire time. We had never been together for that duration, and I was surprised at how easy it was. We read; we went off to different rooms to work; we swam; while I cooked dinner, he made drinks, opened wine, changed records, and set the table; and at night we went to bed in his big tester bed. Afterward, I slept deeply, wrapped in the silky lake-cooled breezes.

We even managed to avoid talking about the war. One evening, sitting on the porch, I joked that he was teaching me temperance.

"I was hoping for tolerance," he said, "but I'll take what I can get."

I KNEW THAT we had become a couple in the eyes of others, but at a party at Gideon Abel's, Frank Tucker brought the fact home with special force.

Gideon was still married to his second and fourth wife and still giving parties in her duplex. Or perhaps it was the same party that he had kept going for the better part of four decades. The room was crowded with familiar faces and some new blood, and I was willing to bet that when he invited the men, he still told them to bring a pretty, leggy girl. The only difference was that I was no longer a pretty, leggy girl. My daughter was becoming one. I was a widow, pushing forty-one. Sonia, who was two years younger, called us women of a certain age. She also said that women of a certain age were just beginning to get interesting, but I had the feeling she was whistling in the dark. Lookers have a harder time aging. The rest of us don't have as much to lose. The fact that two weeks after their weekend at Tanglewood, Miles suffered a mild heart attack in the bed of his twenty-two-year-old secretary made her whistle in the dark sound even more shrill.

I usually tried to avoid Frank Tucker at parties, but that night I sought him out. He had just published a long piece in a popular counterculture—that was the new term—magazine exposing CIA backing of the National Student Association. It had stirred up a hornet's nest in high places. When the CIA found they couldn't suppress it, they scheduled a press conference to scoop it. But Frank and the magazine scooped the scoop by running full-page ads in several newspapers announcing the article. It ended up attracting even more attention. I had seen Frank preening in a television interview.

"How often in life," he asked the interviewer, "do you slay the dragon with a single thrust of the sword?"

I didn't much like his smug air, but I admired, and envied, his achievement, and when he was alone for a moment, I went over to tell him as much.

I held out my hand. He grabbed me in a bear hug and planted a damp sour-whiskey-smelling kiss on my mouth. His tongue made a feint at forced entry. I warded it off. My lower body arched away from his instinctively.

I extricated myself and told him how much I admired the piece.

He grinned down at me. He'd put on weight, and it made his eyes look smaller in his puffy face, like two raisins in a doughy cookie.

"How often in life do you slay the dragon with a single thrust of the sword?" he asked.

"I'm not sure you finished him off, but you definitely delivered a body blow."

He said I was damn right he'd delivered a body blow and asked how I'd been. I said I'd been fine.

"Still scribbling?"

"Every now and then I even manage to get something into print." I regretted the words as soon as they were out. I should not have risen to the bait.

His grin grew wider. "That's the Nell I know and love. And speaking of that, how's your love life?"

The question was intended to provoke, but there was something else behind it as well. The exposé had made him even more of a celebrity, and he could have his pick of younger prettier leggier girls, but I had the feeling some atavistic stubbornness made him regard me as unfinished business.

"Not in need of mouth-to-mouth resuscitation, thank you."

"Then it's true what I hear?"

"What do you hear?"

"That you're sleeping with the enemy."

I stiffened. "The enemy?"

"McClellan. I couldn't believe it when I heard. Not Nell, I said."

"Why not Nell?"

"I told you. Because he's the enemy."

"Charlie and Elliot were good friends."

"Charlie and I were good friends. At least in the old days. McClellan was no friend to Charlie."

"That wasn't the way Charlie saw it." I congratulated him again and moved off.

"What does Frank Tucker have against you?" I asked Elliot a few nights later as we were putting on our clothes. No matter how often I told him that he did not have to come downstairs with me, that the doorman and I were capable of getting a cab without him, he insisted on getting dressed, going down to the street, and putting me in a taxi. Perhaps he knew that, for all my talk, once I was standing on Park Avenue, scanning the sparse late-night traffic for an empty cab, I'd think of him dozing off in a sex-warmed bed and feel a flash of unreasonable resentment.

He sat on the side of the bed and began pulling on his trousers. "What Frank Tucker has against me is you."

"Me?"

He looked up at me. "Coyness does not become you."

"I think the issue is Charlie, not me. He says you were no friend to Charlie."

He stood and zipped his fly. "Do you believe him?"

I had to think about that for a moment. "No."

He shook his head and smiled. "At least it wasn't a knee-jerk response.

"I suppose you know this is ridiculous," he said as we stood in the hall waiting for the elevator.

"You really don't have to come down with me."

"I meant that it's ridiculous for either of us to be climbing out of bed in the middle of the night—"

"Ten thirty is scarcely the middle of the night."

"A figure of speech. We wouldn't have to if we were married."

The idea did not exactly blindside me. In those days, women like me did not sleep with men for protracted periods of time without speculating about marriage. Maybe they still don't. Nonetheless, the suggestion did sound perfunctory. I wasn't a romantic, but laziness did not strike me as grounds for marriage.

"Oh, you hot-blooded Lothario, you. I'm tired of getting up in the middle of the night, so let's get married."

"If I were a hot-blooded Lothario, you would have run for the hills a long time ago. You said yourself how easy that week in Connecticut was. We were like an old married couple."

Clichés usually harbor a kernel of truth, that's why they become clichés, and maybe this one did, but not in my experience. Charlie and I had never been easy. Fanatical, giddy, scrappy, abject with apology, dopey with love, but there was always too much current charging between us to be easy.

"Think about it," he said, as he followed me into the elevator.

"Fine, I'll think about it, and you reconsider in what is called the cold light of morning, when"—I went on as we crossed the lobby—"you're not getting up out of a warm bed to put me in a taxi."

He called me the next morning, though he rarely did that.

"I just wanted to tell you that it's not the middle of the night, I'm not facing going out into the streets, and it still seems like a good idea to me."

"You do know I was on my best behavior that week in Connecticut?"

This time I was not being coy. Elliot did not like drama, and I knew that I could make life a living hell for a man like that, despite my comment about his teaching me temperance.

"Nell, we've known each other for fifteen years. I don't think there are a lot of surprises left."

I told him I had to discuss it with Abby. He said he knew that.

I HAD EXPECTED Abby to be in favor of the idea. She hadn't been entirely facetious when she'd talked about redistributing the wealth in fathers and stepfathers. More than once, I had caught her watching girls and their fathers in museums and movies and restaurants. A few weeks earlier, we had walked up Columbus Avenue behind a girl about thirteen and a man in his forties. They were holding hands, and laughing, and bouncing phrases and jokes and teasing taunts back and forth like tennis balls. My ungenerous heart had shriveled at the sight.

But when I asked her what she thought of my marrying Elliot, she ducked her head so her long hair fell over her face. She had begun doing that when she wanted to hide her face. My lovely daughter was beginning to come up spotty. The British term sounded less ugly than *pimply,* though the terminology didn't seem to make a difference to her. She also did it when she wanted to conceal her emotions.

"You don't like the idea."

"No. I think it's a good idea. Only . . ."

"Only what?"

"I wouldn't have to call him Dad, would I?"

"You do, and I'll wash your mouth out with soap."

WHEN I TOLD Sonia the news, she was more girlish about it than Abby. The three of us were having brunch on the sidewalk terrace of an Upper West Side restaurant, and the clattering of dishes mingled with the gunning of engines and the blare of horns to shatter the soft Indian summer day. Charlie and I had always hated dining outside in New York City. Eat your food before it gets dirty, he used to say. But Abby and Sonia had insisted.

"What are you going to wear?" Sonia asked.

"If I know my mom, a trench coat over a nightgown," Abby cracked.

"Are you impugning my sense of style?"

"I think she was talking about your sense of occasion," Sonia explained. "You're so determined to play this down that you're probably not even going to buy something new." She turned to Abby. "What do you want to bet she's planning on city hall?"

"It's the city clerk's office, not city hall, and we're not going there."

I had intended to at first. If the city clerk's office was good enough for Charlie and me, it was certainly good enough for Elliot and me. But that was the point. I hadn't cared where I married Charlie. The way I'd felt that day, the dusty soulless municipal room was as good as the cathedral at Chartres. But I was clear-sighted about this marriage, or so I thought, and the office of the city clerk was too depressing when seen without a softening scrim of euphoria.

"A judge who's a friend of Elliot's is going to marry us in his chambers."

"I'm the only guest," Abby said, "besides a couple of secretaries he'll haul in to act as witnesses. I'm not old enough to bear witness."

"Don't forget to take rice," Sonia said.

"Raw or cooked?" Abby asked.

"I'm glad the two of you are having such a good time with this."

"Someone ought to," Sonia said above the roar of a truck going by.

"What do you want me to do, hire a ballroom, wear white, and toss a bouquet?"

"What we want you to do," Sonia answered, "is to stop acting as if this is some shady undertaking you're ashamed of."

"I'm not ashamed," I insisted and signaled for the check.

Abby came back to the subject after we had said goodbye to Sonia and were walking up Central Park West.

"You know what I think?"

"What do you think?"

She ducked her head to let her hair fall forward. "I think Daddy would want you to do this."

I reached my arm around her shoulders and gave her a hug. "We'll never know, but thanks for trying."

Twenty

A HANDFUL OF DATES are etched in my mind.

January 24, 1948: the night I met Charlie.

June 10, 1949: the day I married Charlie.

August 20, 1953: the day Abby was born.

November 22, 1963: the day Charlie died.

March 13, 1967: the night I grew up. How did Elliot put it? In this world, naïveté is irresponsible, but willful naïveté is criminal.

He was wrong about the willful part. I never suspected. I could imagine that Elliot would do something like that, but not Charlie.

I'm not sure what made me turn on the television early that night. I didn't usually tune in until the eleven o'clock news. I know one thing for sure. It wasn't a sixth sense. I hadn't an inkling.

The first thing that caught my attention was the huge prop. Mike Wallace stood in front of three columns of blocks, each block connected to various other blocks in the other columns by a tangle of crisscrossing lines. The camera angle was a long shot to give viewers an idea of just how big the apparatus, and therefore the story, was. The distance of the shot made the lettering on the blocks impossible to read, and since I had missed the first minute or two, I didn't know what the program was about. Only when it broke for commercials did I find out.

"We return to 'In the Pay of the CIA,' a CBS News Special, after these messages."

As the commercials unspooled, I got up and moved to the foot of the bed to get closer to the screen. Finally Mike Wallace returned.

"This is a report on a fantastic web of CIA entanglements, an almost comical intelligence debacle that reached into every corner of American life—academia, student organizations, labor unions, magazines, newspapers, and more."

Some laugh. All I could think was that Elliot was wrong. *The Thames Review* had been on the take from the CIA. I had been duped.

Wallace pointed to the first column of blocks and explained that they represented tax-free foundations set up by the CIA. As the camera moved in, I read the lettering and recognized a few names. He followed the crisscrossing black cords to the second column of blocks. Those, he said, represented legitimate tax-free foundations into which the CIA poured money through the first group of foundations. The camera panned down them. The Independence Foundation. The Sidney and Esther Rabb Foundation. The Drinkwater Foundation. I leaned closer to the screen, squinting to make sure I had read the name correctly, but the camera was still panning.

"Go back," I pleaded.

The camera didn't go back. It focused on the front of the building where, Mike Wallace explained, the Drinkwater Foundation had its offices, then jumped to the large brass-framed glassed-in index of the firms located in the building and panned to the words DRINK-WATER FOUNDATION. Under them, in smaller letters, was DIRECTOR, ELLIOT J. MCCLELLAN.

"Mr. McClellan," Wallace said, "declined to speak to our reporter."

The camera showed two other buildings and their lists of companies. Two more men, Wallace said, had refused to speak to CBS reporters.

The program broke for commercials again. I reached for the phone, pulled it onto the bed, and began dialing Elliot's number. I had no idea what I was going to say. Perhaps I wanted to hear him deny the story. Only he wouldn't, because it was true. And it explained everything, the times he had tried to get Charlie to water down pieces in the magazine, the articles he had fought me about over the years. I had thought he was merely cautious. Now I knew he was toeing the Agency line. There was only one thing Elliot's affiliation did not explain. The world was full of women who wouldn't mind getting in bed with the devil. Why had he taken up with one who did?

Mike Wallace was back, standing in front of the third column of blocks. I hung up the phone. These, he explained, represented the publishing houses and magazines that received money, considerable amounts of money, from the CIA through the secondary foundations. Their task was to use the written word as a weapon in the battle against Soviet influence.

As the camera panned the blocks, I waited for the words *Thames Review* to appear. Sleeping with one enemy and writing for another. I felt dirtier than when I'd gone to bed with the scatological screamer.

The camera focused on a block. The word PRAEGER was printed in bold letters. Wallace explained that over the years the CIA had paid Praeger to publish a variety of books that were nothing more than CIA propaganda. "It is against the law to propagandize the American people," he explained.

I knew several editors at Praeger. I wondered if they'd been in on the secret or snookered, as I had been. The camera moved to another block. The letters jumped out at me.

COMPASS.

"*Compass* is a journal of culture, ideas, and politics," Wallace was saying. "According to tax records, the Drinkwater Foundation has been funneling CIA money to *Compass* since late 1948. We spoke to Gideon Abel, the former publisher of the magazine."

Gideon sat in a leather wing chair in front of a wall of books. His manner was patrician and impeccable. He explained, with an air of polite regret, that he had left the magazine in late 1952, as soon as he discovered that the funds from the Drinkwater Foundation came from the CIA.

"And you didn't know before then?" Wallace asked.

Gideon looked several million viewers in the eye. "I hadn't an inkling."

Now Wallace was back on camera, still standing beside the block with the word *Compass* on it.

"In early 1953, Charles Benjamin replaced Gideon Abel as the publisher of *Compass*. During his tenure, the magazine continued to receive CIA funds, channeled through the Drinkwater Foundation. Mr. Benjamin died in 1963, at which point the current publisher, Walter Dryer, took over. Mr. Dryer has denied any knowledge of CIA funding."

Wally's face with his big black-framed James Joyce glasses filled the screen.

"For years I'd heard rumors, but I was never able to confirm anything. If I had, I never would have taken the job. If these allegations are proven, I will resign."

The program was winding down now. Justice William Douglas appeared on the screen.

"What we were doing was aping Soviet methods. The program did irreparable damage to the legal and moral fabric of the country."

Now Allen Dulles stared out at America.

"As the former head of the CIA, you're known as a master spy," a reporter said.

"I don't like that title particularly." His smooth smile gave lie to the words.

"Do you feel that by using the same methods as the Soviets, you were undermining America?"

"They weren't the same methods. The Soviets were trying to destroy. We were trying to build. When you meet a fellow that's trying to destroy, you have to use techniques that are appropriate for that situation."

"Even if they're illegal?"

"Our methods were appropriate for the situation we found ourselves in," he insisted.

Wallace was back on-screen now, talking about the future of the CIA. I switched off the television, picked up the receiver, and began dialing.

"You lied to me," I said as soon as Elliot answered.

"I didn't lie to you. We never discussed it."

"You mean I was supposed to ask you, 'By the way, Elliot, is Drinkwater a CIA front?'"

"It isn't a front. It's a legitimate foundation."

"It was a legitimate foundation until you went to work for the CIA. But I don't care about you or Drinkwater. The only thing that interests me is Charlie's reputation. I'm going to sue goddamn CBS."

He didn't say anything for what seemed like a long time. "For what?" he asked finally.

"Libel. Slander. Defamation of character. I don't know. That's what lawyers are for."

"You can't libel a person who's not alive."

"I'll find something." I was trying to whisper, because I didn't want to wake Abby, but my rage turned the intended hush into a hiss.

"Calm down."

"CBS just called Charlie a CIA agent, and you want me to calm down."

"They didn't call him an agent."

"Close enough."

"I'll be right over."

"I don't want to see you."

"I know that. But I think you and I should straighten out a few matters."

"There is no you and I. Not anymore."

"I know that too. But there are some things you ought to know."

"Anything you have to tell me, you can say over the phone."

"I'll be there in fifteen minutes."

The apartment buzzer rang in ten. The doorman had stopped calling up to announce that Mr. McClellan was here some time ago. When I opened the door, I was struck by how disheveled he looked, for him. His coat was misbuttoned. When he opened it, I noticed he was wearing no shirt beneath his crew-neck sweater. His hair was mussed. He pushed back the shock that fell over his forehead with the heel of his hand. It tumbled forward again. He stepped into the foyer and started to take off his coat.

"Don't bother. You're not staying."

He turned back from the closet and faced me.

"You can't sue CBS."

"Just try and stop me."

He stood staring at me for a moment. "You can't sue," he repeated quietly, "because the charges are true. The foundation was funneling CIA money to the magazine while Charlie was publisher."

"That doesn't mean he knew. Gideon said he quit as soon as he found out. Wally said if it's true, he'll quit."

"And you believe them? Come on, Nell, in this world, naïveté is irresponsible, but willful naïveté is criminal."

"All right, so they're lying. I don't care about them. Charlie is the only one I'm interested in. The program implied that he knew, and he didn't. He never would have gone on at the magazine if he had."

"Charlie knew. He was fully witting."

"Goddamn it, I know Charlie was witty. What does that have to do with it?"

"I didn't say *witty*. I said *witting*. That's the term the Agency uses. The handful of people who know where the money comes from are witting. The rest of you who don't know, or at least aren't officially informed, are unwitting."

"I don't believe you. Charlie would never have taken money from the CIA. Not even to keep *Compass* afloat."

"He didn't do it to keep *Compass* afloat. He did it for his country. Things were pretty scary in those days, if you remember. Anti-Americanism was rampant all over Western Europe. Communist parties were taking over in France and Italy. Communism was on the march in India, Africa, South America, you name it."

"Maybe with good reason."

He raised his eyebrows. "Do I have to remind you of Leningrad? You think that woman Darya was an exception? Charlie knew how dangerous the situation was. He was a realist. That's why it didn't take much to persuade him that what we needed was a good left-wing anti-Soviet magazine."

"I still don't believe you. If he'd known, he would have told me. He would never have kept something like that from me."

"He wasn't allowed to tell you. That was part of the deal. The hardest part for him."

"Is that supposed to make me feel better?"

He shrugged. "It's the truth."

"What would you know about the truth? You've been secretly funneling CIA money to do god knows what."

"I was funneling CIA money to help a lot of people do what they wanted, whether it was to write books, paint pictures, play music, or edit magazines. And I loved every minute of it."

"Because you were pulling the strings of a bunch of puppets?"

"I wasn't pulling Charlie's strings. I was giving him a chance to put out a serious magazine that took on serious issues, even if it wasn't every serious issue you wanted, the way you wanted it. He let you and a lot of other writers have your say. He fought communism, which, as you learned in Leningrad, isn't quite the altruistic force for equality and social justice their propaganda would have you believe. What was the harm in that?"

"How many times do I have to say it? The harm was in the lie. *Compass* was supposed to be searching for the truth, not shilling for the government."

As he stood watching me, his cool blue eyes turned wintry. "Are you angry that he took money from the CIA or that he didn't tell you he took money from the CIA?"

"He didn't just lie to me; he lied to everyone."

"You think no one knew? I'm not so sure. A lot of people must have guessed. But they were having too good a time basking in their own success, not all of it, I might add, deserved. Some second-raters did pretty well off the funding, if they happened to have something to say that the Agency wanted said. Do you actually believe that when those people got an assignment for an article or a contract for a book they asked themselves if they were really that good?"

"So I have you and the CIA to thank for getting my book about Russia published," I said, though I hated myself for the statement. This was not supposed to be about me.

"No, we had nothing to do with that. All I'm saying is that a lot of people found it more convenient not to know."

"Now you're talking about my ignorance of what Charlie was doing."

"No, again. I believe you didn't know."

"Because I'm so dumb?"

"Because you couldn't believe Charlie would do something you think is so wrong."

"You ruined him."

"I gave him a chance to make a difference."

"I know the kind of difference you're talking about. Ousting Arbenz in Guatemala. Overthrowing Mossadegh in Iran. The Bay of Pigs."

"I could counter with the Hungarian uprising, and the Berlin Wall, and the gulags, but that's not the point. Charlie was a publisher. He never had anything to do with operations. In Agency parlance, he was an asset, not an agent."

"I don't care what the Newspeak term for him was. He worked

for the same people. And he lied to me about it." Elliot was right. No matter which way I turned, that fact stood blocking my escape.

"Okay, he didn't tell you where the money for the magazine was coming from. Was that so central to your marriage? It wasn't as if he was cheating on you with another woman, and, believe me, he had the opportunity."

"Thanks for the information."

"I'm not telling you anything you don't know."

He was right. I had known it. And now I was thinking that I would have preferred a moment of physical weakness to an ongoing lie that shammed fourteen years of marriage. And one more thing. A sexual slip would have evened the score.

I told him I'd heard enough. He started for the door, but when he reached it, he turned back to me again.

"Maybe you've heard enough, but Abby hasn't."

The words shook me. How do you explain to a child that her father was not the man she thought?

"I'd like her to hear about Charlie from someone who still thinks he wears a white hat," he said. Then he was gone.

I DID NOT go to bed that night. I sat in the living room, like the watchers who, in the days when the ability to measure life signs was more imperfect, kept all-night vigils beside bodies, on the look-out for a twitching muscle or blinking eye. In those days the fear of being buried alive was not unreasonable. But I knew the cadaver of my marriage was not going to show any signs of life. Rigor mortis was already setting in. Charlie's smile was becoming a mocking rictus. The sweetness I'd struggled to hold on to after his death was carrion.

As the night wore on, the memories came back turned inside out. I wasn't too late with the article on the coup in Guatemala; Charlie didn't want the CIA cover blown. He wasn't courageous when he published the piece on McCarthy; he hadn't run it until McCarthy was finished. How had I misread Charlie so completely?

The tender memories hurt even more. I was standing at the sink in the kitchen, filling the ice bucket, and he was behind me, his arms around me, his mouth on the nape of my neck, binding us together against the world.

We were lying in bed, spooned, breast to back, stomach to buttock, thigh to thigh, holding our breath for the other shoe to drop in Washington, holding on to each other for survival.

He was grinning at me from the big carved bed, beneath a painted ceiling shimmering with reflected light from the canal, while his mouth, still swollen from our lovemaking, lied reassurances.

He had even put it in writing.

I was on my feet, racing down the hall, pulling open the small top drawer of my dresser, rifling through the pearls he had bought me for our tenth anniversary, the only piece of jewelry in the small velvet compartments that wasn't fake. Surely there was some irony in that; the pearls weren't fake, but Charlie was. I pulled out the envelope. The outdated airmail stamp and the Leningrad address weren't even faded, but the letter inside was beginning to come apart at the folds. I had taken it out to read too many times in the past three and a half years. I knew it by heart, but now I sat on the side of the bed and read between the lines.

You are my love. And my conscience. And my touchstone. You keep me honest, or as honest as I can be.

He had written a confession in camouflage.

I tore the letter in half, then fourths, and kept going until it was nothing but bits. They lay on the quilt like confetti. I curled on my side in a fetal position on top of the fragments, my knees drawn up, my arms wound around myself. I had lain the same way after my first miscarriage, hugging the pain to me, and Charlie had come into the room, found me, and curled himself around me. I don't know how long we stayed that way, bound together in our shared loss, his tears running down my cheek.

Now, as the windows faded from black to gray and the world lurched toward a new day, I huddled in the same position, trying to hang on to the memory of that closeness. But it was already seeping away. By the time the buzz saw of Abby's alarm shattered the morning silence, it was gone. My marriage had become a figment of my imagination.

Twenty-One

I WENT INTO THE bathroom to wash my face, brush my teeth, and comb my hair. I did not want Abby to see me this way. The first thing I noticed when I came out was Charlie. He was grinning at me from the silver frame on my dresser. I crossed the room, picked up the photo, and dropped it in the wastebasket. The sound of glass shattering jerked me back from the edge. I bent to take the picture out of the wastebasket. When I straightened I saw Abby standing in the doorway. Her hair was tangled, and her pajamas were twisted, but her face was wide-awake.

"What are you doing?"

"I knocked over Daddy's picture."

As I stood it on the dresser, a sliver of broken glass sliced my thumb. Now my bloody fingerprint stained Charlie's cheek.

Abby went back to her bedroom, and I went into the bathroom for a Band-Aid, then down the hall to the kitchen. Outside the window, gray clouds foamed like toxic sludge. The room lay in shadows. I switched on the overhead light. The flare of white enamel and stainless steel made me wince. There was nowhere to hide.

I began taking things out of the refrigerator. I poured juice, dumped cereal into a bowl, sliced a banana over it. All over the city people were going through similar morning rituals. Some would be discussing a special news report. Some might be parents of Abby's friends. Charles Benjamin. Wasn't he the father of that girl in Susie's, Annie's, Marjorie's class? I heard Charlie's name murmured, disdained, spat. I saw Abby's classmates sitting at their Cheerios and Rice Krispies and cornflakes, suddenly alert to the pitch of adult voices, attuned to the undertones and innuendo of a conversation they hadn't been paying attention to a moment earlier. And I remembered the cruelty of teenage girls.

Abby shuffled into the kitchen and slid into her chair without looking at me. She knew I had not dropped the picture accidentally. I turned my back to her and began making coffee. After a while, I heard the click of her spoon against the bowl. Maybe I was overreacting. Maybe she believed I hadn't meant to drop the photograph. But she'd guess the truth when I told her the rest.

I stood watching the coffee perk. When it was ready, I filled a mug, carried it to the table, and sat across from her. Suddenly I was sitting across from Charlie again, swapping sections of the paper, passing butter and jam, not minding his humming. We'd been in perfect complicity, I'd thought. I felt my face collapsing like a house of cards, like my life now that Charlie had knocked the struts out from under it.

She looked up from her cereal with Charlie's eyes. "Why are you looking at me like that?"

"I was just thinking how nice you look this morning."

She screwed up her face. "In my uniform. Get real, Mom."

She returned to her cereal. I sat searching for words. There was a program last night. It had something about Daddy. No, don't whitewash it. He lied to me. He lied to all of us. She'd ask what he had lied about. I heard myself trying to explain to a thirteen-year-old the nuances of taking money secretly from a clandestine organization, of undermining the underpinnings of democracy; trying to educate a child about the crosscurrents of trust and betrayal between the written word and its readers, between a man and a woman. I was a writer, but I had no words to tell her the truth without taking her father away a second time.

I pushed my chair back from the table. The wooden legs scraped against the linoleum. My scuffs whispered over the floor as I crossed to the counter, refilled my mug, and carried it back to the table.

Perhaps no one had seen the program. Perhaps everyone had been glued to a *Perry Mason* rerun. Even if people had seen it, they wouldn't think it was important enough to discuss over breakfast the next morning. As Elliot had pointed out, not everyone viewed Charlie's actions as an ethical lapse. Most people were probably like Allen Dulles, the head of the CIA, who pretended he did not want to be called a master spy. *You have to use techniques that are appropriate for that situation.* The end justified any means.

"You'd better get a move on or you'll be late for school," I said.

She looked up from her cereal in surprise. I usually nagged her about finishing breakfast, not leaving it. She was on her way down the hall before I could change my mind. I let her go, without a word of warning. I might as well have neglected to vaccinate and inoculate her in infancy.

THE FIRST CALL came at nine o'clock. The timing was a pretense of consideration. If you were calling a woman to gloat, the least you could do was let her have her coffee. The wife of an editor who had always resented Charlie's success told me how sorry she was.

"For what?" My voice was innocent as a child's. It stopped her for a moment, but only for a moment.

"It must have come as quite a shock to find out Charlie was working for the CIA. Unless of course you were too."

The words surprised me. For the past ten hours, I'd been thinking of myself as a betrayed woman, but suddenly I realized I had a choice. I could admit to Charlie's faithlessness or own up to my corruption. I could be a marital cliché, the wife who was the last to know, or a CIA stooge. I'm ashamed to admit that I even hesitated.

"I wasn't," I said, told her I was on deadline for an article, and got off the phone.

Next came a writer whose submissions Charlie had turned down more than once. Elliot was the fifth caller of the morning. I told him I had nothing more to say and hung up. A moment later the phone rang again.

"Now you know what I meant about sleeping with the enemy," Frank Tucker said. "And about McClellan being no friend to Charlie."

I admitted he was right.

"Didn't you ever wonder why I stopped writing for *Compass*?"

"I thought you'd moved on to greener pastures, as in more green matter per article."

"You always did underestimate me." I knew from his tone what was coming next. "Now that you can tell your friends from your enemies we ought to have dinner."

I had loved Charlie for his integrity, and now that I'd found it a sham, I didn't know what to do with the love. Frank Tucker's convictions were the real thing—he had gone to prison for them—but I still found him repugnant. The contradiction was one more cosmic joke, like Yeats's line about love pitching his mansion in the place of excrement.

I told Frank that in view of my track record as a judge of male character, I was thinking of taking the veil. After that, I left the phone off the hook.

I spent the rest of the morning huddled in my study, still in last night's clothing, reliving my life with a stranger I had thought I'd known. At noon, I put the phone back on the hook. It rang immediately. It went on ringing as I headed down the hall to shower and dress. I had a lunch date with Sonia. I figured I might as well start with a friend.

WE HAD AGREED to meet in the dining room of the Metropolitan Museum. She was reviewing a show of William Blake's illuminated manuscripts. Either I was early or she was late. I wasn't sure because after I'd showered I'd forgotten to put my watch back on. I sat waiting at a small table beside the long reflecting pool, feeling as naked and exposed as the bronze nymphs splashing in it, pretending to study the menu for fear of looking around and seeing someone I knew.

"Are you all right?" she asked as she slid into the chair across from me.

"So you saw it."

"In a state of shock. Charlie was the last person I'd suspect of something like this."

"That makes two of us."

"He never told you?"

I shook my head no. "According to Elliot, he wasn't allowed to. In other words, loyalty to a clandestine agency trumped loyalty to me."

Surprise flickered across her face, and something else behind it. Satisfaction. I didn't blame her. She'd spent too many years envying our marriage. I'd spent too many years flaunting our happiness. She was entitled to a little schadenfreude.

The waitress came and took our orders.

"That must have been hard on Charlie," she said when the waitress left. "Not being able to tell you, I mean."

"Apparently not."

She narrowed her eyes as if she were putting me in focus. "You're angry at him."

"Wouldn't you be?"

She thought about that for a moment. "I'm not sure how I'd feel. I'd be disappointed that he agreed to take CIA money. It's so out of character, so at odds with everything he stood for."

"Everything we thought he stood for."

"I suppose it was pretty shabby."

"Pretty shabby! You praise with faint damnation. He sold out. He adopted the methods we were fighting to fight those methods."

"That's true, but . . ." Her voice trailed off.

"But what?"

"Given all that, I'm still not sure how I'd feel in your place. I've never been married to anyone. I've never even been with anyone for a protracted period of time. Miles was my record, and let's not talk about what happened with him. I guess what I'm saying is what you used to tell me about my hectic love life in my misspent youth. You could put what I know about trust and loyalty between a man and a woman on the head of a pin and still have enough room for a couple of hundred angels. I admit what he did offends me. But I'm not sure I have your scruples."

"What does that mean?"

"If I had to choose between a husband I loved and political purity, I have a feeling I'd go for the husband."

AS IT TURNED out, some of Abby's friends' parents had seen the program, as I'd feared. Some of them had even discussed it at breakfast, though not in the way I'd imagined.

"You tell Abby," Lauren's father had said to her, "that she ought to be proud of her dad."

Lauren did not ask for an explanation. She was a thirteen-year-old girl. Of course you ought to be proud of your parents, and most kids were, except when the parents were committing hopelessly embarrassing acts or saying really dumb things. And a dead parent couldn't do that. You could be especially proud of a dead parent. And most of the time Lauren felt really sorry for Abby anyway, because she didn't have a dad. She relayed her father's message without thinking much about what he'd meant.

When Abby got home from school that afternoon, she came straight to my study.

"What did Mr. Dreyfus mean?" she asked after she'd repeated the comment.

"There was a program on television last night."

"About Daddy?"

"It mentioned him."

"Why didn't you tell me?"

"I didn't know it was going to be on. And you were asleep by the time I found out."

"What did it say about him?"

"It talked about the magazine and Uncle Elliot's foundation."

"Then why did Mr. Dreyfus say I should be proud?"

Ask Mr. Dreyfus, I wanted to shout, because I sure as hell don't see anything to be proud of in taking money from a suspect secret organization, and lying to your friends, and deceiving your wife.

She shifted from one foot to the other, but kept her eyes on me.

"I guess because Daddy thought he was doing something for his country." My conscience inserted the word *thought*. My maternal instincts cringed at it. But she didn't seem to notice.

"You mean like President Kennedy said, ask not what your country can do for you, but what you can do for your country?"

"Exactly like that."

They were two of a kind, all right. World-class con men.

ELLIOT CALLED TWO or three times more. Each time I refused to talk to him. I'd had my fill of justifications as well as lies. Finally he gave up and wrote me a letter. In it, he said he understood that I did not want to see him, but he would still like to talk to Abby about her father. I didn't answer the letter.

I HAD FINESSED telling Abby about Charlie's betrayal, but I could not avoid explaining why I wasn't going to marry Elliot. I kept remembering another conversation between another mother and daughter that had occurred a few weeks earlier. I'd overheard only one side of it, but I'd been able to imagine the other.

It was a Friday night, and Abby had invited three friends for a sleepover. Around nine o'clock, one of the mothers had called and asked to talk to her daughter. A little overprotective, I'd thought, as I'd gone down the hall to Abby's room to get Maud.

She followed me back to the kitchen, where I'd left the phone off the hook.

"He'll call, Mom," Maud said. "You'll see."

I turned the flame under the hot chocolate back on.

"He said he'd call, didn't he?"

I lowered the flame. I didn't want scalded milk all over the stove.

"Yeah, I know men don't always mean what they say. I'm not a baby."

I wanted to snatch the phone from her hand.

"But you said he said he had a good time. He didn't have to say that."

I took four mugs down from the cabinet.

"You know what I think? I think he probably has his kids for the weekend, and when he said he'd call you on Friday, he forgot he had them."

The conversation went on that way for a while longer. It was a cautionary tale if ever I heard one.

On the Saturday night after I'd sent Abby off to school unprotected, I announced I had something to tell her. We were sitting at the kitchen table having dinner.

"You're not going to marry Elliot."

"How did you know?"

She shrugged. "He hasn't been around all week."

"He could be away on business."

"He hasn't called. You haven't mentioned him. And the giveaway. I saw the dress Sonia finally convinced you to buy in a Saks bag in your room, which means you're going to return it."

"I'm living with a latter-day Sherlock Holmes."

"What happened?"

"We disagreed about some matters."

"S.O.S., as Daddy used to say. You and Uncle Elliot have been disagreeing about some matters ever since you've known him."

"I wish you'd reminded me of that a few months ago."

Her lower lip jutted out the way it used to when, as a little girl, she was scolded for something.

"A joke, kiddo. It's not your job to take care of me."

"Maybe you'll make up."

"It isn't the sort of disagreement you can make up."

She didn't ask me what kind of disagreement it was, and I was glad, not only for myself, but for her. Adult intimacies were none of her business, and she wanted to keep it that way. But after dinner she said she didn't feel like going to Lauren's with a bunch of other girls from her class.

"You don't have to take care of me."

"I'm not taking care of you. I just thought we could go to a movie."

I told her I was game, and she went down the hall to get the newspaper for the listings.

"How about *A Man and a Woman?*" she said when she came back.

"How about *The Sound of Music?*"

"You're kidding, right?"

"Right. But I figured if you were shooting for steamy, I'd counter with saccharine, and we'd compromise somewhere in between."

We settled on *Doctor Zhivago,* which was being revived. I'd seen it when it had come out two years earlier, but she'd been too young.

I had trouble sitting through the movie that night, not because I'd seen it before, but because I suddenly remembered the review I'd written for *Compass* when the book was published. Since I was the only one at the magazine who had been to Russia, Charlie said I was the logical reviewer and assigned two thousand words, which was longer than most of the reviews *Compass* ran. Now I understood why. The novel painted such a brutal picture of the Bolshevik state that it could not have been more to the CIA's purpose if it had been dictated by one of their agents. Once again, Charlie reached back into the past and strangled a memory.

DURING THE DAYS and weeks that followed the television broadcast, I felt as if I had been plunged back into the turmoil of the McCarthy years. Accusations and recriminations flew, feuds broke out, and on two different occasions, two different people snubbed me. Sonia witnessed the second incident at a book party.

"Smug little prig," she said after the man had ostentatiously turned away from me.

"I can't really blame him. In his shoes, I'd probably do the same thing."

She shook her head. "No, you wouldn't. You'd intend to, but at the last minute, you'd start feeling sorry for him and go out of your way to be nice. Then you'd end up getting angry at yourself for your lack of moral fiber."

Nonetheless, I found myself lifting my chin and straightening my shoulders as if girding for battle before I walked into a room full of people. But I did not have to worry about the school dance that Friday evening. Except for a handful of other parents, everyone there would be underage and uninterested in me.

Three Friday nights during the academic year, the seventh, eighth, and ninth grades from several private girls' schools and their counterparts from boys' schools met in the gym of one of the schools or the rented basement of a church to eye one another warily, feign indifference, and shuffle sweatily around the floor. When the request for chaperones had gone out in September, I had agreed to act as one at the last dance in May.

The night was soft and still, but as I cut through the gated garden of a church on Lexington Avenue, I could feel dirty weather brewing. Boys shouted, shoved, and hit one another. Girls giggled, clung, and oohed and aahed over one another's dresses, shoes, and hair. Abby was among them, but I kept my distance. The only adult worse than a chaperone was a chaperone who happened to be your mother.

I parked myself behind a table spread with trays of pastel-iced cookies and a foul-looking pink punch and tried to keep my back to whatever part of the room Abby fetched up in. Once, I caught sight of her dancing with a skinny boy who came up to her nose and looked as if puberty were a distant horizon. My heart ached for both of them. Fifteen minutes later, I got a glimpse of her in the arms of a six-footer whose dark shadow of burgeoning mustache was visible halfway across the room. Something in his grin when he caught the eye of another boy made me think of Frank Tucker. My sore heart turned to stone.

I was looking at my watch and calculating how much longer I had to stand there grinning stupidly and pretending not to look at the only person in the room who interested me when Lauren's father joined me behind the table. Bill Dreyfus was a handsome man with chiseled features who looked every inch the white-shoe lawyer he was, but something about him gave off a whiff of those hot-air balloons. Maybe it was the intensity of his gaze. It pinned you in place with a wild glitter, as if he were a mad scientist and you were a specimen on a dissecting board.

"I'd sell my firstborn for a good stiff scotch," he said as he leaned into my face.

I took a step back. "I have only a first, but I'd probably trade her in for the same."

We stood side by side then, watching kids shuffle around the room, skulk in corners, and, in two or three cases, cling together precociously. Another parent moved in to break up the clingers. Bill Dreyfus leaned toward me again, and when he spoke, his voice was quiet but urgent.

"Charlie should have gotten a medal."

My head swiveled to him. "What?"

"The guys who gave their lives in the shooting war got recognition."

Maybe it was the amateur band's lugubrious rendition of "A Hard Day's Night," or the heat from the jumping, dancing, hormone-pulsing bodies, but I didn't understand what he was saying, and the confusion must have shown on my face.

"I'm sorry." He shook his head. "I shouldn't have said anything, but I just think it's a damn shame. Instead of pillorying him on television, they should give him a medal for service to his country."

I went on staring at him. He thought Charlie deserved a medal for turning a reputable magazine into a CIA front? Charlie had always said he was a bit of an ass.

Twenty-Two

I COULD NOT STOP reliving my life backward. Not backward in time, but backward in perceptions and emotions. Everything was the opposite of what I'd thought it was.

Charlie sits across the table from me in the flickering candlelight of La Cave Henri IV, brimming with promise, effervescing with hope as he tells me about his lunch with Elliot, and I want to cry because of what he isn't telling me. Or am I missing something? Is he aching inside with the secret? But I will not flatter myself. A man does not ache for more than a decade. He gets used to the pain. Perhaps it even begins to feel like pleasure. If knowledge is power, secrets are dirty tricks, and this one was on me.

We lie in bed later that night, sweat-slicked body to sweat-slicked body, then he rolls away, raises a long arm toward the glass ceiling, and points out Orion, Leo, and Virgo. His ability to spot constellations always dazzled me. Either I couldn't see them at all or I found them everywhere I looked. One night when he was trying to teach me, I found three Big Dippers.

"If it's a boy," he whispers on this night, "we'll name him Leo."

I ask him what he's talking about, and he tells me, with absolute conviction, that we just made a baby.

"Didn't you feel it?" he asks.

And I believe him. Who knows, maybe he was even right. But

now I know what he didn't tell me that night, and I think about how Abby was conceived in duplicity.

My memory prowled, distraught and dangerous, and I'm back in the big shadowy room with reflected light from the canals lapping at the painted ceiling. He closes the door behind us, and without a word we begin shedding clothing, peeling down to ourselves, in perfect accord. We do not even have to speak, I think. Now I knew how much he was not allowed to say.

I saw the rest of it too, though the scene looked different when not viewed through the rosy haze of Venetian glass. He is sprawled on the bed, his dark lashes lying like fringes on his sunburned cheeks, his breathing peaceful as a crypt, and I shake him awake to ask a question. He doesn't even need time to think. The lie comes as quick and easy as a reflex. The lie is who he has become. What does that make me?

The tension between the life I thought I had lived and the revised history of it threw me off-balance. Maybe that was why it took me so long to realize that I was an accomplice, or at least a beneficiary.

The recognition came one morning at the end of May, when a Wedgwood blue sky hung outside my study window. I was sitting at my desk, writing a check for the rent. I could not believe I hadn't thought of it before. The money Abby and I were living on came from the life insurance policy the CIA had bought for Charlie. I was worse than Charlie and Elliot and all of them. They had taken money for an idealistic, if wrongheaded, end. I was using it to live well.

The solution, no, the retribution was obvious. I should have thought of it sooner. I would give away the money. There were hundreds of good causes, but I did not need more than a minute to think of the best under the circumstances. I would give the money from the insurance policy to the antiwar movement. Abby and I did not need an eat-in kitchen, study, and formal dining room in a prewar building with a view of the park. We would get along just fine in a small two-bedroom with a galley kitchen in one of those ugly new white-brick buildings. We would be more comfortable morally if not physically. And she'd be better off in public school, learning about other kinds of people as well as literature and math and science.

I went down the hall to the kitchen, found the morning paper, and carried it back to my desk. The timing was perfect. The lease on the apartment had to be renewed in two months. I turned to the real estate pages. Reality struck. I had not looked at the listings in years. People who lived in rent-controlled apartments rarely did, unless they wanted to gloat. The only way we could save money was by moving into a studio apartment. I pictured myself closing the Murphy bed Abby and I shared into the wall. Where would I work? She could never have a friend sleep over. Even my mother had made a better home for me than that, until Mr. Richardson began to notice me and she decided I should leave it to join the Army.

I dropped the real estate listings into the wastebasket, pulled my Rolodex toward me, and began flipping through it. If I couldn't cut back on expenses, I'd increase income. I spent the rest of the morning calling editors. I didn't bother with the little magazines. They already knew me. And they paid nothing. I called editors at fashion, women's service, and interior design magazines, at general-interest periodicals and glossies. By the time I got up to make myself a sandwich, I had two assignments. I carried my lunch back to my desk and sat down to work again. That was when I remembered that on several occasions *Holiday* had asked me to write travel articles on the cities where I'd attended conferences. I'd always refused. I rarely read travel writing. I could not imagine I'd be any good at writing it. But now I thought of the hefty fees the magazine paid and dialed an editor I knew there. He said he had the perfect assignment for me. How soon could I be ready to leave? For the second time that day, reality threw cold water on my plans. I could not fly off to exotic places at the snap of a suitcase lock. I could not fly off at all. What would I do with Abby? I thanked the editor and got off the phone. The idea didn't come to me until I'd carried the plate from my sandwich and my tea mug back to the kitchen. School was about to let out for the summer. I called the editor back. He asked if I wanted to go to Buenos Aires. I told him I could be ready to leave in two weeks.

Abby turned out to be a game traveler, gobbling up sights and impressions, trying exotic foods, and striking up conversations with total strangers. At a tango performance in a square one afternoon, when the dancers fanned out to take partners from the crowd, one of the men reached for her hand to lead her into the plaza. I expected her to shrink back. She accepted his hand and sailed out among the dancers. My daughter turned out to be a born tango dancer and a shameless ham. I stood watching and thinking how proud Charlie would have been. It was, I realized with a start, the first time since the night of the television broadcast that I'd thought of him without bitterness.

I opened a second bank account. The manager of my local branch disapproved. I don't know why I was surprised. After Charlie died, I'd had to fight to get our Diners Club card transferred to my name. Now, the manager couldn't imagine why a respectable widow would want a second checking account. I thought of explaining that one account was for the funds I earned writing, the other for blood money, but didn't.

I continued to write for the serious journals as well as the more popular magazines. That was why one morning in early September I got a call from Frank Tucker. It was Abby's first day of ninth grade— she was still in private school, thanks to a partial scholarship and my new willingness to write just about anything that paid well—and I had been wandering the apartment in an elegiac mood. In four years she would be going off to college. Four years was a lifetime to her. From where I stood in the empty echoing apartment that morning, it was the blink of an eye.

"I have a proposition for you," Frank said.

"You usually do."

"No, I mean a professional proposition. Can we have lunch one day this week?"

"Couldn't you just tell me over the phone?"

"I mean it, Nell. This is pure business. But if you don't trust me, bring Sonia along."

"And have you ogling her all through lunch?"

"I detect a note of sex envy. It's a good assignment, I promise."

"For whom?"

He mentioned a new left-wing journal. I asked him why the editor didn't call me directly.

"Because he knows we're friends."

That was how upside down my world had turned. Frank Tucker, who had teased and taunted and tried to put his penis in my mouth, was my friend. And Charlie, whom I had trusted with my life, was my nemesis.

We lunched in the garden of a small Italian restaurant in the Village. A lemon sun filtered through the trees, warming the air that had started the day crisp as a just-picked apple. Every now and then a breeze rattled the leaves like rain, though the sky was cloudless. I wished I were there with someone else, though I couldn't imagine whom, except the old Charlie, the one who had never existed.

Frank started talking about the piece as soon as I sat down. The idea was his, he said, but Phil Winters, the editor of *Barricades,* was high on it.

"I can't do it," I said when he finished describing what he had in mind.

He put down his glass of wine and looked at me across the table. This was the sincere moment.

"Look, Nell, I know I haven't always been easy on you. I mean, hell, how could I resist? You always rose to the bait. But take it from me, you're the only one who can do it."

I shook my head. "It's too personal."

"That's the point. The piece will be a prism. You write about how Charlie snookered you, and we see how the CIA screwed the country. Like you gals say, the personal is political."

Even when he was trying to be persuasive, he couldn't help being insulting.

"That isn't what the statement means. And this personal is a little too close to the bone."

"I thought you were a writer."

"That's not the song you usually sing."

"I'm serious. Either you believe that words can pick this rotten world up by the scruff of its neck and shake some sense into it, or you think they're just pretty beads you string together for effect. Which is it?" He sat waiting for the answer.

"I think words can shake the world, but I still can't write about this."

"I'm not asking you to do a piece about having been dumped or cheated on like those sob sisters."

"Sensitivity always was your long suit."

He shook his head. "I mean it, Nell. This is important. Will you at least think about it?"

I told him I would, though I knew I wouldn't.

He didn't mention the article again during lunch, but as we stood in front of the restaurant saying goodbye, he came back to the subject.

"If nothing else, it would be a vindication of Charlie's death."

"How does my writing about Charlie's duplicity"—I had never spoken the word aloud, and it sent a chill down my back despite sunlight spilling over us—"vindicate him?"

He stood looking down at me, and for a moment the fleshy face turned almost kind. "It doesn't. Forget I said anything. Just think about the piece."

I did not think about the piece. I knew I couldn't write it, if for no other reason, and there were others, than Abby. I did not want her to know that her parents' marriage had been a fraud. I did not want her to go through life thinking that, as Frank had put it, her father had snookered me and screwed the country.

A FEW WEEKS after I had lunch with Frank Tucker, Abby got a school assignment to write an essay about a modern hero.

"Define *hero*." I had been late getting home from a literary awards reception and was trying to warm up the previous night's meat loaf and bake a potato, two processes that can't be rushed, but I was as adamant about not living on delivery pizza and Chinese take-out food as I was about sitting across the table from each other and carrying on a conversation over dinner. I tried to limit my evenings out, but the recipient of the award was a translator I'd known since my first job in book publishing, and I'd had to show my face.

She thought about that for a moment. "Someone who fought, maybe even risked his life, to make a difference in the world."

"Margaret Sanger."

"Who's she?"

I looked up from the green beans I was trimming. "And to think I pay good money to send you to a high-minded all-girls school. The mother of birth control. She went to jail for the cause countless times."

"Mom!"

The sexual revolution was under way, but the days when Abby's daughter would learn to put condoms on bananas in that same school were still in the future.

She didn't spring the suggestion on me until the potato had baked, the meat loaf was warmed through, and we were sitting across from each other.

"Do you think it would be too weird or conceited or whatever if I wrote about Daddy?"

I was careful to keep my voice even. "What would you write about him?"

"I'm not sure. But before you got home I was on the phone with Lauren about the assignment, and her dad walked in and said I should write about my dad."

I did not understand Bill Dreyfus's obsession with Charlie.

"Forget it," Abby said.

"No, I think it's an interesting idea."

"Sure you do. You should see your face."

"I can't help that, kiddo, it's the one I was born with. What would you write about Daddy?"

"I don't know. That's what you'd have to tell me."

"Okay, interviewing 101. You have to figure out what to ask to find out what I have to tell."

"Why does Lauren's dad think he's a hero?"

"Wrong question, or rather right question but wrong interviewee. Why do *I* think he was a hero is the one you ask me."

"Do you? I know you used to."

I thought about that for a moment. "Maybe *hero* is the wrong word. It doesn't sound human, and he was. But he was extraordinary too. He had an intriguing mind, at least to me. He cared about social justice. He was"—I hesitated for a moment, but only a moment—"deeply moral. He made me laugh. And he was loving. God, was he loving." The last two sentences surprised me. I hadn't meant to say them. I hadn't even known I was thinking them.

"But don't you have to do something to be a hero?"

"He published an awfully good magazine."

"That doesn't sound heroic."

"Try it when you're older and you'll see. But seriously, years ago, when you were a baby, he was called down to Washington to be investigated, and he stood up to some pretty dark forces."

She leaned back in her chair and shook her head. "I guess you're right. I guess it isn't such a good idea."

"Let's just say you might be better off writing about someone you don't know. When the assignment is a personal memoir, you can write about Daddy, but when it's a modern hero, maybe you'd better stick to more conventional choices."

"Like who?"

"Like whom."

"Like whom?"

"It's your assignment, kiddo, but I promise to give it some thought."

After she helped me clear the table and I stacked the dishwasher, I wandered down the hall to her room. The desk lamp turned the cascade of hair that fell forward over her cheeks to a polished mahogany.

"Rosa Parks," I said.

"What?" she asked without looking up.

"Rosa Parks. That's your modern hero."

She looked up. "Who's she?"

Now I really was beginning to worry about the school.

"The woman who refused to move to the back of the bus in Montgomery."

"Oh, yeah, I forgot."

"She made a difference in the world, and what she did was pretty risky."

"Thanks."

She went back to her book. I went on standing in the doorway.

"Would you like to talk to someone who was involved in organizing the whole thing?"

She looked up again. "What do you mean organizing? I thought she just refused to give up her seat."

"She did, but she wasn't the first, which doesn't make what she did any less heroic. For years negroes had been beaten and even killed for defying white bus drivers' orders to move to the back of the bus. A little while before Rosa Parks made her stand, a fifteen-year-old girl was arrested for the same thing. But when civil rights leaders, who were looking for a test case, found out that the fifteen-year-old girl was pregnant, not to mention hotheaded, they decided they needed someone beyond reproach. That was where Mrs. Parks came in."

"I thought she just got fed up."

"I'm sure she did, but there was more to it than that. There always is. That's why I think you ought to write about her and the incident. It's a lesson in civil disobedience as well as heroism."

"And you know someone who was involved?"

I couldn't tell if she was excited by the possibility of touching history or by the prospect of having to do less research.

"I used to. I can probably track him down."

I KNEW WHAT I was up to, and I wasn't proud of it. I had seen divorced women, broken on the wheel of disillusion, make the same mistake. Before the decree was even final, they began looking up old lovers and boyfriends, working their way back to college romances and high school crushes, searching in phantom memories for an innocence they had lost, a gullibility no grown woman in her right mind should want. I had prided myself on not being like them. Now I was.

Abby went down to Woody's office to interview him. A few evenings later, I met him uptown for dinner. When I'd called to ask him if he'd speak to her, I'd been pretty sure he would suggest it.

Appearing in public with Woody was a crash course in America's snail-like but steady evolution toward racial equality. The first time we'd gone for coffee, we'd had to find an out-of-the-way diner on the border between the campus and Harlem, and even then we'd gotten dirty looks. In Russia, we had made the rest of the troupe uneasy. But now, as I approached the table and Woody stood and leaned over to kiss me on the cheek, the other diners ignored us ostentatiously. In certain circles, and the Upper West Side was one of them, interracial was in fashion.

The first thing I noticed when we sat was the pale glow of gold on the third finger of his left hand. That's what I mean about the phantom memories of disillusioned women. In my mind, Woody would always be unmarried and just a little in love with me, even if he wasn't willing to upend his life for it.

"You're married," I said. "Congratulations."

"The least you could do is sound a little heartbroken."

"I am, but I'm hiding it well. Tell me about your wife."

"She's negro."

"That's not what I meant."

"Sure it is. Or at least part of what you meant. I met her on a protest march. It's where all my best affairs begin."

I changed the subject and thanked him for seeing Abby. He said she was a nice kid and I ought to be proud. I liked him for that.

I asked him about his work; he inquired about my writing. If he'd seen the CBS News Special, he didn't mention it. We went on that way through his osso buco and my veal piccata. The conversation never flagged, but there wasn't a lot of heart to it. Finally, we stood on the sidewalk in front of the restaurant, bathed in a circle of light from an overhead lamp, and my sadness. He said something about staying in touch, and I agreed, but we both knew we would not stay in touch, unless professional exigencies brought us together again. He started to hail a cab for me. I told him I wanted to walk. It was only a few blocks to my apartment.

"You're sure you'll be all right?"

No! I'm not all right, and I won't be.

I told him I'd be fine, leaned over, and gave him a cautious kiss on the cheek. Then I turned and started up Broadway, my spine straight, my shoulders back, my chin raised. No casual observer, not even Woody, who I had a feeling was watching me go, would guess that every human encounter I had these days was nothing more than a brutal collision that made me feel more alone.

Twenty-Three

I HAD RAGED AGAINST JFK and the nation for turning Charlie's death into a footnote. Now two more assassinations threatened to drag Charlie out of the shadows, where these days I wanted to keep him. On April 4, 1968, a sniper in a rooming house across the street from the Lorraine Motel in Memphis, Tennessee, shot Martin Luther King, Jr., dead. Two months later, on June 6, a Palestinian immigrant gunned down Robert Kennedy in the kitchen of the Ambassador Hotel in Los Angeles. A month after that, on a July morning when the air conditioner in the window of my study coughed and sputtered its hoary breath, I got a call from someone who identified himself as Sean Keller. He said he was a reporter. He sounded about twelve. He also said the two recent assassinations had gotten him thinking. I didn't tell him they had gotten most of the country thinking. I had just finished a piece on our violent society.

He said he wanted to talk to me about my husband's murder.

I told him I did not talk to the press about my late husband and got off the phone, but the conversation rattled in my head all morning, as noisy and distracting as the air conditioner. I tried to work, but it was no good. I finally gave up and sat staring at the picture of Charlie pushing Abby on the swing. I told myself I kept it out for Abby, but I kept it for me too.

The realization hit me suddenly. It was the recognition of the tainted CIA money I'd been living on all over again. I could not imagine how I hadn't seen it before. I'd had enough hints. Bill Dreyfus's words about Charlie deserving a medal, like the men who had given their lives in the shooting war. Frank Tucker's comment outside the restaurant about vindicating Charlie's death. And the clincher. How had I missed that? The obscene life insurance policy. The foundation hadn't taken out a policy on Charlie's life to keep him from leaving *Compass*. It had taken it out because Elliot and the CIA knew they were putting Charlie in harm's way.

Or maybe the CIA wasn't worried about the Soviets. Maybe the CIA was the culprit. As I turned off my typewriter and stood, I noticed a letter on my desk. It was a request from a woman who was writing a biography of Richard Wright. She wanted to talk to me and to see the notes from my interview with him. She said she understood there was also a handful of letters. He and I had stayed in touch after the interview, because I had hoped to do another piece on him. I opened the filing cabinet, took out the folder labeled *Richard Wright,* and began riffling through the papers.

"The white West cannot forgive my blackness. It blinds them to who I am. It colors the way they read my books. Even while I battle communism abroad, they stick a knife in my back at home," he wrote in one letter.

"There is a plot against me. I have proof," he said in another.

"To the Americans, I am more dangerous than a communist, because my color speaks to the colors of Africa and Asia as neither they nor the Soviets can."

There were also notes from interviews with some of his friends. One woman just back from seeing him in Paris had told me he'd looked dreadful. She did not trust his doctor, she had added, a Russian émigré who lived mysteriously well in a large apartment on

Avenue George V. "Has Wright on massive doses of bismuth," I'd scrawled.

I didn't bother to put the file away. I was in too much of a hurry.

COMPASS WAS LOCATED in the seedy Broadway building owned by the Drinkwater family, but the foundation itself was in a more respectable skyscraper on Madison Avenue. I could count the number of times I had been there on three fingers, once years ago with Charlie, twice after-hours when I'd picked up Elliot to go to dinner. And I had always been careful not to call him at his office. We had been so circumspect that his secretary had no idea who I was.

She asked if I had an appointment.

"He'll see me."

I sounded like something out of a grade B movie, but I was right. He even came out of the inner office to get me. His voice was cordial. His face gave away nothing.

"I want to know about Charlie's death," I said as soon as he closed his office door behind me.

His face remained impassive. "Why don't you sit down?"

"I'm fine the way I am. I want to know about Charlie's death."

"I thought Charlie's death was the one thing you didn't want to know about." He hesitated. "I'm sorry. That was unfair. What do you want to know?"

"I want to know everything, who did it—them or you—and why."

"So the kid reporter called you. The one who wants to write a piece on what he calls assassinations and foul play."

"It's a good enough term."

"It doesn't wash. Charlie was a publisher. I told you, an asset, not an agent. He had nothing to do with operations. The Soviets had no reason to take an interest in him."

"Then what about you and your friends?"

"You think our people would do that to Charlie?"

"If 'our people,' as you call them, killed Richard Wright, another asset, not an agent, and lots of people think they did, why wouldn't they do the same to Charlie? I have letters from Wright saying he was sure the Americans were out to get him."

"Wright was paranoid."

"It's not paranoia when there's good reason for the fear."

"What would be the motive for killing Charlie?"

"He wanted to stop cooperating. He wanted to go public about what you people were doing. Wasn't there a rumor about someone who tried to stop working with the Agency? He was supposed to have committed suicide by jumping out of a window, but his wife insisted he hadn't even been depressed."

"Who told you about that?"

"Frank Tucker."

"Of course, Tucker, the source of all wisdom."

"He may not be a sterling human being, but he generally gets his facts right."

"Nell, listen to me. Charlie was mugged. End of story."

"What about the life insurance policy?"

"What about it?"

"Why did the foundation take it out if he wasn't in danger?"

"I told you, to keep him happy. He was worried about you and Abby."

"How many thirty-year-old publishers do you know who are so worried about their wives and children that they threaten to leave a magazine they love unless they get a huge life insurance policy?"

"Not all publishers walk around with Charlie's sense of disastrous contingencies."

"Something happened that day in the park, and it wasn't a mugging."

He sat behind his desk and put his head in his hands. "It was a mugging. Just because they didn't convict Vega doesn't mean he didn't do it. I wish to hell they had convicted him."

"Send someone to prison, anyone, and then you don't have to worry about a guilty conscience."

"I don't have a guilty conscience about Charlie."

"You damn well ought to."

I was still standing, and he was sitting, staring at me across the expanse of uncluttered desk.

"I'm not sure you want to cast the first stone," he said quietly.

"What's that supposed to mean?"

He stood. "Nothing, forget it. I'm sorry, but you get me so damn angry."

"The feeling is mutual. What was that supposed to mean?" I asked again.

He hesitated, then sat behind his desk again, opened the top drawer, took out a key, and bent to open the bottom side drawer. He straightened and put a notebook with a marbled cover, the kind kids use in school, on the desk between us.

"I think you ought to have this."

"What is it?"

"Charlie's journal."

"You have a journal from Charlie and you never gave it to me!"

"The day he died, I went to his office to take care of a few things."

"To destroy the evidence."

"Evidence of what? That he took money from the foundation? You could read that in the books. But I had a feeling this existed." He put his hand on the notebook, then took it off. "It was the kind of thing he'd do. He even hinted at it a couple of times."

"So you just took it?"

He closed his eyes for a moment, then opened them. "That's part of my job."

"Why didn't you tell me about it?"

"Before you found out about the funding there was no reason to."

"Charlie was my husband. It's not up to you to decide what I should or shouldn't know about him."

"I was trying to protect you."

"Bullshit!"

He flinched.

"Why didn't you give it to me once I knew?"

"I wanted to. But that night in your apartment, after the television broadcast, I said I'd tell you the rest when you were ready, and you said you'd already heard enough."

"I didn't know you had Charlie's diary."

He shrugged. "His account isn't so different from what I would have told you."

"Then you read it."

"That's part of my job too."

"You really are a bastard."

He shook his head. "I'm just like everyone else, part bastard, part idealist. Just like you, for that matter." He stood, picked up the notebook, and held it out to me. "Why don't you read this before you make up your mind?"

I took the notebook, turned, and started for the door.

"Nell."

I stopped but didn't turn around.

"It was a mugging. I swear to you."

Now I turned. "As if your oaths mean anything."

BOOK THREE

1952–1963

Twenty-Four

*Comments entered later in time

November 18, 1952

I HAVE DECIDED TO keep a journal so that when this is over, when we've ~~vanquished~~ brought down another totalitarian regime, not with guns and bombs but with words (I can see my sixty-year-old self groaning at that, oh, the pomposity), I will recall, without the rosy burnish of memory, what it felt like. And I'm keeping it so I can make Nell understand. I think if I could tell her now, I could make her see it from my point of view—at least I hope I could—but I gave my word. If nothing else, I don't want to endanger anyone. *Jesus, I'd better watch it. I'm beginning to sound like that kid in London who kept changing taxis to make sure he wasn't being followed. 6/1/53 McClellan used the term "eternal confidentiality," but once this is over, and it can't go on forever, I'll try to explain. This is a debt I have to pay. She'll understand that. McClellan did. That was why he came after me. He'd done his homework.

I suspected something was up when he asked me to lunch. Not only the job, but the rest of it. I'd heard rumors about *Encounter* and other magazines. And occasionally Gideon dropped a hint. Once, when we were sharing a taxi, he started to say something about the foundation's funding. Then the cab stopped for a light, he told me he thought he'd walk the rest of the way, and jumped out. *Now I understand the irresistible urge to confess, the desperate desire to cleanse yourself of the stinking little secret. 5/12/63

I'm writing this now, only hours after meeting with McClellan, because I want to be clear not only about what was said, but about the order in which it was said. That's something else I want Nell to understand. I didn't agree to do this to save *Compass*. I agreed because I think it's the right thing to do. In other words, not opportunism but conviction. *Or was I fooling myself? 12/8/54

By the time the "eternal" in confidentiality has expired and this journal becomes of any use, things will have shaken down. Either we'll have headed off the threat or we'll be living under a totalitarian regime and this diary will be my death warrant. I'm not being melodramatic. I know what we're fighting. And that is what I have to get down, just how frightening the world looks today, Tuesday, November 18, 1952.

I don't know anyone who isn't worried sick about another war, which of course with the bomb will mean total destruction. But it isn't just the idea of a shooting war that terrifies. It's a more subtle insidious battle for the hearts and minds of men and women, for the future. Practically every left-wing journal or newspaper in the world is financed by Moscow. At lunch, McClellan told me that the Soviets spend more on cultural propaganda in France alone than the U.S. does in the entire world. Their fingerprints are all over India, Africa, South America, the Far East. The fact that colonial greed and mismanagement turned those areas into such fertile ground doesn't make the situation any less dangerous. I know Nell agrees with me about that. We've discussed it often enough. So when McClellan asked the question in that bastion of haute Gentile privilege, I was ready to say yes, though I admit to having a bit of a chip on my shoulder by the time I got into the place. I'm not going to describe the incident with the door that wouldn't open, because time isn't likely to cast a rosy glow over that. McClellan was standing in the hall, but I don't know whether he saw what happened. He doesn't give away much.

I'm still trying to sort out my take on him. Can I trust him? My initial response is yes. I wouldn't have agreed to this otherwise. Do I like him? That's a more complicated question. We make strange bedfellows, the old upper-class Yalie with O.S.S. credentials and the poor Jewish former fellow traveler from Brooklyn. But I gather from what he told me at lunch, there's a lot of that going around. If the old boys' club wants the anti-Stalinist magazines to be liberal, they have nowhere to turn but the left-wing Jewish intellectual mafia.

I won't bother to record the early stages of lunch. I was being courted, and I knew it. He wooed me with allusions to my vanished grandparents, uncles, aunts, and cousins. He almost overdid it there. I didn't like his bandying about my dead relatives. He lured me with a reference to that shadowy cousin lurking somewhere behind the Curtain, whom, thanks to Uncle Joe Stalin, I'll never know. He reeled me in with reminders that my parents and I were the only ones left, and that was due to the magnanimity and values of the United States of America. Not, as I said, that I needed much persuading. Then he came out with it.

"Would you like to do something for your country?" *Every time I hear that inauguration line, "Ask not what your country can do for you . . ." I'm back at this damn lunch. If I ever do get up the guts to quit, I can hear Elliot asking Wally Dryer the same question. Maybe he'll even put it in JFK's words. 1/20/61

I started to say that I'd like to know a little more about what he had in mind, but before I could, he went on.

"I should mention one condition." That was when he used the term "eternal confidentiality."

I told him eternity was a long time.

"It goes with you to the grave. No exceptions." He sat staring at me for a moment, and when he spoke again, I knew my face had given me away. Or had he merely done enough homework to know not only about me but about Nell and me?

"That includes your wife."

"What happens if I break my word? You send someone to break my kneecaps?"

He smiled across the table at me, and the old cliché about butter and its melting point in the human mouth came to mind.

"We have more elegant methods than that." Then the smile slid from his face. "The division I work for is known as the campus. Most of the men are Harvard, Yale, or Princeton, and half of them write poetry, paint, or play the violin. In other words, they're nothing like those gun-toting cowboys who are still fighting the war, their finest moment. If that makes you feel any better."

It did, but I told him that all the same, I would not toe an editorial line.

"That's the last thing we want," he said. "The whole point of this operation is to promote freedom of expression. Unlike the Soviets, who dictate what people can think and write and paint. All you'll be doing is helping people say what they would have said anyway."

How could I argue with that?

November 19, 1952

Last night Nell and I celebrated the new job. She's over the moon about it, but she kept coming back to one point. Editorial independence. In a sense, I wasn't surprised. That was what I questioned McClellan about at lunch yesterday, but I knew about the arrangement. Does she suspect it?

January 22, 1953

I'm not sorry I agreed to accept the funding. I still believe in the aims. I still think it will permit *Compass* to do some good. But for all McClellan's seriousness of purpose, there's a fun house aura to all this. That's one more reason I hate not being able to tell Nell about it. She'd get a kick out of the ludicrous aspects.

McClellan and I had a curious moment in his office today. His digs are a far cry from ours. His office even smells different. Ours reeks of burnt coffee, stale cigarettes, and ink. The aroma is untidy and vaguely cerebral. His is redolent of expensive leather bindings and furniture polish. Ours simmers with the messiness of inquiry and argument; his lies quiet under the smooth surface of certainty. Appearances, as it turned out, were one of the things he wanted to talk to me about.

He said I had to be wary of what he called governmental extravagance. I thought he was warning me not to be profligate, but it turned out he was less worried about how we spent taxpayers' money than about how it looked to the unwitting. I've already come to hate the phrase, which he keeps throwing around. I'm witting. Everyone else at the magazine is unwitting. Perhaps I wouldn't mind the distinction as much if the second group didn't include Nell. I feel as if I'm cheating on her.

In any event, he sat in front of those shelves of leather-bound books warning me against small touches like leatherette bindings on reports. I told him we didn't write reports, and if we did, I doubt I'd put leatherette bindings on them. He said what he meant was that I had to be careful not to make the magazine look too flush. Parties were another example. I'm supposed to go on giving them, but not make them as flashy as Gideon's. My wife isn't heir to an American fortune. J & B and White Horse are okay; Chivas is not. The last thing we want, he said, the last thing we can afford, is to have people suspect government funding.

So this is the way we fight the cold war, not with guns or words, but with blended whiskey.

May 12, 1953

I'm beginning to understand what I got myself into. Not the funding. I still believe in that. But the lie. I feel as if, in the spirit of altruism, I brought home some harmless stray, and now it's grown into a monster that's eating us out of house and home, fouling the apartment, and keeping me up nights howling at the moon. Note to my sixty-year-old self: that may sound like hyperbole, but it's the way I feel.

We were sitting in my office yesterday evening, Nell, Sonia, Gus, and I. I had just liberated the scotch from the bottom drawer, the one that's designed for files so it's tall enough for whiskey bottles, when Wally came in.

"Now hear this, staff," he announced. "I just got a call from the firm that handles our subscriptions. It seems we're the coming thing in Western Europe and—drumroll please—India. Ninety-seven new subscribers in France, 85 in Italy, 62 in all the Scandinavian countries combined—must be those long winter nights—and, are you ready, 138 in India. A grand total of 382. That brings our foreign circulation to 2196."

Wally said it called for a drink, Gus pointed out we were already drinking, and Sonia lifted her glass and made a toast to our fearless editor. Nell didn't say anything. She just sat looking at me with an expression that shut out everyone else in the room. Under normal circumstances, it would have given me a hard-on. Last night it emasculated me.

If we had been alone, I would have told her, eternal confidentiality be damned. But we weren't, and I didn't. All 382 subscriptions were purchased by the Drinkwater Foundation and sent to unsuspecting but ripe-for-conversion-to-Western-ways readers abroad.

June 12, 1953

This morning McClellan called to talk about Nell's piece in the current issue. The minute he mentioned it, I bristled. I hadn't told him I'd put her on staff. It's no more his business who writes for *Compass* than what they write.

"I have to admit," he said, "I was worried when I saw the title. 'Book Banning in the United States and Russia.' It's not that we don't want you to run anything critical of the U.S. We don't want *Compass* looking like a front organization," he said for what must have been the hundredth time. "But I don't think you can equate the two systems."

"It doesn't."

He laughed. "I know. The title worried me, but the piece was a nice little slice of history. I knew *Uncle Tom's Cabin* had been banned in the Confederacy; I didn't know it was banned in tsarist Russia. Congratulate her for me."

I told him I would, but after we got off the phone, something was still bothering me. If he called to say what he liked in the magazine, was he going to call to complain about what he didn't? *Oh, was I naïve. 12/28/55

September 23, 1953

The stakes have been raised. Note the passive voice. Old Charlie Benjamin didn't do anything to raise them. He's just an innocent bystander. He didn't agree to take the funding. He didn't swear goddamn eternal confidentiality. I'm beginning to sound like some latter-day second-rate Hamlet, awash in indecision and self-pity.

Last night, Abby was fretting about something. She's a tiny mystery, a terrifyingly fragile package of unexpected gurgles and smiles and murderous rages. Last night was one of the murderous occasions. It must have been around one when she started crying. Nell got up and went in to her. The crying didn't stop. It merely went from room to room, as Nell changed her, gave her water, and carried her around the apartment humming a futile lullaby. I must have dozed off, because when I opened my eyes again, the clock on the night table said three ten and the apartment was silent. It took me a moment to realize Nell was in bed and Abby was between us. We know we're not supposed to do that. We've read the books. Not healthy for the baby, the experts insist. Maybe they're right, but there comes a point in the middle of a sleepless night, in a sequence of sleepless nights, that I'd risk Abby's future mental and physical health with a stiff scotch down her sweet little gullet if it would quiet her.

Nell was on her side of the bed with her left arm across the baby. I reached my right arm around both of them. Abby smacked her lips. Nell sighed. I lay in the dark thinking that I was betraying one to protect the other. I hate lying to Nell, but I like to think that I'm doing some tiny part to make the world safer for Abby. Surely Nell will forgive that.

Note to my sixty-year-old self: I hear the fatuousness of the phrase. It was still in my head when I got up this morning. Woodrow Wilson got us into World War I to make the world safe for democracy, and look where that led.

October 1, 1953

Today Elliot and I were having lunch at his club when he announced that the foundation has decided to take out a life insurance policy for me. All I could think of, again, was the young editor from *Encounter* who'd kept changing taxis in London. I'd laughed at his self-importance then, but suddenly it didn't strike me as that funny. I asked Elliot if there was something about this funding arrangement he had neglected to mention.

He smiled, and it occurred to me that, for a grown man, he has very small teeth. He said the Agency valued the work I was doing and wanted to keep me happy.

"This seemed a good way to do it, now that you have a family. We were thinking of three hundred thousand dollars."

I raised my eyebrows. "So if you do send someone to break my kneecaps, Nell and the baby will be in high cotton."

We both laughed, but the joke is wearing a little thin.

March 25, 1954

I had lunch with Elliot again today. It turns out he's a big Housman fan. He said he never would have guessed it of me. Most unmodern, he pointed out. Not in the least, I countered. If you listen carefully, you hear the coming of Hemingway.

It was pretty much a social lunch, little business involved. He even told a funny, well, perhaps not so funny, story about some Drinkwater meddling (my phrase) with a screenwriter in Hollywood. The CIA, through the foundation, has long arms. Apparently, they persuaded the screenwriter to insert a couple of negro characters in a movie, not as servants or slaves or minstrels, but as respectable, if minor, characters. The idea was that when the movie plays overseas, the characters will put the lie to the stories the Soviets sell about racism in America. Not without good cause, Elliot said before I could. The problem is the movie is being shown here too, and now southern theaters are refusing to run it unless the negro characters are cut. Wouldn't Nell love to do a story on that?

April 10, 1954

I lost my temper with Elliot today. He didn't exactly object to the piece on Brecht. He never objects. He just wondered if *Compass* really wanted to heap so much praise on an apologist for Stalin. I pointed out that the article was about Brecht's art, not his politics.

"You can't look at one and ignore the other," he argued.

"That's not what you say when I run something on von Karajan or Furtwängler. Nobody breathes a word about their late lamented Nazism."

He backed down in the end. He always does. But sometimes I wonder if his objections aren't having a more insidious effect. Am I beginning to censor the magazine instinctively? The other night Nell and I had an argument about it. No, not an argument, a discussion.

"That sounds like Elliot talking," she said when I explained that I didn't think the fact that a distinguished Brecht biographer was fired from Brooklyn College after taking the Fifth was relevant to an article on Brecht's art.

She agreed that it might not be relevant to Brecht's art, but it was to the state of freedom in America.

Finally, we both let it go, but her comment about my sounding like Elliot rankled. The idea of Elliot's trying to influence editorial policy is irritating. The idea of my being co-opted without realizing it is demoralizing.

July 22, 1954

Nell was right. It was no accident that Sydney Gruson was pulled off the Guatemala story. Someone at the CIA was spreading rumors around the *Times* that Gruson was a dangerous radical with communist connections and therefore not the correspondent to cover the overthrow of a left-leaning president. By the time the powers that be at the paper realized they'd been had, it was too late. The problem is that I can't run anything on it. I have no proof, only off-the-record accounts from friends at the *Times*. But if they're right, what kind of an organization am I in bed with? I asked Elliot that. He insisted the Gruson incident was blown out of proportion, but he couldn't say any more about it, yet. He must have seen I didn't buy it, because then he brought up the Geneva Accords. "We just signed all of Vietnam above the seventeenth parallel over to the communists, whose dirty tricks make our methods look like playground pranks. Now maybe that doesn't worry you, old buddy, but it scares the hell out of me."

August 1, 1954

Today, Elliot surprised me. He called to talk about the next issue. I suspect he courts Dottie, the new secretary, to get an early look at what's likely to be in it. I expected him to go through the roof at Nell's piece on McCarthy. Maybe I even wanted him to. Nell didn't call me a coward for not running it, but I knew that was what she was thinking. Perhaps that was one of the reasons I decided to publish it. (When did proving my masculinity become editorial policy?) But Elliot didn't even mention the article.

August 28, 1954

Elliot complimented Nell on her piece about McCarthy. That was when I realized why he hadn't objected when he saw the table of contents. He's pleased because now that McCarthy is pretty much yesterday's news, the article proves once again that the magazine isn't a front. It embarrasses me to realize how slow on the uptake I was.

September 7, 1954

The letter came yesterday. I'm to report to something in Washington called the Office of Security, a.k.a. FBI. I went straight to Elliot's office—I didn't want to discuss this on the phone—and asked him what in hell was going on. I'm taking government funds to fight communism, and the FBI is accusing me of being a communist.

Elliot said I'm being called in precisely because I'm cooperating—what an anodyne term—with the CIA. Everyone knows about the fierce competition between the FBI and the CIA.

"It's unconscionable," Elliot added. "Suddenly, Fordham men are deciding whether Yale and Harvard men are fit to work."

I told him, boola boola and all that, but I'm just a Columbia man caught in the middle.

"Don't worry," he said. "The Agency has to let them call you in, but they won't let anything happen to you. The Agency takes care of its own."

When did I become the CIA's own? And if I am, why can't I tell Nell they're going to look after me? She's worried sick about this business, and all I can give her are empty reassurances.

September 8, 1954

Last night I almost did it. I almost said to hell with confidentiality, temporary or eternal, and told Nell.

I'd brought Elliot home for a drink. I think I was hoping that he could find a way to reassure her about this inquisition without telling her the Agency takes care of its own. It didn't work out that way.

When I came back to the living room after going in to see Abby, I sensed they'd been talking about my being called in, though neither of them mentioned it. Then sometime early this morning, lying in bed, bound by the muscle-tense cord of our shared insomnia, she turned on her side and wound herself around me. Under other circumstances, it would have been an invitation, but neither of us was feeling amorous. We're both too frightened. Then she spoke.

"We're the only ones we can trust," she whispered.

I took her hand and held it to my mouth. It was the only way to keep from confessing.

September 15, 1954

I'm writing this in my hotel room in Washington. I just got off the phone with Nell, reporting on my first day of questioning. They told me to come back tomorrow at nine. I have no idea how long this will drag on. There's an eerie Kafkaesque quality to it. I called Elliot out for his comment about Fordham men judging Yale and Harvard men, but the idea that those two semiliterate picklock detectives can get me blacklisted or even sent to jail for reasons I don't know scares the hell out of me.

I'm furious at them, but I'm not feeling too good about myself either. That was the part I couldn't tell Nell. How can I be working for a government that permits this travesty? I signed on to fight totalitarianism, but this is totalitarianism, even if it reads like the Marx brothers' version of it.

December 7, 1954 (The Day of Infamy, all right)

Elliot was right. The Agency takes care of its own. A <u>favorable</u> decision was reached. (In case my sixty-year-old self forgets, I underline for irony.) I got the letter this morning.

I was afraid Nell would want to celebrate the news. She didn't. She said she had no desire to celebrate something that makes her feel dirty. And she knows only half of it.

December 8, 1954

Elliot stopped by the office today to congratulate me on the good news. I told him I'd done a lot of thinking in that hotel room in D.C. It's time for me to get out.

"Who's going to run *Compass*?" he asked.

The question, I'm ashamed to admit, surprised me. I'd meant get out of my connection with the Agency. In my mind, I'd give up the foundation's backing and stay on at the magazine. I knew it wouldn't be easy. We might have to scale back to a quarterly again. But for some misguided naïve reason, I didn't think Elliot and the rest of the board, whom he controls, would dump me. Apparently I was wrong.

I gathered the frayed skirts of my dignity around me and told him Wally Dryer would be happy to do something for his country.

"I have a better idea," he said. "Hang on just a little longer. Now that the Senate has censured McCarthy, the witch hunts are on the way out. The country will right itself. It always has, which is more than you can say for the Soviet Union. And that's what this is about."

Did I listen to him because he made sense or because I don't want to leave the magazine?

October 13, 1955

I can't fool myself any longer. When I took the job, Elliot promised complete editorial freedom. Formally, he's lived up to his word. Occasionally he calls with a suggestion, but he never insists or threatens or forbids. He doesn't have to. He merely talks about what's in the country's best interests. And gradually, I've been co-opted by the arguments. I find myself trimming and shading instinctively. Like the article on Neruda in the last issue. I knew he wouldn't want me to publish it, because of Neruda's connection to the Central Committee of the Chilean Communist Party. I ran the piece and patted myself on the back to boot, but even while I was editing it, I knew I was concentrating on the erotic love poems and conveniently overlooking the political manifestos. Somehow the line about his being awarded the Stalin Prize got cut for lack of space. Guess who pointed out that it wasn't there.

December 19, 1955

I'm just back from a weekend at Elliot's house in the country, and I want to get this down as clearly as I can, because someday when this is over and I finally tell Nell—fuck eternal confidentiality—I want her to know that I would have left earlier, if it hadn't been for her.

I'm not passing the buck. I merely want her to understand. *Just as I'm trying to understand what she did. April 26, 1963

It all started with an article I commissioned Frank Tucker to write on the South Vietnamese president, Diem.

"You can't do a hatchet job on one of our allies," Elliot said. So much for his going through the motions of not interfering.

"He's a murderous thug who stole the election."

"He's better than the communists."

"He's exactly the same as the communists."

It continued that way for a while, until finally he told me he didn't know how much longer he could go on protecting me. I asked what he was protecting me from.

"Don't be coy," he said, and of course he was right about that. I've known for some time that he runs interference for me with the Agency. I never wanted to admit it, but now I have to. I told him it was time *Compass* and I parted company. This time he knew I meant it, and I have to admit the surprise on his face gave me pleasure. Then he said he thought it would be helpful—his word—if I came up to his place in the country for the weekend. "Be good for you while Nell is in Russia. And there's someone I want you to talk to."

I agreed to go to the country but added that I didn't like having the screws put to me. He said no one was putting the screws to me. They just wanted to explain a few facts of life.

No one put the screws to me. Their methods are, as Elliot said in the beginning of all this, more elegant than that. Only one other guest came for the weekend, though Elliot invited some neighbors in for dinner on Saturday night. The pretense was of a civilized weekend in the country, and for the most part it was. The conversation was good, the food excellent, the whiskey and wine aged. The more civilized and gracious things got, the more anxious I became. I don't think I'm cut out for this kind of work.

I arrived on Saturday morning, but we didn't have the conversation until Sunday. No point in spoiling the weekend. It was just the three of us by then, Elliot, a man named Carter Robbins, and I. Robbins must be about sixty with a mane of white hair—why are all these men so hirsute? Am I the only one destined to go bald?— a ruddy complexion, a tobacco-aged voice, and the most god-awful stained and snaggled teeth I have ever seen. Except for the teeth, he was a smooth customer. I wonder why he never got himself to a dentist.

We sat in Elliot's study. The room is wall-to-wall dark wood and leather, but outside a hard metallic sun tinted the snow blue. It occurs to me as I write this that the comment is pure Nell. She's always noticing stuff like that. She would have called this a Courbet snow scene. When I looked past Robbins to the stand of trees in the distance, I had to squint. I don't think it was an accident that he had the light behind him and I was looking into it.

I'm going to try to get the conversation down as accurately as possible. Elliot didn't speak. He said he was there simply as a mutual friend. The word *pimp* came to mind, but I didn't say it. After all, I was the whore in the group.

"Elliot tells me you want to leave the magazine," Robbins began.

I gave a pretty speech about editorial independence.

"I understand." The words rolled out of those crooked brown teeth as round and soft as smoke rings. "And of course you're free to at any time. But I don't think this is the opportune moment."

"Is there ever an opportune moment for a decision like this?"

"I had in mind something a bit more specific. I understand your wife is in Leningrad." He hesitated, and, when I didn't say anything, he went on. "Several journalists posted to the Soviet Union work in close cooperation with us."

I opened my mouth to say that she was not one of them, then closed it. Was it possible that she was? Had she been keeping her own secret? I felt suddenly giddy. Two wrongs don't make a right, my mother used to tell me when I was a child, but in this case they might. I'd be off the hook. I forgot about Diem and *Compass* and editorial independence. All I knew was that a weight had been lifted from me. Then Robbins went on.

"I know Mrs. Benjamin is not one of those journalists . . ."

The boulders settled back on my shoulders.

". . . but our friends in the KGB don't."

"What is that supposed to mean?"

"Our people have been keeping an eye on her. Your wife received a package, amateurish I admit, from a group in West Berlin."

"How do you know all this?"

His smile was as wintry as the landscape beyond the window. "The point is, people over there seem to know about her connection to you and yours to us."

"What else do you know about what's going on over there?"

"Nothing you have to worry about at the moment."

"You have an agent on her?"

"Not an agent, just a member of the touring group who shares our aims. As do you. Isn't that why you signed on in the first place?"

"So what are you saying? If I bow out now, you throw her to the wolves?"

"No one is throwing anyone to the wolves. Mrs. Benjamin is an American citizen. Our job is to look after American citizens. And this man in the touring group is an old friend of hers from their days at Columbia. A negro."

That had to be her old boyfriend, the one she was on the rebound from when I met her. It was odd that she hadn't mentioned that he was with the troupe. Unless there was a reason for her not to mention the fact. I pushed the thought from my mind. Working with these jokers was making me as paranoid as they were.

"He's certainly not going to throw her to the wolves, as you put it," Robbins went on. "But if you resign now, the Russians will hear about it. They hear everything, as do we about them. There's no telling what they'll make of it. They may think it's some sort of ruse. They may think it's a genuine change of heart and try to recruit her, especially since she didn't take the bait from the other side in West Berlin when they tried to scare her away from the Eastern Sector. All I'm suggesting is that, in the interest of her safety, you do nothing until she's home."

And that's where we left it.

Oh, no, there was one more repercussion. Elliot said he's not opposed to a piece on Diem. He just thinks it doesn't have to be quite so hard-hitting.

As I said, whore.

January 14, 1956

Nell is home, thank heavens. Robbins wasn't lying. Somehow people knew who she was. A dissident approached her in Leningrad. Apparently the Russians put a quick and dirty end to that. She's still shaken, but she says fortunately someone from the group turned up and steered her away from getting involved. She didn't mention that it was her old boyfriend. She seems to think he turned up by accident. I didn't suggest otherwise. How could I? An omission, not a lie. When did I begin splitting Talmudic hairs?

February 7, 1956

Nell has been safe at home for a month, but I still haven't resigned.

I toned down the Diem piece. Nonetheless, it caused a bit of a brouhaha. That's why I didn't resign. My voice isn't as loud as I'd like it to be, but I haven't been silenced. Will the sixty-year-old man I'm writing this for believe that, or will he sniff the foul fumes of

rationalization and self-delusion? More to the point, will his wife
get wind of them?

July 7, 1960

I haven't made an entry here for some time. What is there to say except more of the same? Every time I decide to quit, something happens that makes me realize what we're doing is necessary. But we're
just back from Venice, and I think it's important that I record what
happened.

Nell overheard a conversation about CIA funding and asked me
who was paying for our trip. I told her the foundation. Again, not a
lie, merely an obfuscation. The strange thing is I don't feel as bad
about it as I expected. Is it merely the effect of practice? The first
time it's a sin; after that it's a habit. I think in this case there's more
to it than that. It has something to do with our visit to the ghetto.

Venice had the first ghetto in history, the start of a long and hon-
ored tradition. The word even comes from the Italian. A handful of
white lies seems like pretty small potatoes compared to several cen-
turies of bigotry and oppression, culminating in, but not ending
with, the Third Reich. I know she'll be able to understand that.

April 23, 1963

Again, a long hiatus in journal entries. I thought I was getting accustomed to the situation, but something just happened that puts a
new perspective on it. That sounds a lot calmer than I'm feeling.
Fuck, fuck, fuck, fuck, fuck! That's a more accurate description of
my mental state.

This morning I got a call from a lawyer at the NAACP. The name
Woody Jordan struck me as vaguely familiar, but I couldn't place it.
He said he'd been in touch with an attorney at the Southern Chris-

tian Leadership Conference and had something I might be interested in running in *Compass.* The American Friends Service Committee is planning to publish it as a freestanding pamphlet, he explained, but it demands a larger audience. It's called "Letter from a Birmingham Jail."

I knew what he was talking about immediately. The demonstrations in Birmingham, or rather the suppressions of them, have been getting uglier by the day. Hundreds have gone to jail, including Martin Luther King, Jr. They had him in solitary confinement for a while, and I'd heard rumors of a letter he'd written in his cell. Now this Woody Jordan was saying it was no rumor. King started it in the margins of a newspaper with a pen his lawyer smuggled into the jail, continued it on scraps of toilet paper, and finished it on stationery slipped to him by a negro who works at the jail. Then his lawyers smuggled it out page by page. Now they're trying to get as much publicity for it as possible.

Jordan asked if I wanted to see it. I told him I didn't have to. I'd run it in the next issue.

As we were getting off the phone, I placed the name. He was Nell's old boyfriend, the one who'd stopped her from getting involved in that mess in Leningrad.

"Thanks for thinking of *Compass* for the letter," I said. "And thanks for Leningrad too. Nell told me you got her away from that ugly business at the Hermitage." She hadn't told me he was the one, but I couldn't very well say that a CIA handler had delivered the information.

Jordan could have made any number of responses. None of them would have been incriminating. But his silence was. It went on for too long. And it brought to mind an incident I hadn't thought of in years.

Shortly after Nell and I were married, we went to a party in the Village. Gloria Evans, the librarian I'd known after the war, the one the FBI had grilled me about, was there.

"How long did it go on?" Nell asked me on the way home.

"How long did what go on?"

"If that's your story, you stick to it, but the two of you gave yourselves away as soon as you were introduced. The way you both said you already knew each other. *Delicious guilt* would be the operative phrase."

At the time I'd wondered at her perceptiveness. Now I was the one with insight. Sitting there, listening to Woody Jordan's silence, I put it all together. Her failure to mention that he had been on the trip. Her anger at my not being home when she called that weekend. Her constant repetition of *we* in her account of what had happened, as if she was trying to cover her tracks but dying to confess. I knew, because I walked around day and night with the same urge.

After we got off the phone, and I have no idea what we said at the end, I sat at my desk as if in a soundproof cell. I knew the noise was still going on around me—the clatter of typewriters, the ringing of telephones, the horns blaring outside the window—but I couldn't hear any of it. I had gone deaf with anger.

I don't know how long I stayed that way while my mind ricocheted through possibilities. I imagined confronting her. I schemed retaliation with another woman. Not just any woman, her best friend, Sonia. I envisaged calling a divorce lawyer. Then suddenly it came to me. The burden I had imagined being lifted off my shoulders during the meeting with Carter Robbins in Elliot's house really was gone. Perhaps Nell would not see it that way—no two people ever box their moral compasses precisely the same way—but that was how it felt to me. We were even! The cry was infantile, but show me a man with a grown-up heart and I'll show you a cadaver. I was still furious, but I was no longer guilty.

I looked at my watch. It was a few minutes after noon. I had a lunch date in the Village at twelve thirty, and outside my window rain had stalled the traffic to a crawl. I grabbed my trench coat off the coatrack in the corner and began putting it on as I hurried down the hall to the office Nell uses when she's working at the magazine.

As I came through the door, she looked up at me, then at her watch, and said I was going to be late for my lunch date. I stood staring at her, and for a minute all I could see was an image of her in bed with that son of a bitch Jordan. It was ridiculous. I didn't even know what he looked like. But I couldn't blot it out.

"What's wrong?" she asked.

I shook my head. The picture shattered like a mirror breaking, but the anger lingered. I told her I was late because I'd just gotten off the phone with someone at the NAACP. "A fellow named Woody Jordan. You remember, the lawyer who was on the trip to Russia with you."

Her face went still as a mask. If I'd had any doubts, her reaction dispelled them. The image of the two of them in bed returned. I shook my head again to smash it. Then I told her about the letter written in the Birmingham jail.

"Elliot's going to give you hell," she said.

"Elliot's not the publisher, I am." Oh, the bravado of a cuckold.

I will always wonder at what she did next. Was it a confession or a gesture of love, or were they not mutually exclusive? They wouldn't be for me. She got up, came around the desk, and crossed the room to me. When she was inches away, she opened my trench coat and slipped inside it, and there in the overheated office, with rain pelting the windows and the staff wandering past the door, we stood holding each other as we had years ago, when we had been drunk on the newness of us and the limitlessness of a future that had become the soiled, written-in-stone past. That was when I knew that I would go to my grave debating the ethics of what I had done, but I would never forget her lie to me, and I would never forgive myself for lying to her.

BOOK FOUR

1968–1971

Twenty-Five

I SAT STARING AT the last page. He had known, and he had never said anything. I wished now he had. I tried to imagine our life if we had dragged all the secrets out into the open. Would we have absolved each other? Or would we merely have pretended to forgive and carried festering grudges? I'd never know.

I got out the stepladder, carried it and the journal to the big walk-in closet, and climbed to the top. The space was a clutter of boxes of old hats and shoes I would never wear but could not bring myself to throw out. I put the journal behind them. I wasn't sure if I was hiding it from Abby or from myself.

A week later, I got out the ladder again, climbed to the top shelf, took the journal down, and put it in my night table drawer. Some nights I managed not to look at it; more often I found myself opening the drawer, taking it out, and reading through it. After a while I knew the words almost by heart, but the meaning was more elusive. It shifted with each reading. Some nights I raged against him, others against myself. Once, Abby wandered in, and I slipped it beneath the covers. After that, I took to putting it inside another book, as if it were the pornography of my marriage.

Meanwhile, Charlie and I debated. Occasionally, I lost my temper. Even in my head, Charlie was still Charlie. He never raised his voice. When I realized the way I was staging the encounters, I had to laugh. Then I started to cry.

My emotions were on a hair trigger. I blamed myself for the night in Leningrad. I blamed Charlie for the state of the world. Several months earlier, I had sat in my bedroom staring at the television in stunned disbelief as a South Vietnamese police chief raised a revolver to the temple of a Viet Cong prisoner and the prisoner crumpled to the ground. A small shocked *oh,* like the pop of a toy gun, escaped my mouth. A hallucination of Charlie going down went off in my brain like a flashbulb.

One morning I opened the paper and read, in an article seemingly so unimportant that it was beneath the fold, of a Lieutenant Calley, who was charged with the murder of an unspecified number of Vietnamese civilians. When I turned to the inside page where the article continued, I discovered the unspecified number might add up to 109.

This is what you brought on, I told Charlie's empty chair across the table. I did not raise my voice. The horror screamed for itself.

This was in the future, he argued. I didn't see it coming. No one did.

That's the point, I countered. First it's a harmless little fib about funding. Next we're overthrowing duly elected governments, assassinating uncooperative heads of state, and murdering civilians in corners of the world where we have no business being. It's a variation on the domino theory your friends are always talking about. Subvert one safeguard, and the rule of law comes tumbling down.

He was quiet. I had finally beaten him. Pyrrhic victory, once over lightly for breakfast.

But one battle does not determine a war. On autumn evenings when I looked out the window and saw darkness rising from the trees in the park and on soft spring nights when the air ached with a promise that would never be kept, I came face-to-face with my own dishonesty, and not only about Leningrad. I raged at Charlie for the Viet Cong prisoner who slumped to the ground like a rag doll and the 109 civilians, give or take a few women and children, but, and I am not proud of this, his betrayal of me was the pain that would not let up.

You cannot run a magazine devoted to the pursuit of truth, I told him, while you're lying to everyone connected with it, including me. Me, me, me.

What about you? he asked, and a cruel smile played around his thin mouth. What about the lie of Leningrad?

My mistake— I started.

Mistake, he taunted.

My betrayal was a single incident, committed under duress. I don't absolve myself, but it didn't give the lie to our entire marriage.

One withheld fact does not give the lie to an entire marriage, he countered.

Withheld fact, I taunted in return. How about the betrayal of everything we believed in?

Again and again, it came back to that. How had we loved each other so much and understood each other so little?

Twenty-Six

MORE THAN A year after I finally put the journal aside, not in the top of my closet as if I were trying to hide it, but in the drawer in Charlie's dresser where years ago I had found widowed cuff links, old medals from the war, and letters I'd written him, I called Frank Tucker and asked if he was still interested in the piece he had wanted me to write.

"You mean the one about how Charlie snookered you and screwed the country?"

"That's not the way I'll phrase it, but yes, that one."

"So you've finally realized the truth is more important than your girlish heart."

"Are you interested or not?"

"Sure. The topic's still hot. Every day someone spills more beans. There's bound to be a government investigation. More than one probably."

The research for the article was difficult. Few people who had been involved were willing to talk. But I did make one discovery, or at least draw one conclusion, and it gave me such joy that, sitting at my typewriter, I let out a yelp of pleasure. The CIA had not gotten its money's worth. *All you'll be doing is helping people say what they would have said anyway,* Elliot had told Charlie at the first lunch. It was a recruiter's ploy, but Elliot's lie had turned into truth.

The Agency had showered money on magazines and books and art shows and foreign travel, and all they'd gotten in return was a bunch of unwieldy artists and intellectuals going their own way and having a damn good time of it. The recipients shaded issues here and there, but they didn't deliver anywhere near the millions of dollars' worth of propaganda the Agency was paying for. The CIA had been snookered, just as I had.

The second part of that sentence was the painful part. Writing about my marriage was like slicing myself open. I made an effort to explain Charlie's reasoning and motivation, but I didn't try to white-wash him. Any more than in the privacy of my own conscience I tried to whitewash myself. I was past the point in life when I believed people were of a piece. I had learned to live with ambiguity. If you can't, you have no business falling in love.

The response to the article was mixed. Some letters to the editor suggested that Charlie had acted for the good of the country and I'd better grow up. Others railed against him for undermining the American system and warned that the road to tyranny was paved with means justified by ends. One woman wrote that Charlie was a swine, and she wasn't saying that only because she, too, was a wronged wife. The editor said he printed that one for comic relief. I smiled, though I didn't find it amusing.

The responses from people I knew were more surprising. Charlie's parents had never mentioned the television news special, though I was sure they knew about it. Now they said they were glad I had made people understand Charlie's feeling for the country that had saved them. Then his mother mentioned that just the other day she had seen the ghost of her sister in Prospect Park again.

My mother had no interest in the political or moral issues, but she found vicarious shame in the personal implications. In her mind, my having been duped by a man reflected on her. She was also worried about my sullying Abby's view of her father. I told her to look on the bright side. Now Abby wouldn't measure every man she met against an unrealistic image. I didn't add that I was the one who had fashioned that false hero. I had asked too much of Charlie.

A MONTH OR so after the article came out, on a blindingly bright winter Wednesday, I ran into Elliot on Fifth Avenue. I was walking north and he was coming south, and we almost collided. I started to turn away, but he put his hand on my arm to stop me.

"This is ridiculous," he said, and I realized it was. Though I hadn't forgiven him, suddenly face-to-face with him, I was having a hard time hating him. Charlie always said I was an expert at outrage but no good at carrying a grudge, except against my mother.

He asked how I was and wanted to know what Abby was up to. I said we were both fine.

He took off his dark glasses and squinted at me through the glare. "I miss her. I miss you both."

The comment caught me off guard. That was why, standing in the middle of the sidewalk while the midday crowd hurried back to offices, streamed into Saks, and came out of St. Patrick's Cathedral with soot-smeared foreheads—it was Ash Wednesday—I took off my own dark glasses and gave myself away.

"I just want to know one thing. It was bad enough that you corrupted Charlie. Why did you have to come after me too?"

He tilted his head to one side and smiled, not the cool blue-eyed smile that he used to keep people at bay, but an unguarded grin that came and went so quickly I almost missed it.

"Wouldn't it be nice if we only fell for the right people?"

The words were as close to a personal confession as I'd ever heard him make, and suddenly it occurred to me that whatever had been between us was as unfathomable as the love Charlie and I had known. Not as devastating or fly-by-the-seat-of-your-pants fizzy, but inexplicable just the same. I suppose any attachment worth its salt is.

And I knew something else as well. I would always have come

second with Elliot, just as he would have with me. His real love was the secret. I suspect that many in his line of work share the passion. They talk about God and country, but what they mean is I-know-something-you-don't. Charlie had not been one of them. The secret had tortured him. It intoxicated Elliot. As we stood in the merciless light, bound by our long tangled history, separated by what I now knew about it, I finally saw him clearly. And I knew suddenly that he was capable of a lot, but not of Charlie's murder.

Or was I being willfully naïve again?

A FEW DAYS later, I told Abby I had run into Elliot on Fifth Avenue. It was a Sunday morning at the end of February. She was lying on her stomach on the floor, poring over an article in *The New York Times* about the Rolling Stones. Now she looked up at me.

"How did you feel?"

I had to think about that for a moment. "Angry. Sad. Strangely wise. Almost appreciative."

"Not sorry?"

"No regrets, if that's what you mean."

She sat up and hugged her knees to her chest. "Does that mean you're never going to get married again?"

I heard the fear in her voice. She was worried about me, but she was also apprehensive for herself. When she packed her books and records and clothing to go off to college next fall, would she have to find room in her baggage for me?

"You never know," I tried to reassure her. "Maybe I just have to set my sights lower. The woods aren't exactly full of men like Daddy."

"You know what I keep remembering? Something he taught me. Only I didn't know he was teaching me anything when it happened. I was little, like seven or eight. We were in the park, and Grandma Claire was coming for dinner that night. I started making fun of her. This was before she and I became kind of friends. You know, how she called herself a poor widow lady, and always said give her the smallest piece of meat or cake, stuff like that. I was trying to make him laugh, the way you always did when I imitated her, but he stopped me. He said it was okay for you to be mad at her, because she wasn't a good mother to you, but we should try to be nice to her, because she probably went through some bad times herself. Until then, I always thought of her as silly old Grandma Claire. Daddy made me see she was a person with her own story, and it probably wasn't a happy one."

I remembered the time years ago when Abby had defended my mother—"Grandma Claire is all alone," she'd said—and I'd wondered where this child had come from. Now I knew.

"So you see what I mean about the woods not being full of men like Daddy?"

A siren went by in the street below.

"Then why were you so mad at him?"

I started to say that I'd never been angry at him, but she was no longer a child, and I was the one who was always sounding off about truth.

"Life has its ambiguities."

"What's that supposed to mean?"

I stood, went down the hall to my bedroom, and opened the top drawer of Charlie's dresser. His journal was still there. I took it out. For a moment I stood debating. I didn't have to give her the whole diary. I could tear out the final pages, the ones about Woody. I knew some mothers would say I should. But I would not sacrifice Charlie and spare me. I carried the journal back to the living room and handed it to her.

"What's this?"

"You read my version of what happened in that article. This is Daddy's. And it cuts closer to the bone."

"It's a kid's notebook."

"We were young once."

She rolled onto her stomach again, propped herself up on her elbows, and opened the journal. Her long hair fell forward so that I couldn't see her expression. That was all right. That was fine. She was going to have to work this out for herself.

I stood watching her and not seeing her. I was in another living room. Instead of light spilling across the floor, smoke swirled in the overheated air. All around me, girls and men swayed toward one another and back, like a tide dragged by a full moon. Charlie was leaning over me, one hand propped against the wall northwest of my head, isolating us from the others, binding us together. And Billie Holiday was on the turntable, singing about what love could make you do. But Billie had it wrong. She was warning of the transgressions and misdemeanors. I was thinking of the glue that held you, no matter what.

Sources and Acknowledgments

Two first-rate nonfiction accounts of the cultural Cold War proved invaluable in researching this book: *The Cultural Cold War: The CIA and the World of Arts and Letters* by Frances Stonor Saunders, published in the United Kingdom as *Who Paid the Piper?*, and *The Mighty Wurlitzer: How the CIA Played America* by Hugh Wilford. For information about Richard Wright, I have relied heavily on my late friend Hazel Rowley's splendid biography, *Richard Wright: The Life and Times. The Muses Are Heard*, Truman Capote's gimlet-eyed account of his trip to Leningrad with the touring company of *Porgy and Bess*, was a crucial source, though with the exception of Mrs. Ira Gershwin, none of the characters he mentions appear here. Jennet Conant's description of Paul Child's questioning during the McCarthy era in *A Covert Affair* also proved helpful. Mike Wallace's CBS News Special "In the Pay of the CIA" is available on tape, though of course there were no allegations against *Compass* magazine or Charles Benjamin, both of which exist only in my imagination.

I am indebted to Jay Barksdale of the Allen Room of the New York Public Library and Mark Bartlett and the entire wonderful staff of the New York Society Library for help in research and for creating safe harbors for writers.

Many friends and colleagues were generous with information, inspiration, and support during the research and writing. I am grateful to Andre Bernard, Laurie Blackburn, Jane Brodman, Robert Caro, Gilda Delmonaco, Edward Gallagher, JoAnn Kay, Joe Keiffer, Judy Link, Warren Wechsler, and Ann Weisgarber. I am especially indebted to Stacy Schiff and Fred Allen, who are as gifted at editing as they are at friendship.

I have had the good fortune to fall into excellent publishing hands, including Hana Landes, Karen Fink, Annie Chagnot, and all the good people at Spiegel & Grau, and in London, Veronique Baxter at the David Higham Agency, and Paul Baggaley, Francesca Main, Emma Bravo, Camilla Elworthy, and the entire extraordinary team at Picador. And finally, I am deeply grateful to my superb editor and inspired publisher, Cindy Spiegel, and to Emma Sweeney, my cherished friend who turns agenting into an art form.